PRIDE AND JOY

By the Author

Who I Am

Pride and Joy

Pride and Joy

by

M.L. Rice

2012

PRIDE AND JOY

ISBN 13: 978-1-60282-759-2

This Trade Paperback Original Is Published By
Bold Strokes Books, Inc.
P.O. Box 249
Valley Falls, NY 12185

First Edition: November 2012

Credits
Editors: Lynda Sandoval and Stacia Seaman
Production Design: Stacia Seaman
Cover Design by Sheri (graphicartist2020@hotmail.com)

Acknowledgments

Many thanks to Radclyffe and everyone at Bold Strokes Books for all of their dedicated work. I am constantly indebted to my editor, Lynda Sandoval, who always teaches me something new, makes me laugh, and without whom none of this would be possible.

Special and heartfelt thanks are in order for Angie Williams as well as Robin Neuman and many of my fellow Coast Guard Auxiliarists for their support, their knowledge, their friendship, and their advice. I am honored to be counted among your numbers.

Thanks go to my mom and stepdad for always loving and accepting me for who I am. I also want to thank my mom for getting me interested in Broadway at a young age. An appreciation for music and live theater is something that benefits every aspect of my life. As always, I would like to thank my wife for always being there for me, for believing in all that I do, and for being the best friend I could ever hope to have.

Finally, I would like to thank the active duty, reserve, civilian, retired, and auxiliarists of the United States Coast Guard for all that they do and will continue to do to protect us. *Semper Paratus!*

For Mom. Thank you for your constant love and acceptance.

PART ONE

Chapter One

Bryce stared at the perfectly still blue water. There was no breeze to ripple the surface, the sun had begun its rise into the morning sky, and the air was already so warm she was starting to sweat beneath her track jacket. Her favorite kind of day at one of her favorite places on earth. How she ever managed to get any studying done during the week she would never know. School was great and she excelled at it, but the classroom was nothing compared to being in the water.

Of course, it was only a public swimming pool. The locker rooms were kind of nasty and, in two hours, there would be swarms of screaming children trying their best to drown their friends in games of "Shark" and "Marco Polo," so a true sanctuary it was not. Bryce's morning would consist of constantly blowing her whistle to get the kids to stop running on the wet concrete, and her afternoon would hold the joys of bandaging the bloody knees of those who didn't listen.

But for these first hours of the day, the pool was hers. Well, hers and the four students in her beginners' swimming class. She wasn't a natural teacher and didn't take the weekend lifeguard/swim coach job because she was good with kids. She didn't particularly like kids. It just gave her an excuse to get in the water more often than she already did as an athlete on her high school swim team. Even though she had to sit on the lifeguard stand in the hot sun watching other people cooling off in the pool during the day, she had full access to the pool in the off hours. Nothing got her blood pumping like a morning or evening swim, and nothing made her happier than floating weightless in fluid space.

She took off her tracksuit and folded it neatly on the nearby table next to the large beach towel she had brought with her. Despite the warmth of the morning, the sweat that had formed during her walk to the pool caused her skin to prickle with goose bumps. Bouncing on her toes, she swung her muscular arms back and forth to warm up, pulled her long blond hair back into a ponytail, and then slowly lowered herself into the pool. It was always a little chilly the first time she entered the water on these mornings, but she knew that once the school year ended and the blazing West Texas summer sun started its annual slow bake of the land, the cool water would be an oasis to all who sought its refuge.

Taking a deep breath, she submerged herself and sat on the bottom of the pool for a full minute, just listening to the sound of the water swirling around her and using the time as her daily meditation ritual to become one with the liquid world. Eventually the annoying mammalian habit of having to breathe won out over her spirit's desire to become a mermaid and she emerged into the brightening sunlight once again.

When she opened her eyes she startled as she saw two bright hazel eyes staring at her, only inches away.

"Hi, *Miss* Montgomery!"

Bryce smiled and wiped the excess water from her face. "Seriously, *Miss* Cordova. I'm only three years older than you, and I'm just giving you swimming lessons. I'm eighteen, not eighty."

"Sorry, Bryce. You know I'm just messing with you. It's from all those times you babysat Dante. Don't you remember how he always called you that? He was just so happy I wasn't old enough to babysit him myself. Brothers are so frickin' irritating."

"No worries." Bryce winked and flicked excess water from her fingers at her friend. "Get me my towel, would ya? I'm going to swim a few laps and I'll be right out."

Daniela immediately stood up from her crouch and bounded over to the table where Bryce had left her towel, a pleased smile on her face. Bryce swam quickly back and forth across the pool a couple of times, reveling in the feel of water flowing over her streamlined body, and then returned to the edge of the pool, her breath only slightly faster than when she was at rest. She pulled herself out of the water, and as she did, she marveled at how grown up Daniela looked now that she was in high school. She was shorter than Bryce, but even though she never wore makeup—she didn't need it with her complexion and dark hair—people often mistook her for a college student. She looked older than most of Bryce's senior friends.

"Here ya go, *Miss*…"

Bryce raised her eyebrows.

"Bryce."

Bryce playfully punched her friend in the arm. "Why are you here so early anyway?"

Daniela shrugged uncomfortably.

Bryce smiled. "Listen, I know you're embarrassed to be in a swimming class with eight-year-olds, but don't be. I'm really proud of you for finally overcoming your fear of the water and hey, better late than never!"

"Well, when I heard that you'd be teaching...I mean, I'd rather learn from a friend than a stranger, so a little kids' class is just the price I have to pay for being lame and not trying it earlier, I guess."

"Hey, I'd be happy if it was just you in the class, believe me."

Daniela smiled broadly.

"So you want to practice some before the rest get here? We can do that."

"No, actually, I wanted to talk with you about something."

Bryce raised her eyebrows with curiosity. "Let's sit down, then." She led her over to sit on the lounge chairs next to the closed snack bar and wrapped the large beach towel around her own soggy shoulders. "What's up?"

Daniela's smile faltered and she hesitated.

"You know you can talk to me, Dani. How many times have I had to put up with you and Dante running around like demons trying to get me into trouble when I babysat?"

"I never ran around like a demon!"

"You're right. You were always a perfect little angel." Bryce rolled her eyes. "But seriously, you know you can talk to me about anything. We've been friends for as long as I can remember."

"I know. It's just that...this is...personal stuff."

"Well, it's your choice, but you know I'm here for you. Is this something you don't feel comfortable talking to your mom about?"

Daniela winced. "No. Definitely not. I just want the opinion of someone my age. Well, a hell of a lot closer to my age anyway."

Bryce broke into a knowing smile. "This must be about a boy. First year in high school and you're already falling in love. Oh! Is it an older guy? A senior, maybe? Do I know who it is?"

Daniela flushed red and said defensively, "Yes, actually. I *am* talking about a senior. And yes, you know who it is."

Bryce opened her mouth to ask about the identity of the mystery guy, but Daniela interrupted, "And no, I'm not naming names."

"So okay, what do you want to know? I'll have you know, though,

Arati is probably the one to talk to about this. I've always been too busy to date…and most of the guys I know are idiots. But Arati…well, you know Arati."

"I just want to know…if it's normal for me to like someone as much as I do. I'm afraid if I told anyone they'd say that…something is wrong with me."

Bryce paused, waiting for more information, but Daniela just hung her head. Dark silky hair fell over her eyes, obscuring her face. Bryce reached out and brushed the wayward strands behind her friend's ear. "Why in the world would people say that something is wrong with you for liking someone?"

Daniela sighed. "My dad is…protective. He says I can't date anyone until I'm sixteen. That's only two months away, but still. That, and I know he won't approve of who I like."

"What's wrong with him? The guy you like, I mean."

"Well, my dad told me a long time ago that he wouldn't let me date anyone not Catholic and Latino, so that's one thing, and the other… well, let's just say he won't like the kind of person I have a crush on."

Bryce made a dismissive motion with her hand. "Dads are like that, though. You're young and he still thinks of you as his little girl. I don't know why he would be so adamant about the religion and ethnicity thing in this day and age, but I bet he gets over that too. Have you told the guy that you like him?"

Daniela scoffed. "Not gonna happen."

"Why not?"

"A sophomore asking a senior out? How lame is that? No one is ever going to like me anyway. I'm not beautiful and popular like—"

Bryce laughed and interrupted, "Listen, Little Miss No Self-Confidence, I don't think you've noticed how the guys look at you when you walk by in the halls. You know my friend Angela, right? The one in the drama club with you? She told me when you were cast as Rosie in *Bye Bye Birdie* for this year's musical, every guy auditioned to play Albert just to have scenes with you. Before that, everyone had been fighting over playing Conrad. They most definitely think you're hot."

Daniela made a noise in her throat that sounded like she didn't believe that at all.

"Look," Bryce continued, "the point is that no, you are absolutely not weird for being totally in love with someone right now. It's perfectly normal. We're supposed to have crazy hormones, right? And you need to think more of yourself. You're pretty kick-ass, if I do say so myself. Not to mention you're starting to turn the heads of pretty much every guy at school. You'll figure it out soon enough, and when you do decide to tell this lucky guy how you feel about him, I bet you money he'll be groveling at your feet."

Daniela smiled and leaned against Bryce's shoulder. "Thanks, Bryce. You always make me feel better."

"No problem. Now what do you say we get you some extra practice time in the water anyway. I know it's tough being the oldest person in this class, so I'm happy to work with you individually whenever you want. Truth be told, I'm really glad you're here. It's nice teaching a friend instead of snot-nosed little brats all of the time."

Daniela beamed back at her and said, "I want to try it without the kickboard today!"

"Damn right you do!"

"Mom, I'm home! Dani said to tell you hi from her mom!" Bryce yelled as she threw her wet towel on the floor by the front door.

Her mom's voice echoed back from the kitchen, "Pick up that towel! We keep this house presentable!"

How does she always know? Bryce thought.

She picked up her towel and carried it to the laundry room next to the kitchen. "Any letters today, Mom?"

"Not yet, sweetie. Don't worry, it'll get here soon."

Bryce threw up her arms like a child having a tantrum. "It's already April second! The last day they would tell me is supposed to be April fifteenth."

"Patience is a virtue, honey. God will make it happen in His own time."

That kind of response always infuriated Bryce. She was sure God had more pressing matters like ending wars or helping people find a cure for cancer than in making sure she was one of the lucky few to be accepted into the U.S. Coast Guard Academy.

When she had told her parents four years ago about her desire to become an officer in the Coast Guard, they had looked at her incredulously.

"Why in the world would you want to do that?" her Dad had asked.

"Well, I think it would be awesome to join the military, and I like that the Coast Guard has a humanitarian mission rather than just 'blow people up' kind of stuff. That and, if I get accepted into the academy, college will be free! That's got to be good for you guys, right?"

Her mother countered, "But you've never even been on a boat other than to go water skiing at Bison Lake."

"I want to be on the water, Mom. I'm sick of dust and tumbleweeds. Swimming is my life. That has to come in handy in the Coast Guard, don't you think?"

Her parents had paused and looked at each other for a moment before her dad finally smiled and said, "Well, if that's what you want to do, we'll help you get there. I'm actually really proud of you for wanting to serve your country."

Since then, Bryce had immersed herself even more into getting into shape and winning for her swim team. She spent every spare moment she had either in the water or running for miles to get in perfect shape for the trials of academy life and especially Swab Summer, the boot camp she would have to attend in June if she got accepted. Even the spring lifeguard/coaching job was about getting more water time under her belt. The paycheck sure didn't hurt, though.

She was already one of the top students in her school and ranked in the highest percentiles of standardized tests, so she didn't have to worry about her academics, only the essays she had submitted to the acceptance board. Now all she had to do was wait for the letter to arrive. If it didn't, she already had automatic acceptance to her local university, but the thought of staying in Saltus, Texas, made her skin crawl. It was a nice place to grow up and it was the kind of small city where neighbors would always be there to help you out, people banded together to get things done, and everyone genuinely cared about your family. But the wind, dust, odorous feedlots, and conservatism were really starting to wear on her.

Of course, it was true: She was hoping to join the U.S. military—not really a bastion of liberal thinking and open-mindedness. But she wanted to be out on the water protecting the country and saving lives. It was a decision that promised adventure (and an awesome uniform), plus she would get to do something worthwhile for the world. It also seemed like it would take her a million miles from the dry, flat, landlocked part of the country that was currently her home. She would be happy to make a few sacrifices to do that. Now if only the damn letter would arrive!

CHAPTER TWO

The grating screech of her alarm pulled Bryce out of her deep sleep and, without looking, she fumbled to find the snooze button. When the unwelcome noise finally ceased, Bryce let out a groan and slowly sat up. She had been getting up at six a.m. almost every morning for a year to go for an hour-long jog before class, and it was starting to wear on her. It was worth it, though. She was in peak physical shape and it only took a glance at the Coast Guard flag on the wall, her swimming trophies, and her sculpted muscles in the mirror every morning to know she was doing the right thing.

She got dressed, trudged down the stairs, and found her father sitting at the kitchen table reading the newspaper and drinking coffee.

"Morning, hon."

"Morning, Dad."

"Going running?"

"Yep."

"Something new and different," he said in his usual dry, but friendly manner.

"Funny. Going to work?"

"Yep."

"Exciting. What are you building today?"

"A Baptist church down on Seventy-seventh."

"Another church, huh? Saltus doesn't have enough already?"

Bryce's father gave her a warning look over his newspaper.

"You know what I mean, Dad."

Her father put the paper down on the table. "No, I don't know what you mean. You haven't gone to church with your mother and me in months. I've been defending you to her, but if she hears you say something like that she'll get *really* upset. You'd better think about your priorities. God, family, country, remember?"

Bryce's stomach turned, but she nodded. "Yes, sir." He continued to look at her with disapproval, so she smiled halfheartedly and pointed at the back door of the kitchen. "Running time. Be back in a bit."

Once she was outside she leaned up against the B.D. Montgomery Contracting Services label on the side of her dad's silver Chevrolet truck and blew out a decidedly un-Christian curse under her breath. She had found that her faith in what her parents considered religion had been noticeably waning since she had started high school three years ago. It wasn't that she had trouble believing in something bigger than herself or that she wasn't spiritual, she just had a hard time trying to stomach the self-righteous dogma and bigotry that was rife in the church community in which she had been brought up. Her congregation preached unending love and happiness one day, and the next they were spouting hate politics from the pulpit.

So she had stopped going to church.

It hadn't been easy to convince her mother, but she was a young woman and could make her own decisions. It helped that the job at the pool was on weekends and she had the morning shift both days for lessons. She couldn't wait until she was finally able to get out of the house and go to college, where she could study subjects she was actually interested in, experience new things, and form her own opinions rather than having them forced upon her. There was something out there for her to believe in, she was sure of it. But the close-minded evangelicalism of the Bible Belt sure as hell wasn't it.

When she arrived back home after her run, breathing heavily, she walked around with her arms over her head for a few minutes to cool down and worked up the courage to reenter the house. She knew her mom would be awake by now, and even though she only had thirty minutes to get ready for school, her mom would try to talk to her the whole time about the youth group at church, and how much fun they had, and why she should go to their evening meetings. No thanks.

Taking one last deep breath she opened up the back door and sprinted through the kitchen and up the stairs to her bathroom. Luckily her mother was still in her own bedroom, so Bryce immediately jumped in the shower and was able to avoid her mother's barrage of annoying, but well-meaning advice.

After her shower she heard a knock on her bedroom door as she pulled a black Saltus High T-shirt over her head.

"It's open!"

Her father opened the door slowly, afraid of invading his teenage daughter's space. "Can I come in, hon?"

"Yeah, Dad. What's up?"

"I just found this inside my *Field and Stream* magazine that I got in the mail yesterday. Looks like it's for you."

Bryce blinked and stared stupidly at the large envelope in her father's hand.

"What is it?"

He just held the letter out to her, and she could see the edge of his mouth twitch beneath his full russet beard.

Bryce took it from him and her heart jumped into her throat as she saw the familiar Coast Guard Academy seal at the top left corner. She glanced up from the letter to look at her dad just as her mother joined him in the doorway.

"Well? Get on with it!" her mom cried with excitement.

With a shaking hand Bryce tore open the envelope, but hesitated before pulling out the papers tucked inside. This was it. She had studied incessantly and immersed herself in physical training, pinning all of her hopes on getting accepted into the academy.

What if it didn't happen?

What if she had to go to Saltus State University?

She didn't want to sound ungrateful, and SSU was definitely a fine institution of higher learning, but the problem was that it was still in Saltus. She needed to leave her hometown behind and become her own person. She felt constricted here. She wanted the whole world and the open water and, despite the fact that being an officer in the military was definitely regimented, she wanted her freedom.

"Bryce Lee Montgomery. Seriously." Her mother's voice shook her out of her reverie.

Taking a deep breath, she eased the papers from the envelope and let her eyes focus on the words in front of her.

After a pause where she could swear that her heart had stopped for a moment she looked up at her parents and grinned, "Your daughter will be a cadet in New London, Connecticut, starting on June twenty-fifth!"

Bryce jumped as both of her parents let out a cheer and rushed over to wrap her in a congratulatory hug. Her chest swelled with pride as Mom and Dad crushed her between them, and her eyes fell on the Coast Guard flag on her wall. She couldn't believe it. She'd gotten exactly what she'd dreamed of and worked so hard for. The only question now was, could she handle it?

"Bryce! Congratulations! We just heard from Angela!" Jennifer and Arati rushed at her when she entered the women's locker room for an extra swim team practice before lunch.

"Thanks, guys. I'm stoked." Bryce beamed.

Arati pouted a little and said, "I'm so bummed that you'll be going to the East Coast, though. With Jenn going to the University of Texas and me to CalTech, we'll all be on complete opposite corners of the *universe*."

Jennifer, always the calm voice of logic, countered, "Don't exaggerate and don't pretend that we don't video chat every night anyway even though we live just a few blocks from each other."

Bryce laughed and pulled her two best friends into a hug. "I'm going to miss you guys *so* much. We still have another month and a half of school left, though, so let's not think about it right now. Let's talk about happy things. Jenn, has Brian asked you to the prom yet?"

She shook her head. "No, I've been dropping stupidly obvious hints, but he's a boy, and you know how thick boys can be."

"What about you, Arati? Any luck on the date front?"

She sighed heavily. "Not yet. I'm just assuming I'll be going alone. And I really *really* wanted to get laid after the dance. It's just not a prom without it! Do you know how long it's been since I've gotten any action at all?"

Bryce squeezed her friend's shoulder. "I'm going to ignore all of that because it totally icks me out, but you definitely won't be going alone. You can go with me."

Arati looked at her incredulously. "Surely the gorgeous star athlete Bryce Lee Montgomery will get a date. You'll probably even get elected prom queen or something."

"As a matter of fact, I do have a date, *but*—" she cut off her friend before she could protest, "I want us all to go together. Go out to dinner, get a limo, party afterward, all of the cheesy stuff we're supposed to do."

Jennifer chimed in as she placed her glasses in her locker and pushed her long auburn hair into her swim cap, "My parents said I can have a small party at my place. They're going to be at a medical conference in San Antonio that weekend. They trust me to behave, I guess. I totally expect you both to be there."

"Count us in!" Bryce replied, waving Arati's hand for her.

"Don't change the subject, you guys," Arati said, pulling her arm away and glaring at Bryce. "Who asked you to the prom? And why didn't you tell us?"

"Well, I didn't tell you because he just asked me in Calculus two periods ago and I haven't actually said yes yet. But it was Michael Friedman."

The eyes of her two friends widened and they said as one, "Michael Friedman on the diving team?"

Bryce's eyes narrowed. "Yeah. Michael Friedman on the diving team. Why?"

Jennifer shrugged. "He's just…super hot."

Jennifer then looked at Arati next to her, who added, "Yeah. Like, movie star hot. I mean, the way he fills out that Speedo—"

"How do you even know him?" Jennifer asked quickly before her friend could elaborate. "We don't practice at the same time as the divers."

"I don't, really. His cousin, Leah, is a good friend of Angela's, and I hang out with them sometimes. Leah is like, terminally shy, but completely nice, so I assume Michael is cool too. I'm just glad someone asked me, to tell you the truth."

Jennifer shook her head in disbelief. "Bryce, you could've had your pick of anyone in the school. People worship you."

Arati sighed. "You're so lucky."

Bryce laughed. "Not super lucky. I don't even really know him, after all. I talk to him in English and Calculus sometimes, but just about our assignments, swim and dive meets, or about how cold the damn locker rooms are. Nothing heavy." She shrugged. "He seems nice enough, though. I'm going to tell him I'll go with him tomorrow morning. No one else has asked me anyway."

"They think you're out of their league," Jennifer said wisely.

"Come on, guys, you talk about me like I'm a celebrity or something. Don't be stupid."

Jennifer shrugged. "You're not stuck up like the other popular girls. You're nice to everyone. People appreciate that. And it doesn't hurt that you're insanely hot too."

Blushing, Bryce playfully shoved her friend. "Stop it, you'll give me a big head." Inwardly she was very pleased. She had always thought she looked like the nice girl next door, but the way her friends were talking you would think she was a supermodel. "Anyway, enough about me. As far as Michael goes, he has to at least agree to going as a group."

At that moment the swim coach's whistle sounded and the girls left the locker room to swim lap after lap in their practice session.

Bryce kicked at a dandelion in the grass as she leaned against the brick wall outside of the school the next morning. Other students filed past, bleary-eyed and dragging their feet, dreading the start of a new school day and counting down the few remaining weeks until summer break. Bryce, of course, had already been up for two hours, a two-mile run completed and full high-protein breakfast consumed, so she was bursting with energy.

"Michael!" she called as she saw him get out of his black SUV. A smile lit up his face and he waved to her as she approached. He was just over six feet tall, and at five-eight, Bryce only came up to his chin. When she reached where he stood, her head tilted back to smile upward. His teeth were brilliant white and his dark, wind-swept hair shone in the morning sun. Bryce had to admit that he really was a very pretty boy.

She didn't often notice members of the opposite sex. Not like other girls anyway, and *definitely* not like Arati, but Michael was built like a Greek god, and out of the corner of her eye she saw other girls in the parking lot glancing longingly over at the two of them standing together.

"Yes," Bryce said simply.

"Yes, what?" he asked as he smirked, being purposefully obtuse.

Bryce kicked his shoe. "Yes, I'll go to the prom with you." Michael's smile widened and he took a breath to respond, but Bryce continued, "But I want to go with my friends too. Limo…party…the works. Is that okay?"

"No problem. Jeff and Steven want to hang out too. I think Steven wants to ask your friend Arati anyway. Is she going with anyone yet?"

Bryce beamed. "Nope. She'll be really happy if he asks her. He will be too. Trust me."

"Cool. We should all get together soon to plan everything. We'll have a blast." He slung his backpack over his shoulder. "Anyway, we'd better get going. Kafka awaits."

Bryce was surprised when he took her hand in his and she hesitated when he started walking. Michael looked back questioningly, but he smiled kindly so Bryce squeezed his hand and followed him to their first class.

"Who is Gregor Samsa?"

The classroom remained silent.

"Okay. *What* is Gregor Samsa?"

Still silence.

"Mr. Friedman. Answer the question, please." Bryce saw that the English teacher, Mrs. Swift, was getting annoyed. This was advanced placement senior English, but it appeared no one was taking their classes seriously anymore. Senioritis was a nasty virus that spread quickly through the halls of the school as the students saw the brightening light at the end of the interminable grade school tunnel.

Michael was sitting directly behind Bryce. She turned in her chair to look at him as he sat up straighter. He cleared his throat and answered simply, "He's a bug."

"A bug. That's it?" Mrs. Swift asked, obviously unimpressed.

"Yeah, he wakes up as a bug."

There was a long pause before she continued. "Gregor Samsa is a son, a brother, an obsessive worker, the sole means of support for his family, and most importantly, he is a man that is made to feel invisible, unappreciated, taken for granted, and by the end, shameful. And yes, he wakes up one morning to find that he has been turned into a bug, as you so eloquently put it. Now, can anyone tell me *why* he turns into a bug?"

Bryce raised her hand and said, "Mrs. Swift, I think it could just be a metaphor for how he feels once he realizes his family sees him as nothing more than a breadwinner, and the rest of the story focuses on how his parents will never accept him for what he is. He's too different from what they had always known him to be. They're ashamed of him, even after all he did for them."

"That's a good start, Miss Montgomery. Thank you." Mrs. Swift smiled at her. "Who else can tell me more about why a hard-shelled insect may have been used as a metaphor for Gregor's condition?

Remember that there is no wrong answer. Literary analysis depends greatly on the reader's imagination and experiences." Another awkward long pause ensued. "Did anyone actually read this book?"

As the teacher was talking, Michael leaned forward and teasingly whispered in Bryce's ear, "Kiss-ass."

She smiled and raised her hand again.

Bryce was alone in the main school hallway after her end-of-day swim practice when she heard footsteps running behind her. She turned around to see Daniela sprinting in her direction. "Bryce! Wait!" Daniela tried to stop her forward momentum on the slippery floor in time, but instead slammed into her. Bryce laughed as she braced Daniela's petite form until she was able to regain her balance.

Daniela's eyes bulged in embarrassment at her lack of grace, but she said breathlessly, "Ticket."

"What?"

"I have a ticket for you to see me…to see the school musical."

"Oh yeah. Ten bucks, right?" Bryce reached into her pocket and pulled out a messy wad of cash.

"No, this one is free. For you, anyway. Everyone involved in the show gets four free tickets and I have an extra, so I'm giving it to you." She smiled hopefully.

"You don't have to do that!"

"I want to. You…you've always been really cool to me and you spent extra time with me during my swim lessons, so I just wanted to say thank you. Even if it is in this lame way."

"Dude. It's not lame. I really appreciate it. C'mere." Bryce pulled her into a hug. "I'm really proud of you."

It was strangely comforting hugging her friend, but she felt Daniela stiffen at the contact so she held her only briefly. "You okay?"

Daniela squeaked, "Yeah! Of course! Just nervous about the show."

Bryce snorted. "Oh please. Angela said it's really rare for a sophomore to get one of the lead roles in any high school musical. You must be special. You have a real talent for this acting and singing stuff from what I hear. I'll see for myself this weekend."

Daniela looked at her toes with a smile on her face as a distinct red flush colored the tanned olive skin of her cheeks. "Bryce…"

Bryce waited for her to continue, but she could tell Dani was struggling for words. "Yeah?"

Sighing, Daniela finally said, "Nothing. Just thanks for always supporting me. It means a lot."

"Just be sure to thank me when you win your first Tony."

This made them both laugh. Bryce put her arm around her friend and said, "Come on. I'm going home for a well-deserved night off to celebrate getting into the academy. I'm talking a movie with pizza and ice cream. I haven't had something that fattening in about three months. Wanna join me?"

Daniela inexplicably turned a darker shade of red and nodded vehemently.

"So. The acting thing. You seem to really like it," Bryce said as she bit into her heavenly slice of cheese pizza.

Daniela's face lit up. "You wouldn't think that would be something I would get into, would you?"

"Not with your shyness, no. I'm really impressed by how you can get up there and sing in front of everyone."

"Well, I just pretend they're not there. I just try to stay in character and imagine that it's my real life up on the stage."

"Oh, so you're a method actress!"

She smiled. "I don't know about that. I just know it's the only way I can stand in front of all those people and not faint!"

"Do you think this is something you want to do for a living?"

Daniela looked down at her plate. "No. I don't think so."

"Why not?"

"My parents don't really see acting as a real job."

"Does what they think matter? I mean, if it's something you love and kick ass at doing?"

Daniela looked up at Bryce, her eyes narrowed in thought. "Don't you think it's a silly waste of time when I could study to become a doctor or something?"

"Do you want to be a doctor or something?"

She paused. "No."

"Do you want to be an actress?"

After a moment Daniela's mouth broke into a dazzling smile. "Yeah. I think I do."

Bryce stood up and walked around the table to pick up her friend's empty plate. She stopped next to her and said with serious finality, "Then that's what you're going to do. And you're going to be amazing."

Daniela looked up at her with watery eyes. "Thank you."

"I mean it. I totally believe in you. One of these days I'll see you in a movie or something and say, 'Hey! I've known her since she was eleven years old, and I taught her how to swim.' And then I'll wait for the phone call where you'll invite me to your giant mansion in Hollywood where I'll get to lounge by the pool with you and your famous friends, drinking champagne and getting to bum around as part of your entourage."

Daniela laughed. "It sounds like you have my future all worked out."

"Yep. So you'd better not disappoint me." Bryce finished putting the dishes in the washer and walked back over to the table, extending her hand for her friend to take. "Now. Let's go watch a movie and figure out which character you'll get to play in the multi-million-dollar, special-effects-ridden remake in five years."

Chapter Three

The applause was still ringing loudly in Bryce's ears as she and many others made their way to the gym for the party the school had set up for the students and their families to celebrate the opening night of *Bye Bye Birdie*. She walked with Jennifer and Arati and they discussed the show and expressed their surprise at how entertaining it was.

"Angela was so good as Kim, and who knew that Daniela was such a natural! Their duet at the end of 'One Boy' was the best part of the show," Jennifer offered. "Brent was so cute as Conrad too. Can't sing to save his life, though. I wonder why he got that role."

Arati laughed. "Because he's hot, duh. Daniela and Angela were the only two who could actually sing in tune. Daniela especially. They all put on a good show, though."

Bryce just nodded through all of this. Angela was perfectly cast as Kim, but it was Daniela who had really been the star of the show. Her voice was pitch-perfect and soothing, and Bryce really could see her making a career out of the whole acting/singing thing. She looked like she belonged up there while the other students looked like gawky high school over-actors.

After they had waited and chatted in the gym for about twenty minutes the entire cast, crew, and orchestra members walked in and headed en masse straight for the snack table where a giant cake decorated like a jukebox waited for them.

"There's Angela. Let's go congratulate her," Bryce said, seeing her friend from across the room.

After squeezing their way through the hungry performers they finally reached her at the same time as Michael's cousin, Leah Friedman.

"Angela, you rocked!" Leah and Bryce exclaimed at the exact same time, which made them all stop and laugh.

"But for reals, though, you were amazing," Bryce finished.

"Aw, thanks, you guys. I thought I was gonna puke before I went on stage." She then whispered, "Kevin *did* puke and he's only in the ensemble. He had to wear his normal clothes because he ruined his costume."

They all giggled, feeling sorry for him, but unable to ignore the humor of it.

Bryce scanned the room as they laughed, looking for Michael to see if he was here with his cousin, but her eyes fell on Daniela, who was standing alone, her hands clenched together in front of her as if she was nervous about something, staring back at Bryce expectantly. Bryce gave her a thumbs-up and mouthed, "Awesome!" at which Daniela visibly relaxed and walked through the crowd toward them. Bryce lost sight of her and then turned back to her friends as Angela offered, "So what are y'all doing after this? Wanna go out to dinner to celebrate?"

"Sounds great!" Bryce said. "How about Amistad? They have the best burritos."

"What about your super health kick?" Arati asked.

"Hey, I can afford a night or two off. I'll lose anything I gain when I get to the academy anyway."

"You're like, zero percent body fat, Bryce. I don't wanna hear it." Jennifer huffed.

"Let's get out of here," said Angela. "Just let me go say bye to my parents. I'll meet y'all there."

Their group dispersed and Bryce caught sight of Daniela only a few yards away, a huge smile on her face.

"Come on, slow ass." Arati grabbed Bryce's arm and quickly pulled her toward the door. Bryce shrugged and waved good-bye to Daniela and saw her proud smile fall as she was pulled out of the room. She had wanted to talk to her about her amazing performance, but her friends were already gone from the gym and Bryce didn't want to make them wait for her.

"Dani, I'll see you tomorrow!" she managed to shout before the gym door closed behind her.

"Mom, I really need to exercise tonight. I can only stay for an hour. You know I have my most important meet of the year this weekend, plus I have to study for finals. Today in English I found out that I have to write a huge paper on *Crime and Punishment*. I'm not even a quarter of the way through the book!"

Her mother shoved a large box of canned goods into her arms and turned her toward the doors of the church's community room. "Believe me, you'll get plenty of exercise tonight. We have fifty more of these boxes, and you and Daniela are the only young people here to help us carry them. Dostoevsky can wait for a little while. Go." She gestured for her to take the heavy package inside. "And thank you. You know we appreciate it."

Bryce didn't usually mind going to her mother's church to help out with charity or community service, but tonight she was feeling restless. Monday nights her schedule included weightlifting and homework, and with the end of the school year quickly approaching she was starting to feel stressed and like she was falling behind. At least Daniela was going to be here with her. It was almost essential for her to have a friend around to keep her sane as the fiery women of the Saltus Community of Spiritual Women held their monthly fund-raisers and meetings.

The group comprised the most active (and vocal) members of several different religious congregations around town, and while most of their efforts were geared toward helping the needy or supporting the troops, occasionally they would get up in arms about a hotbed subject like abortion or gay marriage. This was when Bryce would have to fake an illness or swim team practice to keep from having to join them. She might not have to go to her mother's bigoted church anymore, but for some reason she was still fully expected to help out with the community group despite her protests about some of their actions.

She walked through the door that had been propped open and set the first of many boxes on the fold-out table next to the far wall. An elderly woman from Daniela's Catholic church smiled and began counting the number of cans inside. Bryce nodded and turned around to see Daniela looking at her with arms crossed over her chest. Bryce had forgotten about not talking to her after the show last night, and since she hadn't run into her at school that day, this was the first time she had seen how her neglect had affected her friend.

Daniela turned and walked away without saying a word.

"Dani! Hey!" Bryce trotted after her until she stopped and turned back. "I'm sorry I had to run last night. Everyone kind of made this mass exodus and I didn't have time to really congratulate you. That was totally rude and I'm really sorry."

Daniela said nothing and Bryce could tell she was hurt.

"Anyway, I wanted to tell you now how incredibly well you did."

Daniela's face softened a little.

"I mean it too. You were honestly the best part of the show. And I really had no idea you could sing that well. You sounded like a professional. I mean, I know everyone worked really hard and the whole thing really was amazing, but…Dani," Bryce paused to think back on how she had felt watching her on stage, "I couldn't take my eyes off you."

Daniela quickly cast her eyes down at her feet, but smiled. Bryce felt a tiny flutter of excitement in her stomach at how her words had affected the young woman.

At that moment Bryce heard her name being called and she turned, upset that this special moment had been interrupted, to see her mother standing at the open front door with Daniela's mother. She could tell the two women had been watching their daughters with irritation.

Daniela's mother called out, "These boxes aren't going to carry themselves, girls. Are you going to stand around talking all night?"

Bryce looked back at Daniela and said, "I mean it. There really are no words to describe how impressed I was. Am. With what you did on that stage."

Daniela nodded and looked back up at Bryce gratefully. "I appreciate that, Bryce. It means a lot to me. You really have no idea."

Bryce put her hand on Daniela's shoulder and could feel her practically vibrating from the praise.

"How many more times do you guys perform?"

"Three more times. Once tomorrow, once Thursday, and our last show is Friday night before Prom."

"Perfect. That gives me a chance to watch the show again."

Daniela's smile widened. "You're actually going to watch it twice?"

"Of course! How could I not want to watch one of my best friends kick all kinds of theatrical ass?"

Daniela laughed. "Now that's one I haven't heard before."

Bryce gestured over her shoulder. "I'd love to gush about how crazy awesome you are all night, but I think our mothers are about to have a conniption fit. I tell you what. You come over and sing for me while I lift weights sometime, and I'll be sure to heap copious amounts of praise upon your deserving self."

Daniela nodded with a pleased and somewhat dreamy look on her face and they walked together out to the waiting boxes stacked in the parking lot.

"I dunno, Mom. That one seems kind of…matronly." Bryce wrinkled her nose at the frumpy taupe dress her mother held out to her.

"You think so?" She turned the dress to look at the front. "What about this one?" She held up the dress she had been holding in her other hand.

"Yes!"

"Really?" Her mother's face lit up.

"No. Do you really think I'd wear a ginormous pink bow on my butt?"

Her mother put both of the dresses back on the rack. "Well, I just don't know, Bryce. You're too picky."

Bryce put her arm around her mother's shoulders. "I just want it to be perfect. That's all. I only get one prom."

Her mother leaned into her and smiled. "Bryce, you'll be perfect no matter what you wear. There's nothing in the world that could ever make you not stand out as the most beautiful young woman in the room."

Bryce laughed. "You're just biased. You have to say that because you're my mom."

Her mother elbowed her in the ribs. "I'm saying that because it's true."

"Well, who am I to argue, then? Come on, this is only the second store. I'm sure we'll find something soon. Of course, I'd be perfectly happy wearing my cargo pants, boots, and a tank top—"

Her mother pulled away and shot her an exasperated look.

"*But*," Bryce continued, "I'm having too much fun shopping with my mom to settle for comfort and sensible shoes."

Her mother's features softened into a pleased smile. "I've been looking forward to doing this with you for years. First your prom dress, then your graduation uniform, then your wedding dress, then baby clothes…" Her mother's gaze drifted wistfully as she spoke.

"Whoa, Mom! Getting a little ahead of ourselves, I think! That is so not on my radar right now!"

Truthfully, the thought of a traditional family life with a husband off at work and children running around her feet scared the hell out of her, but she didn't dare mention that to her mother. Especially not now, when they were having such an excellent bonding day.

"I'm just so proud of you. I can already see the amazing future ahead of you and I get so…excited to think about all that you're going to do with your life. I love you, honey," her mother said, looking at her with unconcealed pride.

Bryce smiled back. "Thanks, Mom. I love you too."

Her mother sniffed. "Well, enough of that. We have to find a dress fit for a princess!"

"A princess, Mom? Really?"

Her mother pushed her playfully out of the door of the shop. "Yes. A princess. Let me have my moment."

Bryce chuckled and led the way to the next dress store in the mall.

The next weekend Bryce stood proudly on the podium as she received the first-place medal for the 100-meter freestyle at her final swim meet as a high school student. Jennifer and Arati stood on either side of her in the second and third place positions. Saltus High had swept the regional competition. She saw Michael, Angela, Leah, Daniela, and her own parents in the stands cheering her on, and wondered if any of them would ever be able to watch her compete as a Coast Guard cadet. It wasn't likely, so she smiled and waved, trying to convey how happy she was that they were all there to support her.

Later, as she, Michael, Jennifer, and Arati compared medals (Michael had come in second on the 1-meter springboard), Angela, Leah and Daniela walked down to meet them from the stands.

Leah was generally pretty quiet and was staring at her toes, so Bryce was surprised when she said shyly, "You looked…really great out there."

There was silence as they all looked at each other. Bryce realized that Leah had been talking to her directly when Leah glanced up to see if she had heard.

Bryce replied with a hesitation of embarrassment in her voice, "Oh! Thanks, Leah. I think we all rocked today. I'm glad you were able to come out and watch." Bryce was used to getting praise, but couldn't figure out why Leah, who rarely spoke when more than two people were around, would compliment her alone. Daniela was looking at Leah with furrowed brows as if there was something she didn't trust about her.

Odd.

"What about you, Dani?" Bryce asked.

Daniela jumped and looked back at Bryce nervously, "What?"

"Did you have a good time? You didn't have to come all the way out here to watch us."

"No! I mean, yes, I had a great time. I'm really glad all of you won something."

"Me too." Everyone stood in awkward silence for a few seconds. "Well anyway, I have to get home since the powers that be were smart enough to schedule a huge swim meet on the same day as the prom."

Michael chimed in, "We're all meeting at your house, right?"

"Right," Bryce answered. "The limo will pick us up at six o'clock and take us to the steakhouse. Then on to the dance!"

"All right. I have your corsage all ready." Michael grinned, obviously pleased with himself.

"I just hope I can get ready in time."

"Even if you went straight from here you'd look beautiful." Michael smiled and put his arm around her waist.

Bryce saw Daniela's eyes widen in what appeared to be utter shock and disappointment as she looked from her to Michael. It looked completely out of place on her normally happy features and with a jolt Bryce realized that Michael must be the senior her friend had a crush on and here she was, going to the prom with him. She felt so stupid and mean.

Trying to salvage the situation she said, "Hey, Dani, I know you can't go to the prom, but you're coming over to Jennifer's afterward, right?"

Daniela slowly turned her heartbroken gaze from Michael to Bryce and smiled weakly. "No. I don't think my parents will let me. They're…strict."

Bryce tried to think of another way to make her friend feel better, but instead Michael laughed and said, "Oh well. It's going to be too crazy for a kid anyway, and I'm sure your *mommy* wants you in bed early. Which bedtime story will she read this time?"

Bryce, Angela, Jennifer, and Leah all stood slack-jawed as Dani's face fell.

"Oh, come on, guys. It was a joke."

Quietly Leah said, "Not funny, Michael."

"Okay, shit. I apologize." No one said anything. "Can we go now? Please?"

"You guys go ahead. I'll see you tonight." Bryce waved at them and they quietly turned to leave. She hung back so she could talk to Daniela to apologize for Michael's random and unexpected comment. She hadn't realized he had a mean streak, and instead of being excited about the night ahead she was suddenly uneasy. Turning around to console her friend, she found that Daniela was gone. She scanned the thinning crowd and saw Daniela's slender form passing through the side doors at a jog.

Shit.

She'd have to talk to her, and soon. Michael would be getting a piece of her mind too. But not tonight. This was her one prom, and she didn't want to ruin it by being petty about one stupid comment. She couldn't help but feel terrible for Daniela, though. Here she was, practically in love with this guy and he had treated her like a nine-year-old. The fact that she looked and behaved older than fifteen apparently made no difference.

Stupid drama. Bryce thought. *Why can't people just get over themselves and be nice to each other for a change. I can't wait till I get out of here.*

Chapter Four

Bryce walked down the stairs slowly, trying not to trip over the long hem of her dress. She never wore dresses, and she worried she might tumble down in the most ungraceful and humiliating manner possible. With Michael, Arati, Jennifer, Brian, Steven, Jeff, Angela, Keiji, and Leah all waiting at the foot of the stairs, a spectacular fall wouldn't be the best start to the evening.

She exhaled with relief as she placed both feet solidly on the bottom landing.

"Made it." She smiled as Michael approached her and put the corsage he had purchased around her left wrist. She saw that the blue hydrangeas and white roses matched perfectly with the royal blue of her strapless gown and knew that the blue of her eyes would stand out even more.

"You look gorgeous, Bryce. And before you say anything else, I'm sorry about what I said to your friend Daniela earlier. I was a dick. Are we cool?" he implored.

"Thank you for your apology, but you need to tell that to Daniela, okay? You really hurt her feelings."

"Yeah, I get it. But guess what?"

"What?"

"There's a frickin' limo in the driveway!"

Everyone laughed and turned to walk outside, but Bryce's parents stopped them.

"We have to get pictures of you kids!"

"Mom!"

"Sweetie, you'll want to remember this moment for the rest of your life."

Bryce's dad was silent and only stared at Michael with fatherly suspicion.

Sighing, Bryce joined her friends in front of the fireplace as her mom took picture after picture.

"Mom. Time. Please."

"I'll upload these tonight and send them to everyone's parents!" Bryce's mother was obviously giddy with excitement about the prospect of being the bearer of such gifts.

"Fine," she said, with playful exasperation. "Can we go now? We have dinner reservations."

"Of course, hon. Come here first, though."

She pulled Bryce into the kitchen so the others couldn't hear.

She spoke in a low, but insistent whisper. "I know you're going to that party tonight and I need to know you're not going to do anything… unbecoming of a young lady."

"Wow. Downright Victorian."

"Don't give me that, Bryce. I just want to make sure you don't drink or…or…" She made uncertain circles in the air with her hands. "Anything else."

"Mom, please," Bryce said as she rolled her eyes.

"I trust you, but unwholesome things happen at parties. Satan will try to tempt you, but always remember that God is watching over you."

Bryce managed a smile, but turned around and tried to stifle the inappropriate refrain running through her head. *He sees you when you're sleeping. He knows when you're awake. He knows if you've been bad or good, so be good for goodness' sake.*

Bryce stared into the blue plastic cup Michael handed to her. The red liquid inside looked like neon-colored toxic waste, an affront to nature.

Michael noticed her appalled look and laughed. "Bryce, it's just vodka, rum, tequila, apple schnapps, and fruit punch. See? Fruit. Practically health food!"

"That sounds soooo disgusting." Her words were slightly slurred.

"Drink it anyway. You've only had two wine coolers, and the night is still young!" With these words he threw back a nearly full cup of what appeared to be nothing more than ginger ale and whiskey. He hadn't stopped drinking since they got to the party (and that didn't even include the gin he had snuck into the prom in a small silver flask—she had taken a drink or two from that herself and had discovered that she really, really hated gin).

Jennifer's prom after-party was a huge hit. Practically every senior in the school was there, out by the pool, in the kitchen drinking horrendous alcoholic concoctions that were never meant to go together, or making out on the couch, in the hallway, even on the piano bench in the living room. Jennifer, usually so down-to-earth and tidy, was clearly trying her best to not freak out about how loud or messy the house was getting. She hadn't realized how big the party was going to get, but was obviously trying to enjoy herself anyway in a last wild night before going to college.

Since she rarely drank alcohol, Bryce was already feeling a little light-headed from her two drinks and didn't want any more, but the frenetic atmosphere, the loud thumping music, the carefree feeling of being young and stupid, if only for a little while, and the gentle goading by Michael drew her in and enveloped her in a hazy trance. She downed the terrible mixture in one long chug and spluttered at the vile taste. Michael just laughed again.

"*Blech!* That shit's nasty!"

"Oh, don't be such a baby," Michael said as he put his arm around her.

"I feel…I feel weird…ish."

"C'mon. Let's go find a place to sit down."

They wandered around, but couples sucking face occupied all of the chairs and most of the corners.

"I've got an idea," Michael said with a smirk. "Let's go upstairs."

"M'kay," Bryce said thickly.

They walked up the stairs slowly, Bryce occasionally tripping on her dress and laughing hysterically each time.

When they reached the landing, Michael turned to his left toward a closed door.

"Michael, no. No, that's Jennifer's parents' room."

Michael chuffed and replied, "They're not here. Nothing's off-limits tonight." With that Michael opened the door. They both heard a gasp and a guy yell, "Dude!"

Bryce's vision was fuzzy, but she saw Arati and Michael's friend Steven in a large bed, frantically pulling the sheets around themselves.

"Sorry, man." Michael laughed and pulled the door shut.

"Oh my God. I didn't think she was *that* serious!" Bryce shook her head, trying to get the disturbing image of one of her best friends naked in bed with a guy out of her brain.

"Aw, let them have their fun, Bryce. They're not hurting anybody."

"You'd better be using protection, Arati!" Bryce yelled through the door. She then hiccupped loudly and any credibility she had as a mature advice giver was immediately lost.

Michael held her hand and led her to the next door. When he pushed it open, Bryce saw a guy she didn't know passed out in the empty bathtub and a girl kneeling in front of the toilet, hanging on for dear life. She had no way of knowing who the unfortunate girl was because her face was obscured by the toilet bowl and the hair that had come down in a mess from the nice up-do she had worn for the dance.

"Nope. Not here either," Michael said with a twinge of annoyance in his voice.

"Let's go find Angela and Jennifer." Bryce was getting tired of playing search the house for whatever the hell Michael couldn't find.

"Nah. I have a better idea. We just…have…to find…a place," he said as he peered into two rooms next to each other. "Ah. Here we go!"

He pulled her into a dark room that Bryce groggily recognized as the upstairs guest room where she had slept many nights.

"What's in here?"

"Just the two of us. Better than being in the middle of all those people downstairs, don't you think?" Michael closed the door and locked it.

Bryce followed his motions with her eyes, an odd sense of unease forming in her chest. Bryce backed into the room and Michael followed. "Come on. Sit down with me."

Not wanting to seem standoffish and rude, Bryce obliged and sat next to him on the bed. He slowly turned her face toward him and before she knew what was happening Michael was kissing her with a rough clumsiness that turned her stomach. She pulled away quickly and put her hands on his shoulders to keep the distance between them.

"Michael, what the hell?" She used one arm to wipe the saliva off her face.

"What do you mean? I just want to get close to you. I've been looking forward to doing that for years."

"But I'm not really…wanting to do that…right now," Bryce said ineloquently.

Michael shook his head sadly. "You don't realize what you do to me, do you? Every guy in school was jealous as hell that I asked you out first. You are seriously the hottest girl in the school. And you're completely awesome too!" he added, placating Bryce when he noticed her furrowing brows.

"Um. Okay. I'm glad you think I'm…awesome—"

Michael leaned forward and kissed her again. Bryce resigned herself to the contact and halfheartedly kissed him back, figuring that maybe if she tried to get into it, she might actually start to enjoy it. He *was* super attractive, after all. Any girl in school would walk across burning coals to be in her shoes right now. So why was she feeling so blah about the whole thing?

Reading Bryce's newfound willingness to give in to his show of "affection," Michael kissed her more intensely and pushed her down onto the bed. He lowered himself on top of her, one leg between her thighs, and slowly reached down to move his hand up her leg under the fabric of a dress that now seemed woefully thin.

The kissing was one thing, but even though her thoughts formed as if they were mired in mud, she knew she wasn't ready to be in this position with him. She pushed up on his chest and tried to turn her head away, but he moved his hand back up to her face and held on firmly so that she couldn't break the contact. His fingertips dug painfully into her cheeks and a fire of real fear ignited in her chest.

"NnnMmphn!" Bryce protested, but it only came out as a pitiful muffled noise. She pushed harder against him, but even though she was pure muscle, he was bigger and determined to stay right where he was. He shifted and straddled her waist to put his entire dead weight on her body to keep her still.

Realizing the situation was about to get immensely worse, Bryce let loose all inhibitions about hurting him and lifted her right knee as hard as she could, connecting forcefully with his genitals.

Michael let out a deep *oof*, rolled off her and, curling up into the fetal position, coughed and tried in vain to catch his breath.

"What the *fuck*, Michael?" Bryce screamed, tears running down her face. She ran to the door and fumbled with the lock. In her drunken and terrified state, she was unable to get it to move, so she banged loudly on the door. "Let me out!"

Michael regained some control over his body and slowly got up from the bed. He wheezed, "You…*bitch!*" Still gasping, he limped over to where Bryce stood.

She turned around to see Michael towering over her, even though his body was still bent forward in pain.

"Don't touch me, asshole!" Bryce pressed her back against the door and defensively raised her fists in a way that might have looked old-fashioned and comical were the situation not horrendously serious.

"What the hell is wrong with you?" Michael's breathing was ragged with pain and rage. "Any other girl would throw herself at me. You're missing out on the best night of your life!"

"Just leave me alone! Get the hell out!" Bryce was shaking uncontrollably.

In a fit of rage Michael lashed out and slapped Bryce full across the face.

The force of the slap threw Bryce to the ground.

"Fuck you, bitch. What a wasted night."

Through the stars popping in her vision, she saw Michael unlock the door and stumble out of the room. She heard some yelling in the hallway, but couldn't make out the words. The next thing she saw was a pair of shiny black shoes and women's dress pants running in to the room, stopping in front of her.

"Oh my God. Bryce, are you okay?" asked a familiar voice.

Bryce sat up slowly, holding on to her head to keep it from spinning around the room like a top. "Ow," was all she could manage before dissolving into tears.

"Come on, let's get you onto the bed."

She struggled to her feet with the support of the girl who had heard her screaming from the locked room. As she walked the few short steps to the bed that had almost been her nightmare, she looked down at the short person helping her, one arm around her waist. It was Leah. She recognized the tight, dark curls of her long hair.

"Thank you."

Leah's voice shook. "I heard you scream and I tried to open the door, but it was locked. When I saw Michael come out and you lying on the floor… What in the hell happened?"

"Michael assumed that I would…that he could…" Bryce sobbed harder.

"Ah. I thought that was it. I'm so sorry. Can I do anything for you? Want me to call the police or something?"

"You would"—Bryce hiccupped—"call the cops on your own cousin?"

"We're not *that* close, Bryce, and I'd call the cops on my own father if he did something like that."

Bryce sniffed and tried to regain her composure. She was sure her makeup was ruined. "No, don't call the police. I'd rather no one else know about this."

"Brycc, this is serious."

Bryce's breathing regulated slowly. "I know. I feel like I shouldn't have put myself in that position, though. I'm such an idiot."

"You're not stupid." She reached out, inviting Bryce to take refuge in her embrace, and even though Bryce had to lean down to do it she rested her head gratefully on Leah's shoulder. "You deserve better than him."

Bryce closed her eyes and enjoyed the feel of Leah stroking her hair. Time seemed to stretch on and Bryce lost herself in the feeling of warmth and safety. In the back of her mind she realized she was surprised that Leah could be so overtly compassionate when they didn't really know each other all that well. A pang of regret formed in her stomach as she realized she probably should have gotten to know her better over the last few years. She was obviously an amazing person.

"Leah?"

"Yeah?"

"Why are you being so nice to me?"

"What do you mean?"

Bryce paused. "Well, we haven't hung out as much as I would have liked and here I am, all crying on you like a baby. I mean, you wouldn't even know who I was if we both weren't friends with Angela."

Leah shifted so Bryce sat up. Leah's eyes were moist and she said quietly, "Bryce, I've known who you were ever since we started fifth grade together."

Bryce felt a twinge of guilt. Leah had been in school with her since fifth grade? She didn't remember meeting her until last year. She decided to keep that damning information to herself.

"Well, anyway, thanks for just sitting here with me. I can't bear to think about going downstairs right now." She sniffed again.

"Don't worry about that. I'll protect you." Leah smiled and tapped Bryce on the tip of her nose.

They both jumped as a loud knock sounded on the door. Bryce looked at Leah with fear in her eyes and Leah hesitantly got up to see who had knocked. When she opened the door, Jennifer was standing outside with a worried look on her face. She blinked at Leah, then peered over her shoulder to see Bryce sitting on the bed.

"What in the hell happened?" she asked with a tremor in her voice.

"Come in first," said Leah.

Jennifer rushed past Leah to sit on the bed beside Bryce while Leah closed and locked the door behind her.

Jennifer moved a strand of loose hair behind Bryce's ear. "Jesus! What did he do?"

Bryce turned her head to look at her reflection in the mirror and saw that her hair was a mess, her mascara had run (even though it was the expensive kind that wasn't supposed to), her cheek was a violent shade of red from where Michael had slapped her, and her lipstick was a large smear around her mouth.

Leah asked, "Is he downstairs saying something?"

"No," Jennifer said, still watching Bryce worriedly. "I just saw him making out with that ho-bag Lucia Dell and knew something must have happened. So…why is he downstairs making out with Lucia while you're up here looking like you've been tumbled in a dryer?"

Bryce looked to Leah for help and nodded. She couldn't bring herself to speak the words to Jennifer. She was too humiliated, not to mention still trying to sober up.

"Michael forced himself on her, Jenn."

Jennifer's eyes widened in horror. "You mean you were—"

"No, no. Bryce is a tough chick. She didn't let it get that far, did you, Bryce?" Leah braved a smile.

Bryce was starting to feel a little better now that her friends were with her. "Oh hell no. And I don't know how he has any desire to make out with *anyone* right now. I don't think his dick will work right for at least a week. I racked him pretty hard."

"I'm going to go downstairs and make sure his dick doesn't work for the rest of his *life*!" Jennifer got up to confront Michael, but Bryce jumped up to stop her.

"No! Jenn, no. It's okay."

"What do you mean it's okay?" she asked incredulously. "He tried to *rape* you."

"He seriously didn't get anywhere close to that. If he had, then yes, I would send you and every other person here to rip off his particulars in the most painful way possible, but he didn't. Let him have his ho-bag. They deserve each other." She shuddered. "I just want to go home. Please don't tell anyone else."

Jennifer stood in angry silence, tapping her foot in the fidgety way she did when she was waiting for test results. She finally let out a breath and said, "Fine. I won't kill him and I won't tell anyone. But I want him out of my house. *Now.*" She then hugged Bryce and Leah and stomped out of the room.

Everything was silent but for the muffled bass coming from the music playing downstairs. With knee-trembling abruptness, Bryce sagged with complete exhaustion. Her surge of adrenaline ebbed, and now she just felt sick and wanted to curl up in her own bed and sleep for days.

"I hate to ask, Leah, but can you take me home now?"

"Of course. Come on, let's sneak you out the back."

As they descended the infrequently used side stairs and made their way toward the less crowded sunroom exit, they heard Michael yell, "Fine, this party is lame anyway. Fuck all y'all!"

Bryce was thankful for Jennifer's loyalty as she unceremoniously kicked Michael the hell out of her house. People would wonder why, and she was sure the asshole would spread some sort of lie around the next day, but right now Bryce just wanted to get away from him and the stifling crowd of people.

They sat in Leah's car next to a park for a good two hours simply talking, calming down, and letting Bryce sober up until she felt somewhat normal again. Bryce marveled at what a difference a good friend could make in such a short amount of time. There was something about Leah that just made her feel safe and comfortable.

When they were back in the driveway to Bryce's house Leah smoothed Bryce's hair and wiped the smudged lipstick and mascara from her face. "There. Now you just look like you're tired from having a good time. They won't suspect anything." She smiled.

Bryce took a deep breath. "Okay. Do I look drunk anymore?"

"Nah. You'll pass. Here, have a mint so you don't smell like a frat house."

Bryce snorted and took the candy gratefully. After it had dissolved on her tongue, she found herself unable to move to open the door. Leah noticed and placed a comforting hand on her shoulder.

"Are you sure you're gonna be okay?"

Bryce's eyes welled with tears again, but she couldn't cry now. She knew her mom would be waiting up for her, and that was a confrontation she just couldn't bear.

"No. I'm not. Leah, can you stay with me? I really don't want to be alone tonight."

Leah paused, her eyes wide, but said, "Yeah. Okay. Sure. Whatever you need."

"I owe you so much."

"No, you don't. I'm here for you." She waited for Bryce to regain her composure. "You ready?"

Bryce took another steadying breath and pasted a fake smile on her face. "Yeah. Let's go."

They entered the house laughing, pretending like they'd just had the best night of their lives. As she knew she would be, Bryce's mother was sitting on the couch, pink rollers in her hair that matched her worn terry cloth robe, reading her ever-present Bible.

"Hi, Mom!"

"You're home early. Is everything okay?"

"Oh yeah. I just got really tired."

"Where's Michael? I thought he was bringing you home."

Bryce faltered so Leah replied, "He wanted to hang out with his friends a little longer, so I offered to play chauffeur."

Bryce saw her mom purse her lips. She knew her mom thought it supremely ungentlemanly to not bring a date home.

"It's okay. I'd rather hang out with Leah anyway. Michael and I don't actually have much in common. I had a great time, so don't worry. Oh, and Leah's going to stay over tonight, if that's okay."

Mrs. Montgomery looked surprised. Leah had only been over to their house once before and she hadn't strung three words together. Bryce could practically read her mother's mind. Why would a mere acquaintance all of a sudden be invited over for a slumber party?

"Sure. You're welcome anytime, Leah."

"Thanks, Mrs. Montgomery."

Bryce started up the stairs. "G'night, Mom."

"Night, sweetie."

Once Bryce was back in her room, the familiar surroundings enveloped her like a warm blanket. She felt safe here. Nothing soothed like the comfort of home. Of course, she still couldn't bear the thought of spending the night alone, so she gratefully looked over at Leah, who was taking in all of the medals and trophies on almost every open space in the room.

"I have some pajamas in the top drawer over there. Help yourself."

Bryce grabbed her own sleepwear and went to the bathroom to change. She began the slow and painful process of removing her prom dress and tsked when she saw a small tear in the bodice.

Oh well. I'd never put this thing on again if you paid me, she thought bitterly.

The simple act of putting on her baby blue striped pajama pants and swim team T-shirt calmed her nerves considerably, as did the routine task of washing her face and brushing her teeth.

When she was done with her nightly rituals, she opened the door to her room and startled as she saw Leah's bare back across the room. She had forgotten to knock.

"Oh! Sorry."

Leah hurriedly pulled Bryce's lifeguard shirt over her head and turned around shyly, her cheeks flushed. "No worries."

Bryce entered the room and closed the door behind her. For some reason her heart was beating fiercely in her chest. She wasn't modest after years of changing in pool locker rooms, but the image of Leah's smooth back seemed to have stubbornly imprinted itself on her brain.

Weird.

They stood looking at each other in awkward silence for what seemed like a full minute before Leah finally said, "You look really tired. Are you sure you want me to stay?"

"Yes! I mean, yes please. I'm sorry. I'm so jumpy tonight. I don't know if I'll even be able to sleep, but it will be nice knowing I'm not alone."

They both moved to the bed and got under the covers, unfamiliar butterflies fluttering in Bryce's stomach.

"'Night. Let me know if you need anything, okay?"

"I will. Good night."

Bryce's mind raced for several hours as she lay in the dark. Images of an angry Michael conflicted with remembrances of Leah's kindness and the shockingly alluring image of her near-naked form. Eventually the images of Leah won out and she relaxed into a healing sleep.

CHAPTER FIVE

Leah ended up spending all of Sunday at the Montgomery household, and by Monday, just in time to go back to school, Bryce was almost back to normal emotionally. Her new friend was a godsend, but Bryce was also fascinated by her and wanted nothing more than to spend as much time with her as possible before she left for the academy. She had never found a guy she liked and now, out of the blue, she was drawn to a girl she didn't even know that well. Maybe she was just latching on to her because of the care Leah had shown after such a shit-tastic night. Either way, she couldn't seem to get Leah out of her head.

Bryce took a deep and steadying breath, trying to work up the nerve to walk into her English class. She didn't know if she would be able to be in the same room with Michael, much less sit with her back to him, not knowing what he would do.

"Bryce."

She jumped about two feet into the air and spun around as she heard Michael's voice behind her. Losing her balance, she fell back against the lockers with a loud metallic crash that made the students filing into the classroom laugh.

"Whoa! Bryce, calm down."

"Stay away from me!" Her body shook.

Michael put up his hands and took a step back. Quietly he said, "Listen. I want to apologize for what I did the other night. I was drunk and I just lost control of myself. I said and did things that were inexcusable. When I sobered up I…I couldn't bear the thought of…" He seemed to choke up.

Bryce stayed silent, still cowering against the lockers, holding her books close to her chest as if they were impenetrable armor.

Michael sighed shakily. "Anyway. I know there's nothing I can do to make it up to you, but I don't want you to be afraid of me. I'm not that guy. And I want you to know how truly sorry I am. I bring new meaning to the term 'epic fail,' and I'll regret what I did for the rest of my life." He hung his head in what appeared to be real shame.

Bryce grappled with what to say. He still scared the hell out of her, but he seemed to be genuinely sorry for his horrendous mistake. She settled on, "Thank you. For the apology. But…I don't want to talk to you ever again."

Still looking at the ground, Michael nodded sadly.

Bryce edged away from him and entered the English classroom. She didn't sit in her normal seat in front of Michael, but instead chose an empty desk at the back of the classroom, telling Mrs. Swift that she had a nasty cold she didn't want to spread to the rest of the students. It was going to be a long day.

Bryce stopped at her house only long enough to drop off her backpack and put on her more comfortable running shorts. This didn't stop her mother from trying to start a conversation, though. Bryce walked quickly through the living room on her way to the front door.

"Hi, honey!"

"Hey."

"How was your day?"

"Fine."

Her mother patted the seat on the couch next to her. "Sit down with me for a while."

"I'm on my way to meet the girls at the park."

"I wanted to talk to you about going to church when you leave for New London."

"Mom—"

"I'm just worried about your spiritual well-being, Bryce. You need to be careful or God will start to take notice."

Bryce didn't know what to say to this. Her mother's voice had taken on a slightly threatening tone. "Um. Okay. Can we talk later? Jenn and Arati are waiting for me."

Her mother glared. Bryce could tell she wanted to force her into an unwanted conversation, but her mom nodded curtly, ending the tense silence. Bryce took the opportunity to hug her good-bye and then left to jog down to the park that was situated conveniently in the center of the neighborhood where she and her friends all lived.

The dry grass crunched as Arati walked ahead to the picnic table next to the small lifeless pond. Hanging back, Jennifer whispered in Bryce's ear. "Are you going to tell her about what happened?"

Bryce was surprised. "I assumed that you already had!"

"No way. I said I wouldn't tell anyone and I won't. But I think you should tell her, you know? She's our best friend."

Sighing, Bryce nodded, and sat down with Arati to do just that.

"He did *what*?!" Arati exclaimed from across the concrete table as Bryce recounted the terrible night.

"Yeah. But he apologized today. For what it's worth."

"Not very much, in my opinion!" Jennifer sniffed.

"Well, I'm glad he did. It doesn't change anything between us, but at least I know he regrets it and hopefully will never do it to anyone else again. Maybe another girl couldn't have fought him off like I did. But seriously, Arati, I don't want you to tell anyone else, okay?"

Arati scowled. "I won't if that's what you want, but *I* think we should get a posse together to nail his balls to the diving board."

Jennifer barked a laugh. "Sorry. Weird visual. Gross."

"So that's why you left the party early, huh?"

Bryce shrugged. "I couldn't stand to be there anymore. I felt so… dirty."

"Ya think?" Jennifer rolled her eyes. "I can't believe he turned out to be such a creeper."

Arati shook her head. "I feel so damn lame that I was just down the hall and didn't hear anything and wasn't there to help you. I'm so selfish."

Bryce threw the dead leaf she had been systematically tearing apart at her friend. "Shut up, Arati. I'm glad you had a good time. Don't you dare blame yourself for anything." She paused and started picking at chips in the table before she continued, "I'm just glad Leah happened to be there."

Arati looked at Jennifer and then back at Bryce. "Leah?"

Confused, Bryce glanced at her friends and said, "Yeah. Leah Friedman. She's the one who heard me yelling and found me on the floor. She was brilliant. She got me through the night."

Arati and Jennifer looked at each other with sly smiles.

"What? What's so funny about Leah? Seriously, guys, she stayed with me all night, and all day Sunday. She got my mind off everything and it turns out she's really, really cool. It's too bad she's always so shy around us. You guys would love her too."

Inexplicably, the grins of Arati and Jennifer had grown even wider as they heard her talk enthusiastically about her new friend.

Bryce huffed. "Okay. Out with it. What's going on?" She was starting to get irritated. They'd better not make fun of the girl who had kept her sane after the worst experience of her life.

Arati looked at Jennifer with barely contained glee. "It's just that…Jenn, you tell her."

"No way. You're the one who's good with the gooey stuff."

Arati turned back to face Bryce. "Okay, Jenn and I are *pretty* sure Leah has been, like, totally in love with you since elementary school."

Bryce's stomach flip-flopped. "What, Leah's like…gay?"

Jennifer shrugged. "She's never said anything. I mean, can you imagine? In this town? This isn't exactly ground zero for tolerance. Most people aren't as open-minded and cool as us." She beamed proudly. "It's just that…well, you can tell she totally digs you."

Bryce sat in stunned silence.

Jennifer continued, "So, we just thought it was…you know… interesting that she spent the night at your house."

Bryce could tell that there was a question hanging in the air that her friends were too polite to ask.

"She didn't…*do*…anything, if that's what you guys are wondering."

Arati looked disappointed. She loved hearing juicy gossip.

"And anyway, how in the hell do you know she has a crush on me? She's never shown it."

Jennifer smiled. "Bryce, you've never really *seen* her. She's always been 'Angela's friend.' The way she looks at you…well, I only wish that any of the guys at this school would look at me that way. That, and she never talks when you're around."

"Right. She's super shy," Bryce added.

"Yeah, she's shy, but she actually talks to other people more than you'd think. Just not while you're anywhere near her. You make her nervous."

"And she's not the only one!" Arati offered.

Jennifer turned to look at her incredulously. "Arati! Seriously? One isn't enough for her right now?"

"What? What do you mean she's not the only one?" Bryce asked, annoyance on her face. What was with the secrets being revealed today? Despite her irritation, though, she felt a kind of pleasure knowing there were people out there who were into her. She knew people thought she was pretty, but she had just never had the time to think about dating.

And she'd never thought about…girls.

After a prolonged silence Jennifer poked Arati in the side. "Well, you're the one who opened your big mouth, so go ahead."

Arati's made an "oops" face and said, "Stewart."

"The sweaty guy from Biology? Ew. I mean, no offense. I'm sure he's a lovely person on the inside, but…ew."

"Antonio."

"I don't believe this. You guys are seeing things."

"Dani."

"Danny who?" Bryce asked.

"Daniela Cordova. Duh."

Bryce's jaw dropped. "No way, guys. That one you got wrong. Dani is just a friend."

Jennifer shook her head. "We see the same look on Daniela's face that we see on Leah's. That girl totally idolizes you."

Bryce's head was reeling. Daniela was so young. But even as she had that thought, she realized Dani really wasn't the same little girl she had always known. And three years wasn't a big deal when you reached high school and beyond. But still. She was like a little sister. Wasn't she?

"Okay. I'm freaking out a little. What is this? *Bryce's Sapphic Adventure Hour*? Why didn't you guys tell me this before?" Her ears were hot, but she couldn't tell if it was from anger or something else.

Her friends looked at each other and shrugged as one. Jennifer spoke. "We didn't think it was a big deal. We just thought it was cute. Why are you so upset?"

"I'm not…upset. I just…don't you think it's weird that *two girls* would have crushes on me? You just don't see that out here."

Arati beamed. "I don't think it's weird at all. You *are* a hottie, Bryce. I think half of the school probably has a crush on you. Guys *and* girls. Hell, even I wouldn't kick you out of bed."

Bryce rolled her eyes. "Come on, Arati. I've only ever had one boyfriend, and that was Chris Yamada in junior high. We held hands in a movie *once* and that's about it. He wasn't even a boyfriend really. No one, except…except you know…the 'M' guy, has even asked me out since then."

Jennifer looked at her sagely and said, "Boys are intimidated by you. You're pretty badass, you know. And the girls…well, I just assume they don't even realize that they have a crush on you yet. It takes time for certain people to figure out their own sexuality." Bryce could have sworn that Jennifer gave her a knowing look before continuing, "And even if they already have, they probably don't feel comfortable expressing it in a place like Saltus."

"Well thank you, Dr. Fowler. Damn, you're going to be a shrink, aren't you?"

Jennifer smiled. "Zoologist, actually. But it doesn't take a shrink to see you're so into your grades, your swimming, and pretty much anything else that piques your interest that you wouldn't know if someone was madly in love with you unless they dropped down on one knee and proposed on the spot. Even then you'd think they were just asking you to go to a football game or something."

Bryce didn't know what to make of this observation, so she just stayed silent, trying to filter and process all of this new information. As far as Daniela was concerned, Bryce thought it was sweet. She knew Daniela had always liked her a lot and she thought it was cool that she could be a role model for her. But Leah…she had slept in the same bed with a girl who had a crush on her. That felt a little odd. But Leah hadn't tried anything…weird. She had just been there for her when she needed it the most. She knew she couldn't let something like this get in the way of their friendship.

A flash of Leah's bare back flashed into her memory. Shivering slightly, she shook her head to clear it of the image. Why in the hell would that come up now? And what was up with the butterflies trying to make a daring escape from the confines of her stomach?

She realized Arati and Jennifer were staring at her, trying to gauge her reaction, and she wanted to make damn sure they couldn't see the confusion that was bubbling up from the inner depths of her psyche.

"Well, I guess it's good to know that *nice* people like me too and not just overly horny assholes." She tried to smile as if the news she had just heard hadn't rocked her, but she knew it must look forced.

CHAPTER SIX

Forty, forty-one, forty-two, forty-three... Bryce counted in her head. Her arms were shaking as she repeatedly lowered herself to the floor in full-on push-up mode. A bead of sweat dripped from the tip of her nose onto the tan carpet below.

50! She collapsed onto the ground, breathing heavily. She had been working out in her room for a full hour, trying to exercise through all of the crazy thoughts going through her head. It had been two days since she had learned about Leah's crush, and she couldn't think clearly. Every time she saw her in the hallway at school she would smile awkwardly, her heart would skip a beat, and she would purposefully take whichever hallway got her away from Leah as fast as possible.

She found herself repeatedly thinking about the kindness Leah had shown when she had been feeling so low, and the thought of being physically close to her was disconcertingly appealing for some reason.

What was going on?

Exhausted, she finally got to her feet and flopped heavily onto her bed where she meditated in silence for a while, just trying to piece her thoughts together. She didn't know how long she was there, but she jumped as her ringtone blared from her iPhone. She fumbled for the device on her bedside table. She didn't recognize the number.

"Hello?"

"Bryce? Hey, it's Leah."

"Oh! Hey!" Her voice cracked as it hit about an octave higher than normal. She cleared her throat and overcompensated by speaking in a low, breathy whisper. "I mean…hey." Bryce smacked her forehead in embarrassment at her extreme uncoolness. She heard what might have been a chuckle on the other side of the line.

"Hey. I'm in your neighborhood and just wanted to see if you were okay and maybe wanted to hang out. Go to a movie or something."

Bryce was silent for a beat too long.

"Or…or not. Just, you know, I was in the neighborhood and bored so…yeah, never mind. I'm sure you're busy. Don't worry about it."

"No!" Bryce said quickly. "I mean, yes, let's do something. Are you nearby?"

Bryce swore she could actually hear Leah smile.

"Yeah, I'm just around the corner. I'll come over. See ya in a bit."

"Yeah, see ya."

Bryce hung up and sat stunned by her emotions. When Leah's voice had drifted out of her phone, adrenaline had shot through her body with a mixture of excitement and anxiety. If she didn't know any better she'd think she was crushing on Leah too.

Faster than she had been expecting it, the doorbell rang downstairs and the sound of her mother welcoming Leah into the house forced Bryce into action. She looked at her reflection in the mirror and jumped to her feet in a panic. She was sweaty, her hair was a tangled mess, and her tight tank top was damp from her workout.

She tried to put her hair into a more presentable ponytail and was able to shove her free weights into the corner, but before she could put on a clean shirt there was a knock at her door.

Shit.

She opened the door slowly, peeking through the crack.

"Hey, Leah."

"Hey."

She realized she was being rude as she stared in silence from inside her room, so she sighed and opened the door all of the way.

"Come on in. Sorry about the mess. I was working out."

Bryce couldn't help but notice the up-and-down look Leah gave her. She swore she saw appreciation in her eyes. Bryce's embarrassment quickly shifted to confidence and she was suddenly more proud of her body than usual. An overwhelming urge to strut around the room and show off fell upon her.

That had never happened before.

Instead, Bryce said, "Sorry about this." She gestured to her clothes. "Let me go take a shower and I'll be ready to go."

Leah's eyes were wide and she swallowed hard, but she tried unsuccessfully to look relaxed and just nodded. Maybe there was something to what Jennifer and Arati had said after all. Now that she was looking for it, Leah did act differently around her. Bryce's heart leaped. She pulled a clean T-shirt out of the closet and turned to Leah, holding it up to model it off as she did. The shirt had an image of an old-fashioned microphone on it and Bryce asked, "How's this? I got it at that music festival last year." She held it close to her chest so that every curve could be seen.

"Fine. It's cool," Leah answered quietly.

Okay. That was it. She was *flirting*! With Leah. She had never overtly flirted in her life, and here she was, flirting with a *girl*! What in the world had come over her?

"Shower! Showering now. Be right back," she said as she hurried out of the room.

"So. Now that I don't smell like a dirty locker room, what do you want to do? Movie, right?"

"Whatever you want. I was just completely bored at home. Angela spends all of her time with that douche bag Jeff ever since they hooked up at Jennifer's party. Ugh."

"Well, I'm trying to save money, but I do have a decent selection of movies. If you don't mind hanging out here again." Bryce gestured to her far wall where a bookshelf stacked full of DVDs stood.

Leah smiled. "Why do I have an online movie account when I could just come over here all of the time?"

There was a soft knock on the door. Bryce yelled out, "Yeah?"

Her mother's voice could be heard muffled from the other side. "Do you girls need anything? Snacks or something?"

Bryce looked at Leah, who shook her head and said, "No, I'm good. Already ate."

"No thanks, Mom."

"Do you want to join your dad and me for a movie in the living room?"

"No, we're okay."

"Are you sure? We're watching *The Robe* for our Bible study."

Bryce grimaced and looked at Leah, her cheeks flushing. Leah only smiled kindly.

"No, Mom. We're good. Thanks. Go away now, please."

"Okay, just let me know if you need anything."

"Bye!"

They heard her mother walk back down the stairs and Bryce shook her head in embarrassment.

"Sorry about her."

"Why? She seems nice."

"Yeah. She's nice. As long as you think the way she does. So anyway, what do you want to watch?"

They settled on *Bringing Up Baby*, a 1930s-era romantic comedy from Bryce's collection of classics, and got comfortable on the bed, her portable computer set up between them to show the film.

Bryce found she was having trouble concentrating on Katharine Hepburn's witty banter because she could practically feel Leah's warmth so close to her. By the time the movie ended she discovered that she had unconsciously shifted to sit so close to Leah that their legs were almost touching.

"So. Did you like it?" Bryce asked nervously. For some reason she was desperate for Leah's approval of the choice.

"Totally." She smiled sincerely. "Anything with Katharine Hepburn and a big cat is a winner in my book."

Bryce closed her computer and set it on her bedside table. As she turned back to Leah, she settled into a cross-legged position.

"Do you need to go home now?"

Leah's mouth twitched. "Not really. I already wrote my last paper for Economics yesterday. I'm pretty much done for the year. Ready to graduate and get out of the house, you know?"

Bryce sighed. "I do indeed. I'm so damn excited to get to the academy that I could just spit."

A melodic laugh escaped from Leah's lips. "Elegant, Bryce."

She shrugged. "That's me. Perfect pretty princess. Born and raised."

Leah laughed again and Bryce's mouth went dry as she watched her run her slender fingers through her dark curls. She tried to speak, but instead only croaked, "Where?"

"What?"

Bryce tried to cough demurely before saying, "Sorry. Where are you going to college?"

"Oh." Leah smiled. "SSU. I mean, I got a full ride for my GPA, so that's hard to turn down, you know? My parents have promised not to pry once I start living in the dorm, but man, do I wish I was going to be in a different city."

"You know what?" Bryce tilted her head to the side.

"What?"

"I'm really going to miss you."

Bryce saw Leah's chest rise beneath her thin T-shirt as she started breathing faster.

"I mean, don't get me wrong, but I'm bummed that you've always been so shy."

Leah paused. "I'm going to miss you too. I've always…liked you."

Bryce tentatively reached out and took Leah's hand. Leah was trembling.

"Promise you won't forget me?"

"I could never forget you, Bryce."

They stared into each other's eyes for a while before Bryce finally asked, "What are you thinking?"

Leah took a deep breath. "I don't think you want to know."

"Come on, Leah, we're friends now. You can tell me anything."

"I'm thinking…I'm thinking that I really want to kiss you."

That was all Bryce needed to hear. She leaned forward and placed the softest of kisses on the corner of Leah's mouth.

When her lips felt the impossible softness of Leah's, her body shuddered and she found that she couldn't pull away. Leah's mouth formed a surprised "Oh!" but even as she gasped she moved her head to kiss Bryce back.

They wrapped their arms around each other and tentatively explored each other's lips. This was what Bryce had been hoping to feel with Michael before he had so blatantly overstepped her boundaries. And she was having these feelings for another girl! This wasn't the rough, forceful kiss of Michael; it was a gentle, loving caress that was more amazing than she could have ever imagined. It felt…right.

So slowly that the movement was almost imperceptible, Leah leaned into the contact and kissed Bryce with even more hunger and desperation. Heat coursed through Bryce's stomach and she leaned forward to press herself against Leah until they were lying together on the bed.

With gut-wrenching suddenness, the image of Michael forcing himself on her popped into Bryce's head and she jerked away from the contact. She rolled off Leah and sat hugging her knees on the far side of the bed. Leah immediately jumped up from the bed and ran to stand in front of Bryce, putting her hands on Bryce's shaking shoulders.

"Bryce? Are you okay?" Her voice was unsteady.

Bryce's eyes were full of tears, but even so, when she looked into

Leah's face she saw worry, hurt, and confusion. "I'm so sorry, Leah. I didn't mean to…"

"No, Bryce, I'm sorry. I shouldn't have said that. I didn't mean to freak you out. I won't tell anyone about this, I swear. I'm so so sorry." Desperation poured from her like a heavy fog.

Bryce shook her head, looking down again. "No, it's not that. I just…I thought about Michael…" Her voice trailed off.

"Oh my God, Bryce. Damn it, I'm sorry." Leah pulled her into a careful and hesitant hug. "Let me know if there is anything I can do. I feel so stupid. You just got assaulted and here I am—"

"No! Leah, this is *not* your fault. You were…you *are* amazing." She pulled away from the hug and looked up into her friend's green eyes. "You're…you're beautiful, Leah."

Leah's face broke into a wide smile and she gently stroked Bryce's cheek. "*You're* beautiful and amazing, Bryce." She sat down gently on the bed beside her. "You know, I've had a crush on you since junior high. You have no idea how you make me feel."

Bryce sniffed and laughed. "I'm starting to figure it out."

"What do you need me to do?"

"Can you…just hold me for a little while?"

Leah nodded as if that were the easiest request in the world.

CHAPTER SEVEN

Bryce trudged downstairs the next morning, only minutes before she had to leave for school. Leah hadn't spent the night, but Bryce had been unable to sleep because of the hurricane of emotions swirling around in her head. She hadn't been able to make herself get up for her run since "the incident," and when she saw her parents downstairs waiting for her, she felt a cold ball of ice form in her stomach.

"Morning," she said, trying to act nonchalant as she reached for a cereal bar from the cupboard.

"Bryce, sit down, please." Her father was sitting in his normal chair at the kitchen table, but this time he didn't have his usual cup of coffee or newspaper nearby. His hands were clasped in front of him and he sat up straight with a look on his face like that of a CEO about to discipline an underling.

"I have to leave for school in like three minutes, guys."

"Bryce…sit down."

She did as she was told.

Her mom spoke. "Honey, what's going on with you?"

"What do you mean?"

"You've been acting strangely ever since the prom."

Bryce's mind raced. Yes, she had been on an emotional roller coaster for the last five days, but she couldn't for the life of her remember acting differently around her parents. She honestly didn't think that they could be that observant anyway.

"What do you mean?"

"You haven't gotten up for your run in almost a week, and you haven't said two words together to us until this morning. Arati and Jennifer haven't been over in a while either. Did you guys get into a fight? Does it have something to do with that Leah girl? We're worried about you."

"I'm fine, Mom and no, I'm not fighting with anyone. I'm just ready to graduate and get to the academy."

Bryce's parents stared at her without speaking. She shifted uncomfortably in her chair. Finally, her mother said, "We're not blind, Bryce. Something is going on and we want you to know that you can talk to us. We're praying for you and you know that God has a plan for your life. Let Him in to your heart and you'll feel so much better."

Bryce suppressed a shudder. She hated it when her parents did this. She knew that they cared and were only saying these things because they loved her, but she still couldn't stomach it.

"Okay, Mom. Can I go now? I'm going to be late for school."

"Bryce?" Her father pinned her to the chair with his stern gaze. "We mean it. If there's something bothering you, we want to know about it."

"I'm fine, Dad. Seriously. I just have a bad case of senioritis. Is it not okay for me to take a break from my routine for a while?" She shrugged. "So can I go now? Please?"

"Go on, sweetie." Her mom stood up with open arms, inviting Bryce into the embrace. "Remember, always trust in God and you'll have nothing to fear."

"'Kay. Bye, guys. Love you."

Bryce pulled away from her mother and practically ran out the back door. As she drove her grandmother's hand-me-down Cadillac to school, she replayed her every action from the past week, trying to determine how her parents had figured out that something was going on in her life. Sure, she hadn't gone out for her runs, but so what? And it wasn't like she had long, sit-down chats with them every night usually, so what was the deal?

Her grip on the steering wheel tightened. She was dealing with her own crap right now. She did *not* need her parents meddling in her life too. She sighed heavily and tried to relax before she ran the car into a telephone pole and added even more complications to an already strange sequence of events.

"Hey, Bryce." A small, shy voice that she knew all too well roused her from her musings as she walked from her car to the school doors.

Bryce looked to the girl now walking beside her. "Hey, Dani. What's up?" Her cheeks grew warm. This was the first time the two had spoken since Jennifer and Arati revealed that Daniela might have a crush on her too. Bryce realized she was staring at the soft skin of Daniela's cheek. "Shit."

"What?" Daniela replied, confused.

Bryce sighed. "Nothing. I'm just realizing…never mind. It's nothing."

"Oh. Okay." Daniela looked anxious and shifted uncomfortably. "Well anyway. I just wanted to say hi. I haven't seen you much since Saturday at the swim meet. Will you be back to work at the pool this weekend?" She smiled hopefully. "That guy you had sub for your swimming class is kind of an idiot."

"Yeah, definitely. They just gave me the weekend off for the meet and the prom." She shivered unconsciously every time she thought about that night. "And Dennis isn't *that* bad. He's just your normal, everyday high school stoner."

"Yeah, and he's not you."

Bryce stopped mid-stride before walking up the stairs toward her English classroom.

Daniela took a few more steps and then stopped and turned around, flushed. "I mean you're a much better teacher. He just had us kicking on the side of the pool for an hour. We're way beyond that." She hesitated before saying, "Anyway, gotta go. Bye!" She hurried off in the opposite direction, shaking her head. Bryce thought she heard her mumble, "Stupid, stupid, stupid…" as she walked away.

Bryce felt the breeze from behind before her two friends cornered her at her locker before lunch. "Geez, guys. Were you actually running?"

Jennifer and Arati stood staring at her, hands on their hips. They looked like twins despite the obvious difference in their ancestry. "We just heard Leah talking with Angela."

Bryce felt faint. What had Leah let slip? "Yeah, so? People are known to talk with their friends on occasion." She knew she was being overly defensive and that pointed out guilt more than anything.

"Okay, Miss Hides Things from Her Best Friends in the World Even Though They Tell Her Every Little Detail of Their Own Boring Lives. Talk." Arati was fighting the urge to smile.

"What do you mean? What did Leah say?"

Jennifer took the reins. "She was just gushing about how much fun she has had hanging out with you, how you two seem to be getting a lot closer, and how she was looking forward to the next time you ask her over."

Bryce let out the breath she had been holding. "Is that all? What's the big deal?"

Arati answered, "Listen, Bryce. We're not stupid. We tell you that she has a crush on you and now you're inviting her over…alone?" She paused for effect. "You like her."

"Yeah, of course I like her. She's really nice."

"Don't act dumb, Bryce Lee Montgomery. We've noticed you acting differently."

Crap.

"I'm so not talking to you guys about this in the hallway of Saltus frickin' High School. Come on, let's go to lunch."

Arati and Jennifer shared a victorious look and then nodded in unison.

They sat down to eat at the taco fast food restaurant a block from the school and Bryce stayed silent, focusing on her bean burrito as if it was an incredibly complicated work of art. She couldn't get away with it.

"Bryce. Talk." Arati had finished her quesadilla in record time, in what Bryce assumed was full preparation for a lengthy discussion.

Bryce slowly swallowed her bite and then let out a sigh before saying quickly, "Okay. So, yeah. You guys told me that Leah has a crush on me. For some reason I couldn't stop thinking about it and… well, I think I might like her too. There. Happy?"

Bryce jumped as Jennifer and Arati squealed as one. That wasn't the reaction she'd been expecting. Of course, she hadn't known what to expect.

"Come on, guys. It's not that big a deal. I'm not saying I'm… gay…or anything."

Jennifer tsked. "Labels are limiting—"

"Have you told her you have a crush on her too?" Arati interrupted, clearly excited by the news.

"Well, not in those words, but…" Bryce felt her face slowly heating. The blush didn't go unnoticed by Arati, who lived to revel in the affairs of others.

"Oh my God, Bryce. Give us *all* the details. What did you guys do?"

Jennifer elbowed Arati in the ribs. "Arati! Calm down. This is obviously freaky for her. Stop being so nosy!"

Bryce smiled sheepishly. "No, it's okay. If I can't tell you guys, who can I tell?" She took a calming breath. "We…made out a little."

Yet another squeal from Arati.

"*But* it didn't turn out so well."

Arati's squeal cut off with comical suddenness. Bryce could practically hear the expected scratch from the record needle.

Jennifer looked concerned. "Why? What happened?"

"I thought about…him."

The faces of her friends paled as one. Bryce lowered her head.

"Oh, Bryce, I'm so sorry." Jennifer reached out and laid her hand on Bryce's clenched fist.

Bryce's breathing was ragged, but she continued. "So anyway. I don't know if this is going to be a problem or not. I mean, they're cousins. She does look a lot like him, now that I think about it. I don't think I have the time to work through it, either. I'll be leaving for Connecticut so soon…"

Jennifer let go of Bryce's hand and sat back in her chair with a sigh. "You don't have to figure out anything right now. This is a new experience for you, and you have the rest of your life to sort it out. If you want my advice, which I know you do because I'm always right, just let things happen. Don't force yourself to do anything and don't freak out if you get confused. This is totally normal after what you've been through. And, you know, maybe you should talk to your mom."

"Oh, *hells* no! What do you want me to say? 'Hey, Mom. I was almost date-raped at prom and now I'm making out with the dude's cousin and, gosh darn it, I think I might be a lesbian!' Yeah. That'd go over really well. She's not the most liberal person, you know. She'd probably call for an exorcism."

"But you're not Catholic."

The very Jennifer-like statement was so matter-of-fact that Bryce had to laugh. "Trust me. She wouldn't care. But anyway, lunch break is almost over. Let's get back, but *please* don't tell anyone about this, okay, guys?"

"Bryce, you know us better than that." Arati got up from the booth and the others followed. "We're just happy that you're finally interested in something other than school and your gorgeous physique, aren't we, Jenn?"

"Absolutely. We were starting to think that you were going

to become a Coast Guard nun or something." Bryce looked at her incredulously. "Oh, come on. You *are* pretty one-track-minded. It's about time you got to hook up with someone and feel raging hormones like us lowly humans."

Bryce turned suddenly and pulled both of her friends into a hug. "I have no idea what I'm going to do without you both while I'm at the academy."

The next three weeks passed in a blur. Bryce had started running again, she did copious amounts of homework, and almost every day after school she spent a few hours with Leah at one of their houses. Despite what Arati insinuated daily, they spent most of their time together studying for finals, listening to music, or watching funny cat videos on YouTube. Her friends didn't really need to know about the make-out sessions, did they?

Her every thought was of Leah. Her every waking moment was spent thinking about her, wishing she was kissing her, dreaming about what they would do together when they finished college. This was what always stopped the blissful thoughts cold. After college? What about during college? Bryce was a realist, and she just couldn't see how their new relationship could survive such a long distance. Maybe it wasn't meant to. Maybe this was just the universe's way of setting Bryce on her proper path. Maybe it was just a brief moment of pure joy that would form the basis of her future relationships.

Her logic was failing her for the first time in her life. Never had her emotions dominated her so completely. It scared and thrilled her at the same time. Her reason warned her against getting too attached. Her heart stubbornly ignored it. This was her time. She'd enjoy it for as long as she could.

"I can't believe it all ends tomorrow," Leah said wistfully as she flopped down onto the bed after hitting *play* on her iPod. A quiet and baleful male voice accompanied by an acoustic guitar soon drifted dreamily from the speakers.

"It's not ending. It's beginning," Bryce said as she rolled onto her side and draped her leg over Leah's.

"It's weird to think about, though. All we've ever known is parents, school, home."

"I know what you mean. But graduation is just the start of the rest of our lives. And it won't be so different really. We'll obviously still have school, at least for a while, and our parents and home aren't going anywhere. You especially. You could see them every day if you want. I'll be all the way on the East Coast."

Leah laughed. "Don't you dare say I'll see my parents every day. I love 'em to death, but I so don't want them anywhere near my college years. It's going to be majorly sucktastic to still be in the same city. What if their friends at SSU see me doing…something bad?"

"Something bad? Perfectly behaved little angel Leah? Right," Bryce teased.

Leah punished her for it with a light swat on her backside. "Hey. I plan on making the most out of my time at college. Nothing crazy like drugs or rampant sex orgies—"

"Damn well better not!"

"But I plan on…I don't know. Having a good time, I guess."

"Sounds like a plan. I don't know how many parties, rampant sex or otherwise, will happen at the academy. Doesn't seem like kegs, Solo cups, and late-night benders would be easy to come by when everyone lives on a military campus. I'm still excited, though. Parties aren't really my style anyway." Bryce unconsciously curled up closer to Leah's warm body.

"Well, I guess we'd better make sure you have enough fun now to last you all four years." Leah raised herself from the bed and repositioned herself directly above Bryce.

"That," Bryce said, pulling Leah down to rest on her, "is the best idea you've had all day."

CHAPTER EIGHT

Bryce threw her mortarboard into the air as the auditorium burst into applause and the orchestra played "Pomp and Circumstance." Her gold honors sash swung on her shoulders as she joyously ran around hugging all of her friends. She knew her parents were watching from the balcony, and as she thought of them, her cell phone buzzed. Sure enough, her dad came up on the screen as the caller. She answered, having to yell over the crowd. "Dad, meet me outside by the car…No, by the car…I can't hear you. I'll be out in a little bit."

As she tucked the phone back under her robe she was nearly knocked over as two pairs of arms wrapped around her from behind.

"We did it! We're outta here!" Arati yelled gleefully as she bounced up and down, still holding on to Bryce and Jennifer.

Bryce just laughed and reveled in the excitement of the moment. The fear of change and the sadness at the separation from her friends lingered in the back of her mind, but she was determined to ignore it.

Her friends finally let her go and pulled her toward the exit. Before they could get through the crowd of people and around the discarded caps that littered the floor, Bryce was stopped by a tap on her shoulder. She turned around to see Leah beaming at her.

"Hey there." Bryce smiled back.

Arati and Jennifer were pulled to a stop when Bryce turned around, and now she could hear them moving away politely, giving her a chance to talk to Leah alone.

"Congratulations!"

"You too!"

"Your salutatorian speech was amazing!"

Bryce grimaced. "I thought I was going to pass out!"

"Well, nobody could tell." Leah leaned forward and whispered in her ear, "Yours was way better than Jonathan's valedictorian speech. His was so damn boring. 'Your future is a winding road. Don't forget to take the scenic route every once in a while. Life doesn't always have a working GPS.' Blah blah blah. Yours actually excited me."

"Oh, I excited you, hmm?" Bryce smirked and Leah's cheeks reddened.

"Can you come with me for a sec?"

Bryce glanced back at her two friends and held up a finger to get them to wait for her. They nodded and started taking pictures with some of their fellow graduates.

Leah took hold of Bryce's hand and led her through the blinding pops of hundreds of camera flashes, out of the auditorium through a side door, and into a deserted hallway. The noise from the main hall was instantly muffled as the door closed behind her. Bryce leaned back against the wall, thankful for the relative quiet.

"Wow. That was intense," Bryce said as she relaxed.

"I know what you mean."

"So. What's up?"

Leah paused. "Are you going to the senior lock-in at the SSU rec center tonight?"

Bryce had been avoiding the subject with her friends. "Um, no. No, I don't think so. I'm all partied out this year, if you know what I mean."

Leah nodded understandingly.

"Why, did you have something else in mind?"

Instead of answering Leah leaned in slowly and kissed Bryce softly on the lips. Her heart immediately felt like it was going to jump through her chest. Despite having spent the last three weeks of school in Leah's company, every time they kissed it felt like the first time. Yes, this was indeed what it was *supposed* to feel like.

Bryce reacted by pulling Leah into a fierce hug and kissing her back with all of the energy she could muster. The adrenaline of the afternoon only fueled her reaction. She didn't feel the need to pull away from Leah anymore. Not since that first time. A thought of Michael appeared in the back of her mind, but then floated away as if it had never existed.

Eventually they relaxed and drifted apart.

"Wow," Bryce said succinctly.

"Yeah."

"What was that for?"

"Why not?" Leah smiled slyly.

"Good point. So. Do you want to hang out at my house instead?"

"That sounds perfect." Leah smiled with what appeared to be relief. Bryce guessed that Leah's shyness made hanging out at crowded parties low on her list of things that she wanted to do.

"Perfect. Call me in a few hours. My parents are taking me to an early dinner at Madame Josephine's to celebrate. Their béarnaise sauce is to *die* for."

"Will do. My parents are taking me out too, so I'll call you when we get back."

Bryce squeezed Leah's hand and turned to go, but stopped suddenly to turn around and place a last quick kiss on her cheek. Leah beamed at her as she walked away.

Bryce paced back and forth in her room, picking up her phone every few minutes to make sure the battery hadn't died. She had eaten a delicious dinner with her parents, but all she could think about now was having Leah back in her arms. Warning thoughts continued to sound in her head, but she tried her best to fight them. Still, what was she getting herself into? She would be leaving for school in only one month. Did she really need to have a long-distance relationship to worry about? And what about the whole lesbian thing? *That* had been a shock to her, but in normal Bryce fashion, she had taken it in stride and would own it as best as she could. She wasn't one to shy away from a challenge and was comfortable enough with herself to accept any new self-discoveries with an enviable matter-of-fact confidence.

She jumped as her familiar ring tone played at full volume, and she almost tripped over her own feet rushing to pick it up.

"Leah!" She heard a laugh on the other end.

"Hi, Bryce. Are you done with dinner? My parents and I just got back from eating at the country club."

"Yes, I'm home. Come on over!"

"Cool. Be there in ten."

Bryce pressed the End Call button and sat down on her bed. She put her hands over her face, trying to force herself to keep it together. Years of studious learning, practicing, working out, and a single-minded will to succeed had caused this sudden flood of emotion to take hold stronger than she suspected was normal for a young woman her age.

"Don't let this get away from you, Bryce," she said out loud to herself. "You don't want to get hurt right before you finally get out of here."

Still, the urge to see Leah again and bury herself in her embrace overrode all rational thought.

Before she knew the minutes had passed, Leah was knocking on her door. Bryce sprang to her feet to let her in. She had changed from her dress and graduation gown into her favorite pair of ripped jeans and a faded concert T-shirt. When she opened the door she saw that Leah had also gotten more comfortable and was wearing soft cotton cargo shorts and a Saltus High Orchestra shirt. She had forgotten that Leah was a viola player. She would have to get her to play something for her some time.

"Hey." Bryce couldn't help the smile that formed.

"Hey."

"Come on in. I picked out some movies if you want to watch something. I have something from almost every genre because I didn't know what you'd be in the mood for." Bryce led Leah to the stack of DVDs on her dresser as she rattled off the names. "I picked out *Poltergeist* for horror, *My Fair Lady* for musical, *Romy and Michele's High School Reunion* for comedy, *The Cutting Edge* for romance," Bryce blushed as she said it, "*Queen Christina* for classic, *The Fifth Element* for sci-fi, *Heavenly Creatures* for just plain weird, *Glory* for war—"

"Bryce," Leah interrupted.

"Yeah?"

"While I totally appreciate all of the thought that went into these excellent selections, I kind of just want to sit and…talk for a while." She smiled hopefully.

"Oh! Yeah. Sorry. Here, have a seat." Bryce moved to her bed and sat with her back against her headboard. Leah sat at the foot of the bed facing her.

There was a brief lull, but finally Leah said, "So. We're high school graduates now."

"Yeah. It's kind of a relief, but at the same time, I'm scared to death."

"I bet it's even harder for you. Going off to the East Coast, joining the military, leaving your friends and family."

Bryce rolled her eyes. "Don't remind me. I've worked so hard to get to where I am and now I'm terrified. I mean, I'm excited too, but just…you know. It's scary."

Leah paused again, biting her lip like she was afraid to say something.

"What's wrong?"

Leah glanced at Bryce and then stared down at her clasped hands. "I just can't help but think about how bad this timing is."

"What timing?"

Leah moved her hand in a sweep between herself and Bryce. "This timing. Us. I mean, I don't want to put a label on this, but are we dating? Are we girlfriends? Is this something we need to think about with you going away?"

Bryce thought about it for a few minutes before saying, "You know? This is just as new for me as it is for you and I'm worried about the same things, but I'm thinking we just take it one day at a time and see what happens. All I know right now is I can't stop thinking about you. You've made me feel things that I've only seen in movies and read in books. That's cheesy, but it's true. And the weird thing is it has all happened so fast!"

Leah laughed. "It may be fast for you, but I've been wanting to kiss you since junior high. Never in a million years did I think it would actually happen."

Bryce's eyes widened and she shook her head in disbelief. "I can't believe I never knew that."

Leah raised her eyebrows. "Like I would have ever said anything!"

Bryce took her hand, "Hey, I kind of wish you had. We'd have had more time."

"I don't want to think about time."

"How about we just agree to enjoy what we have right now? Whatever happens, happens. Deal?"

"Deal."

Leah crawled forward and straddled Bryce's legs. Bryce brushed Leah's brunette curls from her face and pulled her forward, running her hands down her back and kissing her gently.

The next morning Bryce woke up to the sound of her phone ringing. It was Jennifer.

"Hello?" Bryce mumbled.

"*There* you are."

"Yeah, here I am. What's going on?"

"Nothing. Arati and I just assumed you were going to the lock-in with us last night. We didn't see you there and when we called you didn't answer."

Bryce remembered turning her cell phone off as soon as Leah had agreed to sleep over. Then Bryce remembered that Leah had slept over! She turned her head to see Leah asleep on top of the covers, a Coast Guard blanket draped over her. Curls lay gently across her cheek and her mouth was slightly parted as soft snores escaped her lips. Bryce smiled.

In a whisper she said, "Oh. Yeah. I didn't feel like going. Being with that many people isn't my thing right now."

"Hmm. Makes sense. I just wish you would've told us. We were worried about you. Angela couldn't find Leah either." Jennifer paused. "Wait. Oh my God. Bryce!"

Bryce tried to ignore the warmth in her cheeks. "What?"

"Is Leah with you?"

Bryce shrugged even though Jennifer couldn't see it. "Yeah. So?"

"Oh my God. Did you guys…No, sorry. None of my business. I'm not Arati."

"*No!* No, we just hung out. I'm not ready for…*that*…yet. I mean damn, I just figured out that I like chicks. Give a girl time, yo!"

Jennifer laughed. Bryce could tell she was pleased that she had finally found someone she was really interested in and was comfortable talking with her about it.

"Okay. But you have to let us know *everything*. Arati is going to have a damn conniption fit when she finds out! She'll be so happy for you too!"

"Well, what are you guys doing today? Why don't we all go have lunch in the park? I'll bring my football."

"Bryce, as per usual, you're the only one who wants to throw that stupid football around. But lunch sounds great. Twelve o'clock?"

"Sounds good. Can you bring the sandwiches?"

"Yep. Okay, see you soon. I'll call Arati."

Bryce hung up the phone and gently patted Leah's shoulder. "Hey. Leah. Time to wake up. It's almost noon already!"

Leah shifted and slowly blinked her eyes open. "Oh. Hey." She smiled sleepily. "Thanks for letting me crash here. I was too tired to drive home."

"Making out until three a.m. will do that, I guess."

Leah's smile widened even more. "Yeah, I guess it will. I'm sure as hell not complaining, though."

"Me either. But come on, let's get ready. We're going to meet Jenn and Arati in the park for lunch. If you want to, I mean."

"Absolutely. I like them. They've always been really nice to me."

Leah and Bryce entered the kitchen and found a pair of blue eyes staring at them suspiciously.

"Morning, Mom."

"Don't you mean 'afternoon'?"

Bryce looked at her watch.

"Nope. Have ten more minutes until afternoon."

Her mother turned her attention to Leah, who stood slightly behind Bryce. "How are you today, Leah?" Despite the greeting, her eyes remained steely.

"I'm well, ma'am. Thank you for letting me stay over last night. My parents say thank you too. They don't like me to be on the roads too late."

Her mother nodded curtly. Bryce felt a chill in the air that had nothing to do with the air-conditioning vent directly above her. Why was her mom acting so strangely? She was normally extremely welcoming to all of her friends, and right now she was on the verge of being downright rude. Out of the corner of her eye she saw Leah shrink to hide behind her even more.

"Are you okay, Mom?" Bryce asked tentatively.

"Yes. Of course I am. But I do need to talk to you about something. Leah, may I borrow my daughter for a few minutes?"

Leah stuttered, "Y-yes, of course."

Bryce swallowed and followed her mother to her father's office. The door was closed firmly behind them.

"What's up? You're acting all weird."

"Your father and I are still worried about you. You haven't been yourself lately. We're wondering if…" She paused, trying to find the right words. "We're wondering if that Leah girl has something to do with it. We think she might be a bad influence on you."

Bryce's jaw dropped. "Uh, no, Mom. Leah is amazing and one of the nicest people I've ever met. And why would you single her out? Arati does way more crazy things than Leah or any of my other friends combined, and you love her."

"Yes, but Arati hasn't been joined at the hip with you…alone…in your room…since you met her."

"Look, Mom. Leah is not a bad influence. It's just that I'm about to leave for the academy and I don't have a whole lot of time to spend with a new friend, you know? I'm trying to make it count." What Bryce said was true, of course, but she knew her mother would see past the innocent face she was desperately trying to show. She could already feel the heat starting to scorch her ears, a sure sign that she was either lying or leaving out important information.

It's a damn good thing I don't play poker, Bryce thought wryly as she held her breath, wondering what her mother would say next.

"Bryce…just…be careful. The devil has many disguises, and some of them seem like good things on the surface. He waits for you to get comfortable with his lies and then he has you. Just like that." She snapped her fingers.

"Are you seriously saying Leah is the devil? Really?" Her face fell in disbelief. "That is so incredibly insulting and backward."

Her mother shook her head. "No, I'm not saying that. Leah seems like a good person, but even good people can be led down the wrong path and can take others with them. I mean, look at it from my perspective. She shows up out of the blue and now you're with her all the time. You're acting strangely, you're secretive, you've left poor Dani to help out at the SCSW charity events alone. Her mother says she's been really depressed for the past month. I think she misses you. It just seems like this Leah girl is…leading you astray. It might be best if you don't see her anymore."

Bryce's brow furrowed in anger. "Mom, I'm going to go now before you…throw holy water on my friend or something. Leah and I are meeting Arati and Jenn at the park for lunch. And don't worry, if she sprouts horns and a tail, you'll be the first to know." She spat out the words.

"Bryce Lee Montgomery! Don't you take that tone with me!"

Bryce opened the door and slammed it as she headed back to the kitchen. She saw Leah sitting in one of the kitchen chairs and grabbed her arm as she made a beeline to the back door. "Come on. We don't want to be late. And we sure as hell don't want to be here anymore."

Leah followed along silently in Bryce's turbulent wake.

❖

Arati was already at their usual picnic table in the park when Bryce and Leah arrived. Jennifer joined them with the sandwiches only a few minutes later.

"Here you go. Turkey for Bryce, egg salad for Arati, PBJ for me, and Leah, I didn't know what you wanted so I made you two. Egg salad or turkey?"

Leah smiled shyly. "You didn't have to do that, but I'll take the egg salad."

"So are y'all girlfriends now or what?" Arati burst out.

Bryce almost choked on the bite of turkey sandwich she had just taken. Leah patted her on the back as she coughed and spluttered. She was grateful when Leah answered, "We're not really thinking about things like that right now. Things are too up in the air, you know?" Leah looked at Bryce for approval.

Bryce nodded. "Yeah, we're just enjoying each other while we have the time. We don't know what will happen next."

Arati smiled widely and spoke to Leah. "Well I'm just happy you got our rigid little Bryce out of the closet."

"Hey!" Bryce objected.

"Oh, come on, Bryce. Jennifer and I have been waiting for you to figure it out for years, but you're just so damn determined that you haven't been able to see past your own ambition."

Bryce, wide-eyed, stared at her.

"It's true," Jennifer said plainly. "Aw, look guys, she's blushing!"

"Am not." Bryce pouted. Her friends laughed happily.

CHAPTER NINE

The next day Bryce started the summer schedule at the pool, working Monday through Friday. Taking time off for graduation had been fun, but she was glad to finally get back in the water. Well, next to the water, watching little kids try, with admirable persistence, to avoid the splashes and dunks of their friends. She'd only had to rescue someone once since starting the job, but she couldn't count the amount of times she had blown her whistle or yelled for kids to stop being morons in one fashion or another. Still, she enjoyed it and was happy in the knowledge that she was there to protect people.

The class she had taught on the weekends had ended that morning, and she was fairly confident that none of the children—or Daniela—would harm themselves in the water.

Daniela.

Before this last morning session she hadn't spoken with her since their class two weekends ago, but every time she saw or thought about her she remembered Arati and Jennifer's revelation that Daniela might also have a crush on her. That was stupid, though. Daniela obviously had a crush on Michael. It had been so obvious at the swim meet. For some reason the thought of Daniela liking someone else caused her to prickle with jealousy.

Bryce shook her head to clear it. It seemed like she just couldn't stop thinking about girls. She must really be desperate to explore her new feelings. She thought about it logically. She really had been so focused on school and swimming (and she had never found many guys attractive—go figure) that she hadn't allowed herself the same leeway of other teenagers in the love department. Now her hormones seemed desperate to play catch-up. That, and she now knew with certainty that she was indeed gay. She wasn't one to second-guess herself for long, and the events and feelings of the last few weeks left no doubt in her mind. That fact alone didn't bother her at all, but the timing couldn't have been worse.

What am I supposed to do now that I'm leaving for school in a month? I can't start a serious relationship. It's not fair to Leah, and it's sure as hell not fair to me. I won't have time to sneeze with the workload I'm about to have.

Maybe she'll wait for me...

As soon as the thought entered her head, she knew it was absurd.

Right. Because people never find love or explore their sexuality in college. *God, this sucks.*

She supposed she'd just enjoy it while she could, making it absolutely clear there were no strings attached. And, oh, there were so many things left to enjoy.

With her thoughts wandering in an entirely inappropriate direction considering her location and duties, she saw a teenage boy slip and fall as he was running, yanking her out of her tantalizing daydream. She'd already warned him twice. She sighed as she descended her ladder, first aid kit in hand. Back to reality. Her inner musings about Leah would have to wait.

Leah elbowed Bryce as they walked slowly through the park that evening. "What's got you so quiet tonight?"

"Sorry. Just thinking."

"About what?"

"About myself. About us."

Leah was silent.

"I love spending time with you and...and the other stuff," Bryce's face flushed, but she doubted Leah could see it since the sun had almost completely set over the horizon. "But I just don't know how we can make it work once we go off to college."

Leah stopped and kicked at the dead grass before finally replying, "I've been thinking about that too. I don't want you to feel like you have any obligations to me once we're separated. I respect you too much to tie you to me...to this town...when you'll be off in the world adventuring."

"Hey, you'll be having a blast at SSU too, you know." Bryce turned to Leah and smiled.

"You bet your hot ass I will!"

Bryce laughed and presented her backside for Leah to smack, which she did with glee.

"We're still good with 'whatever happens, happens' right?" Bryce asked hopefully.

"Yeah. I'm good with whatever quality time I get to spend with you."

"Speaking of quality time, I think it's about time we get back to my room." Bryce didn't need to elaborate.

The next morning Bryce awoke to a soft tapping on her door. It took her a moment to realize it was her Mom trying to wake her for her morning shift at the pool. She fumbled for her iPhone on the bedside table and realized with a jolt that she had overslept. She had been so busy with Leah, she had forgotten to set her alarm. As soon as the thought formed she also noticed Leah draped over her. The covers had been kicked down to the end of the bed, and they were both dressed only in their underwear.

Fuzzy warm memories slowly crept into Bryce's sleepy mind. She and Leah had spent hours listening to each other's favorite music, wrapped tightly in each other's arms. Late into the night Bryce had been drifting slowly into sleep when she felt Leah's soft lips brush against hers just as one of her own favorite ballads started to play from the iPod speakers next to the bed. All feelings of drowsiness had fled in a rush of eager passion.

Bryce smiled dreamily at the remembrance of the blissful hours spent exploring each other's bodies and experiencing real intimacy for the first time. She reveled in the warmth of Leah's body next to hers and snuggled in closer to her sleeping form.

Then everything happened in a blur.

She heard her doorknob slowly beginning to turn and with a rush of fear she remembered she had also forgotten to lock her bedroom door. She had to get up before—

It was too late. Her mother was standing in her doorway, looking at her in abject horror. She scrambled out from under Leah's embrace and tumbled onto the floor next to her bed, her eyes never leaving her mother's.

"Mom, it's—"

"Get…*her*…out of my house, Bryce."

"But, Mom—"

"Now!"

Bryce's hand trembled as she turned around, still on her knees next to the bed, and shook Leah's shoulder to wake her.

Leah stretched and smiled as she slowly opened her eyes. Her smile immediately froze in place when she looked over Bryce's shoulder and saw what must have been a terrifying look in the older woman's eyes. Her glance shot back to Bryce, who could hear Leah's frantic thoughts as if they were her own.

"You have to go, Leah. I'll call you later, okay?" Bryce's voice shook.

Leah simply nodded and got up on the opposite side of the bed, trying in vain to hide her nudity. No one said anything as she quickly gathered her wildly scattered clothing and dressed with trembling hands. In less than thirty seconds, she edged past Bryce's unmoving mother, down the stairs, and out of the house.

Bryce shakily got to her feet and put on the workout shorts and T-shirt that had been lying next to her bed. Whatever was about to happen, she didn't want to feel even more vulnerable by being half-naked.

When she was done, she stood and faced her mother, bracing herself for a fight. Her mother's frizzy dark blond hair was exploding from its usually well-crafted helmet style, and Bryce struggled to meet her gaze. She looked like a Midwestern Medusa who wanted nothing more than to turn the whole world to stone. Bryce had never seen such fury. She knew her mom was judgmental and holier than thou at times, but she never seemed to anger quickly. The fire in her eyes scared the hell out of her.

"Mom, Leah—"

"You will never say that whore's name in my presence again." She spoke with livid calmness.

Bryce only blinked.

"We did not raise you to be like…like *this*." Her mother gestured with disgust in her direction. "How *dare* you commit such filthy acts in this house?"

"Mom, we—"

"I don't want to hear it, Bryce!" Her mother's hands flew to her face, covering her eyes to block out the shame she saw before her. It took a minute for her to regain her composure. She unconsciously wrapped her fist around the ever-present gold cross that hung at her

neck. "You know God will punish you for what you have done. You must ask for forgiveness."

Enough. "God will punish me for being born gay?" Bryce couldn't believe that the words came out of her mouth, but out they were determined to pour. "He'll punish me for the way He made me? Mom, I'm the same good person I've always been! The same smart, genuine, hardworking girl you've always been so proud of! Why should it matter that I'm attracted to women?"

"God doesn't create perverts!" her mother screamed. "You will burn in hell if you give in to this disgusting lifestyle!"

Bryce's mouth hung open in shock. She didn't know how to respond.

Her mother advanced on her quickly and Bryce tripped backward, falling onto her bed.

With her finger in Bryce's face she said quietly, "You are joining the United States military. They don't let filthy…*lesbians*"—Her nose crinkled in disgust as she said the word—"into the service. You are about to ruin your life. Throw away everything you've worked for!"

Bryce responded with quiet logic, hoping to calm her mother down. "Don't Ask, Don't Tell was abolished, Mom. It's okay to be gay in the military now. I'll be fine."

Instead of calming her down, this only sent her mother into another frenzy. "I won't have you insisting that you're gay! You were raised to be a good Christian! How can you do this to me?"

Bryce's temper flared and she sat up straighter. "What in the world makes this about *you*? This is *my* life and I'm just trying my best to figure things out! I don't need you spouting religious bigotry in my face just because you're too close-minded to see beyond the evangelical propaganda that has poisoned your brain! I'm your *daughter*, for Christ's sake!"

"Don't you *dare* use the Lord's name in vain!"

Bryce heard footsteps pounding up the stairs. Moments later, her father burst into the room and bellowed, "What in the world is going on up here?"

Bryce's mother turned on him, "I found *your* daughter naked in bed with Leah Friedman!"

Her father's eyes widened and his gaze moved to meet Bryce's, but he didn't say anything. Her mother wheeled back around to face her. "You have broken my heart, Bryce. May the Lord forgive you for what you've done." With the words hanging in the air, she spun around on her heel and left the room, a door slamming in the hallway a few seconds later.

The silence left in her wake was deafening. Tears welled up in Bryce's eyes, but so far, the shock was winning out. She could only sit on the edge of her bed, heart racing, trying to rationalize everything that had just happened.

"Honey, are you okay?" Her dad wore a worried frown. Bryce saw him start to move toward her, but he stopped, as if he were uncomfortable getting too close.

Okay? "Yeah, Dad. Best morning ever." That was it. She couldn't help it anymore. Tears poured down her cheeks and she bent over, holding her head in her hands as she cried.

Still, her father didn't come closer, didn't touch or hug her.

"I'm going to go talk to your mother. See if I can calm her down, okay?" His voice was kind, despite his obvious discomfort with consoling her. He had never been good with the depth of female emotions.

Bryce didn't respond, but only curled into the fetal position, facing away from her father and her bedroom door. She breathed deeply, trying to get her crying under control. She hated feeling weak.

After several moments, she heard her door close quietly behind her.

She was alone.

CHAPTER TEN

Bryce stayed curled up on her bed for most of the day, watching the shadows descend and rise on the wall as the sun rose and set. She waited for someone to come and talk to her again, to apologize, to berate her, to say anything, but no one did. Vaguely she realized she had never called in sick to work. She hoped she would still have a job come tomorrow.

The ring of her phone startled her.

The caller ID displayed the name *Leah Friedman* in bright white letters. At first she didn't want to answer it, but she knew that Leah was probably worried sick.

"Hey, Leah," Bryce said in a monotone when she accepted the call.

"Oh my God, Bryce, are you okay?"

"Peachy. How are you, though? Oh, and please don't fill out the comment card for Casa Montgomery's hospitality. We have a reputation to uphold, you know," Bryce deadpanned.

"Don't worry about me. I'm fine." Her voice softened. "What happened after I left? If you want to tell me, that is. You don't have to."

"No, it's okay. Mom completely lost her shit. She's super conservative and she pretty much damned me to hell."

"Shit."

"Yeah. It's so nice to hear your mom tell you she's basically ashamed of you after one small act despite your whole life of being the perfect daughter and your parents' pride and joy."

"What have you been doing all day?"

"Lying here."

"You didn't go to work?"

"Nope."

"Is there anything I can do?"

"I don't think so. I wouldn't come over here again if I were you, though. I'm so sorry." Anger crested inside Bryce again. "I can't believe she treated you like that! I'm so pissed. Not to mention mortified." She sighed. "I don't know what to do."

"I'll do whatever you need me to do. I don't want to cause any problems."

"I know you don't, Leah, but I also don't want you thinking this is your fault."

"But—"

"No. This has nothing to do with you. I've recently figured out I'm a lesbian and I happen to have a mother who thinks evangelical zealots are too liberal. Yay me."

Leah was silent for a moment. "Maybe my parents could talk to your parents. My mom knows your mom from that community group they're both in. Your mom helped mine collect holiday toys at our temple a few years ago, remember? They know about me. They even know I've had a crush on you for years—"

"They *what*?"

"It's okay! They're totally cool with it. I can have them call—"

"Don't you dare! Anytime anyone tries to express a differing opinion to my mom, she just puts up a wall and shuts people out. They don't need to get in the middle of this. For their sake."

Leah was silent for a while. "I just don't know what to do."

"I don't either, but I'm not up for talking right now."

"I'm sorry."

"It's okay. I'll talk to you later, though. Thanks for calling."

"Take care, Bryce." Leah sounded heartbroken.

Bryce hesitantly made her way downstairs later that evening, the rumbling in her stomach impossible to ignore. Even though the thought of food made her queasy, she knew she had to eat. She hoped she had waited long enough that both of her parents would be in bed. Her chest contracted painfully as her mother's words resurfaced in her mind. Even her father hadn't come to talk to her again that day. She had been left alone in her room, shunned like a pariah in her own home. Tears stung her eyes, but she defiantly fought them off, not wanting to revert to her earlier despondency. She was determined to be strong through whatever happened next.

Tiptoeing silently down the hallway, she paused at the top landing to listen for noises downstairs. Hearing nothing, she continued. She paused again on the top step, but still heard no voices or movement. Finally, she descended the stairs, skipping the seventh one that always squeaked, then froze at the bottom when she heard her father's deep voice speaking softly from the kitchen.

"You can't just let her sit in there alone forever, Cynthia. One of us should go talk to her."

She heard her mother sniff quietly. "I can't even bear to look at her. All I see is her…them…in bed." Her mother's voice cracked. "I just can't."

"That's no way to treat our daughter."

"I know, I know, I know." Her mother's voice became muffled. Bryce could practically see her burying her face in her hands. "I don't know what to do. There has to be some way we can help her."

"The only way we can help is by talking to her. She's not doing this just to upset us, you know."

"I need to talk to Harold. He'll know what to do."

"Well, you'd better do it quick. Who knows what she's thinking up there alone. Will you at least go say something to her? She's our baby."

"Our *baby* would never—"

"Cynthia."

Her mother sighed. "I'll try."

Adrenaline shot through Bryce as she heard her mother's chair slide back from the kitchen table. She spun around and jumped up the stairs as quietly as she could, slipping into her room. She'd just managed to close the door softly as she heard her mother step on the squeaky stair. She scrambled into bed and said nothing as her mother knocked.

When she didn't answer her mother opened the door just enough to let a small spray of the hall light into the room.

"Bryce?"

Her heart thudded. She didn't reply.

"I'm sorry we had this…fight, but I'm going to get you some help. You won't have to deal with this alone."

That was it? That was trying? Bryce waited for her mother to continue, to say something more meaningful, but after a pause the door shut again.

Bryce rolled on to her back and fumed. Get her help? From Harold

Noke? The old-as-dirt pastor from her mother's evangelical church, who preached hellfire and damnation not only for homosexuals, but for anyone who didn't fit his narrow "family values" mold? Bryce could think of nothing worse. He was the main reason she had stopped going to church. His malevolent sermons made her nauseous. She hated that someone like him had turned her away from something that used to make her so happy.

She had always had fun at church when she was younger. She played with the other kids in her youth group, reveled in the otherworldliness when the choir sang, liked hearing about the unconditional love that was supposed to come from something larger than herself, and especially enjoyed the peace and happiness of the Easter and Christmas services.

That all changed when Pastor Harold took over the congregation five years ago. It was a slow transition, but eventually the sermons about loving one's neighbor and helping those less fortunate gave way to more politicized sermons about the evils of atheists, modern-day witchcraft, and downright xenophobia. The most disturbing thing was that she could only watch helplessly as her mother followed like a drugged sheep down his increasingly judgmental path. Her father followed too, but mostly because he followed his wife's lead in almost everything. He might look like a tough lumberjack, but he was more like a loyal dog where Bryce's mother was concerned.

Bryce quivered wondering what Harold's "help" would consist of. What could she do about it? It bothered her to think that she had upset her mother so much, but being gay wasn't something she had just decided to be one day. Sure, the revelation had happened very quickly, but that wasn't out of the ordinary for Bryce. She always took everything in stride and had never encountered an obstacle she hadn't overcome with spectacular ease.

This, however…

She didn't know what to do. Should she fight back? She only had to put up with her mother for three more weeks before leaving for the academy after all. But, oh, how those three weeks would suck! Not to mention the possibility of damaging their formerly close relationship forever.

Bryce smacked her fist ineffectually on the bed. No, she couldn't fight back. It wouldn't help. She wouldn't take everything lying down, of course. That just wasn't in her nature. But she *could* try to ignore everything. Pretend nothing had ever happened, just to keep the relative peace.

She scoffed out loud.

Who was she kidding? Her mother would never forget what she'd seen. And they hadn't even been doing anything *too* interesting. But still…

Maybe she should talk to Arati and Jennifer. They always knew what to do. Well, Jennifer always knew what to do, and Arati always made her feel better about whatever she did. She'd talk to her friends. Tomorrow. She was too tired, too hungry, and too upset to do anything right now.

A soft scraping noise startled Bryce awake. She had been dreaming that she was locked in a giant maze. Every time she thought she had found a way out, she ended up in a bright, empty room that vaguely reminded her of one of the rooms in her house. She spent a long time in each room she entered, hoping someone would find a way in to free her. Occasionally she could hear her parents on the other side of the wall, but their words were muffled and no matter how hard she hammered her fists on the smooth, white plaster, nothing ever changed. She would finally turn around and head back into the dark maze, feeling her way past trash cans and broken brick as if she were in a never-ending back alley in a slowly decaying city of perpetual night.

Roaches ran over her fingers as they slid along the walls and rats ran between her feet, tripping her as she moved, yet she continued, finding one useless room after another. Right before the noise in her room woke her up, she had seen four shadowy figures standing in a doorway. She could tell they were there to help her, but she couldn't make out their faces. She had taken her first step to run to them when her eyes snapped open. She blinked in confusion as her brain tried to make sense of the image of her bedroom ceiling in contrast with the dark maze that had just imprisoned her.

She heard a quiet click and looked over to her bedroom door. A bowl of oatmeal, a plate of buttered toast with grape jelly, and a glass of orange juice sat just inside of her door. She wondered if it had been her mother or her father who had put it there.

Her stomach growled loudly as the smell reached her.

Groggily she eased out of bed and approached the plate. Paranoia struck her as she wondered if her parents had poisoned the food.

"Oh my God, Bryce. Chill," she said quietly to herself before taking a huge bite of toast.

When her breakfast was gone, Bryce found that she was still hungry. She also realized she only had fifteen minutes to get to work. She bounded across the room to change into her swimsuit, thrilled that this would give her an opportunity to get out of the house. Dealing with her mother this morning wasn't something she thought she could stomach. It would also give her the opportunity to go over to Jennifer's house afterward and talk things through. She was feeling more optimistic already now that she had a plan, however weak it might be.

When she was dressed she grabbed her iPhone and keys and quietly opened her bedroom door. She listened, but heard no one. Instead of a silent descent like she had attempted last night, she bolted from her room, barreling noisily down the stairs and out the front door. She didn't even look around on her way out, being focused solely on escape.

She reached the front door and fumbled the lock open, then sprinted for her car in the driveway. The strain in her muscles, still tight from lying in bed for over twenty-four hours, was a welcome pain in contrast to the emotional turmoil she had been through. She reached her car, unlocked and opened the door, and plopped down in the seat in one fluid movement. As the car started, she saw her mother open the front door and stare at her sadly. She pulled out of the driveway and sped toward the waiting refuge of the swimming pool.

When she arrived at the pool house she found that the lock had been cut off her locker and the contents removed. Confused, she walked to the office and found her supervisor sitting behind his desk, typing on his computer.

"Hey, Rob. I'm sorry I didn't call in yesterday. I was really sick."

The middle-aged man in a baby blue polo shirt looked up, his face showing irritation. "I'm sorry you were sick, Bryce, but you didn't call in at all and didn't answer when we called you. We didn't know if you were sick or dead."

Bryce flushed. "I'm sorry. I just felt so awful that I couldn't think about anything else. It'll never happen again, I promise."

Rob sighed. "That's true. Unfortunately we can't have 'no call, no shows' for even one day here. These kids depend on our lifeguards with…well, with their lives. Dennis had to come in on his day off and get a sitter for his little brother because of you. I'm sorry, Bryce, but you know we have a zero tolerance policy about this kind of thing."

Bryce's heart sank to her feet as she realized what he was saying. Her lip trembled. "You're firing me?"

"Yes."

Desperation forced her to put her hands on his desk and plead her case. "But I've been working at this pool without being late even once for months. Dennis is late all the time!"

"Late doesn't equal absent without notification."

Bryce looked into his eyes, hoping to see a change of heart. When she saw none she stood up again and said in a firm voice, "This isn't fair and you know it. I've given hours and hours of service here. I'm the best lifeguard you have."

He leaned back in his chair and nodded slowly. "Yes, you were, which is why I'm so disappointed in you."

Bryce turned to begging. "Rob, I leave for Connecticut in three weeks and I could really use the money. Isn't there anything I can do to make up for it? Work overtime? Take some of Dennis's shifts off his hands?" Bryce was trembling, trying to persuade her boss to give her another chance. She knew she sounded desperate.

Rob sighed and pinched the bridge of his nose. He said nothing for a long time and Bryce was about to beg for her job again when he finally said, "Bryce, you're the only person who I would even slightly consider doing this for."

Bryce held her breath.

"You have one more chance."

Bryce jumped in the air and squealed, something she didn't think she had *ever* done before.

"*But*," Rob continued, "if you are late or have to miss work just once, you're done. Got it?"

Bryce beamed. "Yes! It won't happen again! Thank you, thank you, thank you!"

"Okay, fine. I get it. Now get out there and watch over those kids."

Bryce practically hopped out of the office, grabbing the cardboard box that held her gear as she left. She didn't know why this job meant so much to her, but she figured it might have something to do with getting her out of her house. The thought of spending the next three weeks cooped up in her room sickened her. Now she had several hours almost every day at one of the places she loved most in the world. That was worth more than the paycheck at this point.

She used her time at the pool that day to contemplate what her mother had said about church, about her parents helping her "get through" this, and to figure out how she really felt about it. She realized she had ignored all of the signs of her blossoming sexuality over the years. The way she had become overly fascinated with certain actresses and singers, how she never really looked at guys the way Jennifer and especially Arati did, and how she had just used her schoolwork and sport as an excuse to not have to deal. She hadn't even realized she had been lying to herself. Leah had blown the deceit wide open.

At the end of her uneventful shift, she descended from her lifeguard tower, appreciating it all the more since she had almost lost it forever, and decided that going over to Jennifer's house was definitely the next best step.

Chapter Eleven

Bryce, freshly showered and changed into her most comfortable swim team shorts and Texas Longhorns T-shirt, rang the doorbell of her best friend's house. Jennifer answered with a genuine smile on her face.

"Look who it is! Where have you been for the last couple of days? Oh wait, never mind." Jennifer winked conspiratorially.

Nausea hit Bryce instantly. "Can I come in? I need to talk."

Jennifer's smile fell as she noticed her friend's discomfort. "Of course! Let's go to my room."

Jennifer led the way to her upstairs bedroom and Bryce actually got light-headed as she passed the guest room where Michael had attacked her. Luckily, Jennifer wasn't looking at her and didn't notice.

They entered Jennifer's room and Bryce sat down on the carpet in the middle of the room. Jennifer looked at her quizzically, but joined her.

"What's wrong?"

"You're not going to believe what happened yesterday."

"Try me."

Bryce told her the whole story, up until her near firing that morning. When she was done Jennifer was staring at her, mouth wide in horror. "So anyway. I wanted to hear what you think about it. What should I do?"

For the first time in their friendship, Jennifer was completely silent on the subject. She was a quiet person, but was always ready with sound advice and logic for any situation. Right now, she seemed stumped. "Wow, I…"

"Shit." Bryce leaned over and placed her face in her hands.

"No! I mean, let me think about this. Okay. I just need some clarification. Are you saying that you are definitely, no doubts about it, positively a lesbian?"

"Yes. I'm a lesbian. For sure." Saying it out loud sent waves of uncomfortable adrenaline through her body.

"Do you have a problem with that yourself?"

"No! Of course not. I mean, it's a little unexpected in an…expected sort of way, I guess, but I am who I am." Bryce shrugged. "This just adds another layer, I guess."

"Well, that's a good start." Jennifer patted her knee. "Now. Is this something that you want to lie to your mom about?"

"Not really. I mean, if it makes the next part easier, maybe, but I'd feel crappy about it. We have our troubles, but she's my mom, you know?"

"I know. Does your relationship with Leah figure anywhere in this?"

"What do you mean?" Bryce lifted her head.

"I mean, how serious are y'all?"

"Well, we've talked about that a lot actually. I really like her and I know she's liked me forever, but neither of us can see how this can last when we go to college. I mean, I want to spend every second of every day with her right now, but my practical side knows that this is just an amazing moment that will have to end soon."

"And you're prepared for that?"

Bryce shook her head. "Nope. How can I be? But I've accepted it and that's the best I can do for now."

Jennifer nodded as she looked at the floor, thinking. "Okay. That leaves you two options here. And you're not going to like either one."

Bryce sighed and stretched out to lie flat on the floor as if she were in a psychiatrist's office. "Okay. Shoot."

"One: Lie to your mom and tell her you're not gay, you were confused, and make up something that sounds believable for why you were practically naked with Leah."

"It's too late. I already admitted to her that I'm gay. I don't think she'll believe me if I just pretend like it was a mistake. She'll know I'm lying."

"That's true. The second option is to be yourself and deal with her bigotry in whatever form it may take. Stand up for who you are and risk pushing her away."

Bryce threw her arm over her eyes and growled, "This is all so damn pleasant."

Jennifer sighed and stretched out next to Bryce on the floor. "The next three weeks of your life aren't going to be the best."

Bryce took a moment to gather her thoughts before asking, "What about Leah?"

"You have to decide that on your own. It doesn't sound like your mom is going to welcome her back to your home with open arms, and I still don't see how you guys can continue dating unless it's on the sly. Unless you don't mind the confrontation, of course."

Bryce was quiet for a long time.

"What are you thinking?"

"I'm thinking lots of bad words that I won't say out loud." Bryce paused. "And my heart hurts."

Jennifer stood up and held out her hand. Bryce grabbed it and was helped back onto her feet. Jennifer pulled her into a tight embrace and Bryce's eyes watered, but she was determined to keep her composure.

"What do you do when your mother tells you you're going to hell?"

Jennifer sighed into Bryce's hair. "I don't have an answer for that one. I'm sorry."

After spending the next few hours at Jennifer's house, Bryce realized she would have to go home and face her parents. She left the comfort of her best friend with regret and slowly made her way home, taking the longest route she could think of to reach her house. When she finally pulled up to the driveway, a wave of apprehension washed over her when she saw an unfamiliar Range Rover in the driveway.

Maybe it's nothing. Not everything is about you, you know.

She parked her car and made her way to the front door. She didn't want to risk going in the kitchen door since it was dinnertime. Maybe she could avoid her parents again tonight. She opened the front door quietly and stopped in her tracks as she saw her father standing sentinel in the hallway.

"Bryce, honey, please join us in the living room."

Her heart hammered as she followed him to what she now knew was waiting. Sure enough, as soon as she stepped foot into the living room she saw her mother sitting with Pastor Harold and an unknown woman on the couch.

"You've got to be kidding me. Is this an *intervention*?"

"Sweetie, no." Her mother said kindly, her tone far nicer than when she'd found Leah and Bryce together. "We just want to talk to you about what you've been going through."

"With two strangers? Mom, this is none of their business." The insult of the situation heated Bryce's whole body like a flare.

"They're here to help, honey. Let's talk about this."

Bryce turned to go to her room but ran into her father standing like a redwood tree behind her.

"Sit down." He said it quietly, but she knew by the tone of his voice she would have to obey.

She crossed her arms, scowling, petulant as a little girl as she sat on the love seat alone. Her father remained standing behind her, as if ready to block her if she decided to try another escape.

Her mother began, "Bryce, you know Pastor Harold Noke from the church, and this is his friend Dolores Coulson."

"Hello, Bryce," Harold and Dolores said as one with sugary smiles on their faces.

"Hi," Bryce replied with no emotion in her voice.

"They're here to help you with the problems you're facing with… with your confusion."

"The only problem I have right now is sitting here." Bryce knew she was being obstinate and likely making things worse for herself, but she was just so angry about being put through this when she had so many things to worry about on her own. How dare they make her feel like this! Like something was wrong with her. Like she'd morphed into some kind of freakish monstrosity.

Pastor Harold looked at her with a patronizing grin as he said, "Now, Bryce, please don't take offense to us being here. We're here because we love you and want to help you. Would you please let us do that?"

"Say whatever it is you want to say," Bryce snapped, wanting to get it over with as soon as possible. She couldn't believe how combative she was being. She had never behaved this way to anyone, especially adults. This thought only made her more angry with them for causing her to lose her normally kind and respectful demeanor.

Pastor Harold leaned forward, resting his elbows on his knees and clasping his hands together. Bryce couldn't see past the liver spots that dotted his hands and face. "Your mother told us about your friend Leah and how you two are…experimenting with each other."

Bryce's ears flamed with humiliation.

"I'm here to let you know there's nothing wrong with that."

Her mother's head whipped around to stare at him, open-mouthed.

"But you need to realize experimentation is just that. Soon you'll understand that being with another woman isn't what God wants for you and isn't something you should naturally want either."

Bryce shook with a fury she feared would erupt like lava onto everyone around her. Through the red of her vision she saw her mother visibly relax and turn her concerned gaze back onto her daughter.

Pastor Harold continued, "Now, I'd like to hear what you think about all of this, Bryce. Was it Leah who forced you into participating in lesbian acts?" His voice sounded kind and understanding, but his words sizzled like acid on her heart.

Bryce took a steadying breath before answering. "Leah is an amazing girl and everything I did was because I am attracted to her. No one forced me to do anything. I am an intelligent, strong, and rational young woman who is more than capable of understanding what my body and heart are feeling." She couldn't believe her response had been so calm and reasonable. She wanted to tear the room apart like a wild banshee.

"So you're claiming you are attracted to women? All women?"

Bryce spat out the answer. "Of course not all women. Are *you* attracted to all women?"

"Are you attracted to men?" he countered calmly.

Bryce hesitated and thought back on the years of her life since she reached puberty. She'd had crushes on boys before that, but boys were obviously not grown men. She also remembered her thoughts at the pool today. Women, not men, had always fascinated her. "No. I'm not attracted to men. I'm gay." It terrified her, but felt *so* good to say these words in front of Pastor Harold, the mystery woman Dolores, and her parents. A weight lifted off her shoulders and she couldn't help but smile. Her mother noticed, and she looked horrified.

Silence hung in the room and Bryce could only hear old Pastor Harold's labored breathing and the ticking of the clock above the fireplace.

Finally, Pastor Harold said, "Bryce, my colleague Mrs. Coulson," he gestured to the woman sitting next to him, "runs a therapy program for teenagers in your situation—"

"What *situation*?" Bryce interrupted.

Mrs. Coulson spoke for the first time with a sickly sweet high-pitched voice, "Teens who struggle with being gay, honey."

With eyes aflame Bryce slowly turned her head to look at this woman who had the audacity to speak to her so familiarly. "I'm *not* struggling with it. *She* is." She pointed an accusing finger at her mother. "And please don't call me 'honey.'"

Mrs. Coulson nodded as if she understood. "This is the reaction I get all too often. I know you feel angry. I know you feel like God has abandoned you."

Bryce rolled her eyes and slumped back against the couch. There was no reasoning with these people. They were so mired in their own self-righteousness, they wouldn't accept homosexuality even if Jesus himself descended from heaven and became the grand marshal of the Gay pride parade. The misguided holy smog they had formed around themselves obscured everything.

Mrs. Coulson forged forward. "I'm here to tell you that God *hasn't* abandoned you. He has only given you an obstacle to overcome in order to prove your love of Him. You have received a gift!" She clasped her hands in front of her, full of religious fervor. "You get the opportunity to really prove yourself to your Lord and Savior."

A wave of icy cold doused the heat in her body.

"Now, there are several reasons people develop unwanted same-sex attractions—"

"Who says it's unwanted?" asked Bryce, obstinately.

Mrs. Coulson continued as if Bryce hadn't spoken. "You may not have bonded properly with your mother, you may be too close with your father, or—"

Enraged, Bryce shot to her feet. "What?! Okay, stranger who knows nothing about me, my mom and I have always been close," Bryce looked to her mother, who reluctantly nodded, "and I'm just as close with my dad. Isn't that how it's supposed to be? You think girls shouldn't be close with their fathers? If so, I pity your relationship with your own parents."

"Bryce, sit down." Her father put a hand on her shoulder and urged her down onto the love seat.

"I know people don't always choose to be gay, Bryce," Mrs. Coulson continued. "But you have to know that you *can* choose to change."

"And if I don't want to change? If I want to be true to myself?"

Pastor Harold hung his head and shook it slowly. "No one wants to be gay, dear. It just might take you a while to realize it. That's why we're here to help you."

Bryce's eyes glazed over and a buzzing sound filled her ears. For the next few minutes, although it seemed like an eternity, she only heard snippets of the conversation being directed at her. There was mention of a support group, mentors, a program, and Wednesday and Sunday nights. Eventually Bryce realized the room had gone silent and her eyes refocused to see everyone staring at her.

"What? Are we done now?"

Pastor Harold spoke first. "Yes, we're done for tonight. The next steps are for you and your parents to take." He stood and reached out his hand for Mrs. Coulson. She took it and stood beside him.

"Thank you for coming, Harold. It means everything to me." Bryce's mother's eyes streamed tears.

"I'll be praying for your family, Cynthia. You know where to find me if you want to talk."

"I hope I'll be seeing you soon, Bryce." Mrs. Coulson smiled genuinely and turned to leave.

Bryce watched them walk out of the house and rose to escape to the refuge of her room. Maybe she would even go over to Leah's or Jennifer's to get out of the house.

"Bryce?" Her mother sounded defeated. It broke her heart to hear such pain in the voice that had always been so comforting to her.

Bryce sighed and turned to face her. "What, Mom? You want to make me feel more like a disgusting freak? I thought Pastor Harold and that shrew did a decent job of it already."

Her mother cried harder and Bryce's resolve weakened. "Honey, I just know you can beat this."

Bryce spoke gently, but as firmly as she could. "Mom, this isn't a disease. And the last time I checked the calendar, it's also not the Dark Ages. You're making me feel like I'm on the burning end of a witch hunt."

"You know that's not how we want you to feel, but you have to realize how hard this is for your father and me." Her mom walked over to stand next to her dad, who put a large comforting arm around her shoulders.

"Mom, this is just something else about me. I have blue eyes, I'm an awesome swimmer, I'm not bad-looking, I'm smart, I work hard. And I'm biologically attracted to women."

Her mom winced.

"And I'm a really good person. Just how you two raised me to be."

This time her father spoke. "We're not saying you're not, Bryce. We really just want to help you."

"Help me by supporting my decisions, by trusting me about what's right for my life."

Dad dismissed her words with a quick shake of his head. "The ministry Mrs. Coulson told you about is one of the best in the world for helping young people come back to Christ in the love of a heterosexual relationship."

Bryce's stomach churned. She thought she might vomit on the carpet at his feet. Still, she replied calmly, "Dad, nothing is wrong with me. Try looking on the other side. There are groups that help parents accept their children. How about you guys go talk to them. You'll realize I was born this way and if I 'change' I'll just be living a lie."

"Bryce, please be reasonable."

"Why is this all on me? You guys could do with a bit of education on the subject too, you know. Do you want me to be unhappy?"

"Of course not, honey," her mother said. "But we really want you to at least go to a meeting or two. Talk to Mrs. Coulson. Hear what she has to say. Will you do that for us?"

Bryce remained silent. She saw the pleading look in her parents' eyes and knew she would do almost anything to make them happy, just as she had her whole life. She had never been the rebellious type. Following the rules had made life easier up until now. The thought of disapproval or shame from her family had always terrified her. Looking at them now made her feel like a little girl who was being grounded for doing something awful.

She huffed, "I'll go for you guys, but don't expect anything. And in the meantime, will you talk to some other people? By that I mean not people from your church, to get another point of view on this?"

Her mom's lips pursed, but she nodded slightly.

"Thank you. Now if you'll excuse me, I feel like going to my room." What she actually felt like doing was scuttling under her bed to hide from the world until the day she could get on the plane to New London.

CHAPTER TWELVE

Bryce's normally well-manicured fingernails had been reduced to messy stubs. She couldn't help but bite them when she felt nervous, and sitting in Dolores Coulson's living room surrounded by other depressed-looking teenagers was definitely not calming. The days leading up to this Sunday night meeting had been unbearably uncomfortable at home. Despite her promise to do so, her mother had refused to seek out information from any other sources, her parents barely spoke with her at all, her mother left handwritten Bible verses on her door every morning (several from Leviticus), and Bryce spent all her time either at work or locked in her room. She hadn't seen or spoken with any of her friends in days, and her workouts were limited to swimming at the pool after work or lifting free weights in her room.

I can't do this, she thought frantically, her gaze darting to the motley group of teens stuck at Mrs. Coulson's house. *This is nothing but brainwashing by religious zealots.*

Bryce's thoughts turned back to her mother's desperate face, and a pang of guilt stabbed at her. She could suffer through at least one meeting and then tell her mother it wasn't going to work. That would have to be enough.

As she was having these thoughts Mrs. Coulson walked into the room carrying a tray of fruit punch and shortbread cookies. She situated it on a brilliantly white lace doily draped across the coffee table in the middle of the room. Several of the teenagers pounced on the refreshments as if they hadn't eaten in days. Bryce didn't feel like she ever wanted to eat again.

"Hello, everyone. Welcome back to our weekly Path of the Covenant meeting. We have a new member today. Her name is Bryce Montgomery. Please welcome her to the group, everyone."

"Hi, Bryce," they all said as one.

She didn't answer.

"Because she's new we're going to explain how our group works. It's a good refresher for everyone else, too." Mrs. Coulson turned her sugary gaze on Bryce. "Path of the Covenant is part of what some people call, albeit a bit too crassly, the Ex-Gay Movement. It's a group that caters specifically to teenagers and young adults who are struggling with homosexual feelings and urges."

Bryce couldn't help but roll her eyes and make a scoffing noise. She saw Mrs. Coulson's lips purse. She continued by clearing her throat dramatically. Obviously she thought Bryce was impertinent.

"Bryce, what is a covenant?"

"An agreement."

"Yes, but what does it mean in a religious context?"

Bryce sighed. Might as well play along. "A covenant is an agreement between Man and God to do or refrain from doing something." She paused before adding, "Depending on how God or Man feels about that something at the time."

Mrs. Coulson's eyes narrowed, but she pressed on. "Correct. A covenant is an all-important agreement between Christians and God to act appropriately according to the Gospels. The reason this support group…"

Bryce stifled a groan. A support group? Not when you're force-fed illogical and hurtful propaganda.

"The reason this support group is called Path of the Covenant is because you young people," she gestured around the circle, "have recently discovered things about yourself that go against God's plan. We're here to help! We want you to know God loves you and that, with His help, you can change." She clapped her hands with delight. "This has been proven time and time again, and anyone who accepts this help can go on to live happy, normal, heterosexual lives." Mrs. Coulson had gotten more and more excited as she spoke, clearly reveling in her own piousness. "Bryce, I'd like to introduce you to my husband, Tom Coulson."

She turned to her right, and the unassuming man who had apparently been sitting next to her the whole time stood and nodded. Bryce hadn't noticed him because he had been practically sunken into the couch. When he stood, he cowered as if afraid of being struck. He was the mousiest man Bryce had ever seen. His hair was messily combed over his balding head and he had a graying mustache that looked as if it were trying to make him look manlier, but it failed miserably.

"Hello, Bryce." Tom's voice was so quiet she could barely hear him speak. "I myself am an ex-gay." He waited for surprise or any kind of reaction from Bryce, but she offered none. "I went through this same twelve-step program when I was in college, and through the love of our Lord, I was able to see that my attraction to men had a root in being too close to my mother and sisters growing up. I was the youngest, so they would take me shopping with them and my sisters would dress me up as a girl for plays they put on. When I reached puberty I found that I thought about other boys in a sexual way and I hated myself for it." He took a deep breath. "Anyway, my parents discovered Path of the Covenant at the church in my hometown and they really changed my life. I'm a happily married man now." He glanced briefly at Mrs. Coulson, who gazed lovingly back at him with watery eyes. "And I know this group can help you kids too."

He smiled shakily and sat back down, a little too quickly.

"Isn't…that…*wonderful*?" His wife was still looking at him with pure awe on her face. No one responded.

"Now that you've met my husband, a Path of the Covenant success story"—she beamed—"let's go around the circle and introduce everyone." Mrs. Coulson smiled sweetly and started. "Bryce, we've already met, but again, my name is Dolores Coulson. I'm a daycare provider for children under two and I hold these meetings in my free time in order to give back to society and to help young people such as yourself find their way back to the Lord."

Bryce fought the upheaval in her stomach.

Next to Mrs. Coulson was a frail-looking boy. Bryce guessed he was no more than eleven years old. Mrs. Coulson smiled at him to continue the introductions. In a quiet voice he said, "My name is Benji."

"Benji, continue, please." Mrs. Coulson prodded him.

The boy took a deep breath and said, "My parents think I'm too eff…eff…"

"Effeminate, dear."

"…effeminate and Mrs. Coulson has helped me realize that I can grow up to be a real man if I pray hard enough."

Bryce's eyes were wide with shock and pity.

Next to him was an older girl wearing a T-shirt from Saltus High's rival school, DeSoto. "My name is Amanda and I'm attracted to girls."

"Amanda…" Mrs. Coulson leveled her gaze at Amanda with disapproval.

"My name is Amanda and I'm attracted to girls." She looked defiant.

Mrs. Coulson shook her head and said to Bryce, "Amanda has only been coming to meetings for two months, so she's still working on Step Two: Accepting that she wants to change."

Mrs. Coulson then looked to the next young man, who had a glazed look in his eyes as he smiled too widely with teeth that were unnaturally white. "I'm Corey and I *used* to be attracted to men, but Mrs. Coulson has turned my life around. I have a girlfriend named Sarah and I'm asking her to marry me when I graduate from college in a year." Mrs. Coulter clapped for him, smiling proudly.

"I'm Brandon," said the boy on the other side of Bryce. Apparently they were saving her for last. "This is only my third meeting."

Mrs. Coulter didn't force him to say more. He seemed very shy.

The last person in the circle was a fit and handsome college student who spoke with a heavy accent. "My name is Luis. I moved to Galveston from the Virgin Islands with my parents five years ago, and I just finished my first year of university at Saltus State. I came out to my parents three years ago, and, in order for them to help me pay for college, I have to attend these meetings." He looked disdainfully at Mrs. Coulson.

"Now, Luis, we've discussed this. I can't help you if you won't at least try."

His ebony skin flushed even darker with the rage Bryce knew he must feel.

Now it was Bryce's turn. She hesitated with all of the eyes on her, but finally said, "I'm Bryce, and I don't need to be here."

Mrs. Coulson tsked. "Of course you need to be here, Bryce. You have unwanted sexual attractions to women."

"I have sexual attractions to women, Mrs. Coulson, but they are by no means unwanted."

Out of the corner of her eye she saw Amanda smile.

"Well, coming to these meetings is the first step in acknowledging that you have a problem."

"I'm not an alcoholic or drug addict, ma'am."

"No, but you *are* perverting God's natural plan." Mrs. Coulson's gaze turned to ice as she glared at Bryce. Her tone was knife-sharp. The room fell completely silent. "You think because television shows portray gay behavior as okay that it is. It is *not*. You are not normal, and I'm here to help you get back on the right path to salvation. Without people like me showing you the way, you would be just another lamb to the devil's slaughter. Why can't you see how disgusting your acts, your thoughts, your heretical lifestyle choices are to God? It's here in black and white." Mrs. Coulson thumped her Bible down on the table.

"Your interpretation," Bryce said calmly.

Mrs. Coulson grew more heated as she spoke. "You *will* change, Miss Montgomery, or you *will* spend an eternity in hell as Satan's whore. That is your only option. Choose wisely."

Bryce took a good twenty seconds to slow her breathing before finally replying, "You are not God, Mrs. Coulson. I don't judge you on how you live your life. You seem like someone who honestly wants to make the world a better place, however misguided you may be, but you shouldn't judge me on the way I live mine."

"The Word of God says—"

Bryce spoke louder. "I'm a good person who has never hurt anyone. You don't know who I am. You know nothing about me. And this is the twenty-first century." Bryce swung her arms out to encompass the group. "There's nothing wrong with me and there is nothing wrong with the kids in this room. The only thing wrong in here is you and your hateful, backward thinking." The stunned looks on the faces of the others in the room told Bryce Mrs. Coulson was unaccustomed to people arguing with her.

Mrs. Coulson's face reddened, and her sticky sweet veneer cracked. "We cannot help you, Miss Montgomery, if you refuse to accept your dysfunction and ask Jesus Christ for forgiveness."

"That's not going to happen, and I don't need angry bigots like you trying to change the way I was born just because you find it 'icky.'" Bryce stood to leave.

"Bryce Montgomery, you are damning yourself to eternal hell with this choice!" she yelled.

Bryce stood. Enough was enough. "Being gay isn't a choice, Mrs. Coulson, but refusing to be berated and insulted by people like you is. Good-bye and thank you for your…*hospitality*."

She turned and marched out the front door. How she'd thought she could endure such treatment, even for her mother's sake, was beyond her.

As she stormed down the walkway to her car she heard the door open behind her. She wheeled around, expecting to see a furious Mrs. Coulson, but she relaxed when she saw Amanda running after her with a smile on her face.

"Bryce! Wait!" She took a deep breath. "I just wanted to say thank you. I haven't been brave enough to stand up to her. My parents make me go to these horrible meetings, but seeing you fight back…well, I'm not coming back here ever again. I don't care what they say." She beamed.

Bryce smiled. "You're welcome. Although I'm scared to death to go home now. I don't know what came over me. I guess I've just never been one to take abuse. I'm better than that…and so are you."

"And you've made me realize it, so thank you!" She pulled a scrap of paper and a pen from her pocket and scribbled quickly. "Here, this is my e-mail address and phone number. If you need to talk to someone who can relate, just get in touch, okay?"

Bryce took the information and nodded, doubting that she would ever get up the nerve to call or e-mail this girl and rehash all the terrible things that had been said in this group.

Amanda waved, hopped on her bike, and pedaled off.

Bryce sat down in her car with a huff, wondering where she should go and what she was going to say to her parents. What could they do to her? They weren't paying her college tuition, so she didn't have to worry about being monetarily cut off like Luis did. The Coast Guard Academy was free to all who were accepted. She had also saved up enough money lifeguarding and teaching to easily pay for incidentals for a year or more, and once she graduated, she had a full-time job waiting for her as an officer.

So, what then?

She realized she dreaded her parents' disapproval. They had always been so close, and she had always been such a perfectly behaved child, that the thought of rebelling or living a life that was obviously so disgusting to them pained her. She knew in her heart they were wrong, of course, but that didn't mean she felt like flaunting her newfound sexuality in front of them.

She sighed and picked up her phone. After a few rings Leah answered.

"Bryce! I'm so glad you called. Is everything okay?"

"Well, define okay." Bryce's voice was emotionless.

"That doesn't sound good."

"Can you meet me for dinner tonight at seven thirty?"

"Sure. Where?"

"How about that Greek place next to the mall?"

"Okay." Bryce could hear the trepidation in Leah's voice and she knew neither one of them were going to enjoy the upcoming meal very much.

When Leah walked into the restaurant Bryce's heart leaped and then fell again. She looked beautiful in a bright sundress that hugged her curves in a very pleasant way. This wasn't going to be easy.

Bryce stood and hugged Leah before they both sat down in the booth Bryce had chosen in the deserted back corner of the restaurant. They sat in awkward silence. Bryce hesitated to start what was sure to be an unpleasant conversation.

Finally, she blurted, "Hummus?" and gestured to the warm pitas and dip the waitress had placed in the center of the table.

Leah declined. "It's good to see you." She watched Bryce with obvious concern. "I was so worried about you after…after what happened." She blushed and looked at her folded hands.

Bryce put down the pita she had picked up and said stiffly, "That was embarrassing for you. I'm so sorry."

"Yeah, but I really was more worried about you."

"Well, that's kind of what I wanted to talk to you about."

Leah sat up straighter, as though bracing herself for what Bryce might say.

Bryce told Leah everything that had happened since she had been so unceremoniously kicked out of her house. Leah looked sad for most of the story, but the sadness was replaced with horror when Bryce told her about Path of the Covenant.

"Your parents are honestly trying to convert you to straight?"

"Yep."

Leah spluttered for a moment before finally getting out, "What year do they think this is? I didn't think people actually believed in that crap anymore!"

Bryce smiled wryly. "That kind of backward thinking is unfortunately still alive and well in this country and definitely in Saltus, Texas."

"So what are you going to do?"

"Well, that's why I wanted to talk with you actually."

"I'm not going to like it am I?"

"No, but neither am I. So here's the deal. I'm not going to put myself through the bullshit of that crazy hate group—"

"That's awesome!" Leah interrupted. "Your parents shouldn't be making you feel like something's wrong with you! I'm glad you see that."

"Well, here's the not-so-great part. Even though I know they're being ignorant, I still feel awful about putting them through this—"

"Bryce, you need to stand up for yourself. You're being led like a sheep." Leah was getting defensive on her behalf.

Bryce exhaled with irritation. "Please just let me finish. This isn't easy for me. I'm a born rule follower. It has served me well, and I'm not the kind of person who can just destroy the lives of the two people I love most in the world just because they don't agree with a part of who I am!"

Leah bowed her head. "Sorry. I'm just so pissed at how they're treating you."

"Leah, everything you're saying is something I've already told myself. You are so not wrong. It's just that I can't bring myself to rock the boat any more than I have to right before I leave them for the first time in my life. This wasn't going to be easy for them in the first place. I'm an only child and they're about to send me away not only to college, but to the military." She slapped both palms on the table. "They're scared! And now I spring the lesbian thing on them…I don't know. I'm not going to be emotionally abused by that disgusting group, but I'm also not going to rub my parents' faces in it. I have to keep to myself for the next two weeks and concentrate on getting ready for school." Bryce sat back and folded her hands in her lap. "That's it."

There was silence as Leah thought about what Bryce had said. "So you're saying no more 'us,' huh?"

Bryce slouched farther back into her seat. "Yeah."

Neither of them said anything for a while, but finally Bryce asked, "Do you hate me?"

Leah actually laughed. "Oh my God, Bryce. You don't know me at all, do you?"

Bryce looked confused.

Leah shook her head and smiled as if she were talking to a small child who couldn't understand the simplest of ideas. "I've wanted to be close to you for as long as I can remember. You are the kindest, smartest, most beautiful, and best all-around person I have ever known. No. I don't hate you."

Bryce's face flushed and she started to protest.

"Stop, Bryce. Let *me* finish now. The last month has been the happiest time of my life. Never in my wildest dreams did I ever imagine you'd think enough of me to actually call me a friend, much less…well, get as close as we have. There is nothing in the world that will ever make me lose that friendship. We've discussed this happening and it's not a surprise to either of us. I was just hoping that it wouldn't happen so soon." She made a pained face, but shrugged.

Bryce wiped at her eyes. She couldn't help but feel like she was losing something important with Leah, but she nodded. "I've told you things I would never tell anyone else, Leah. I'm sorry it took me so long to see how awesome you are and I will never, ever forget you. I don't want to lose your friendship either. It means the world to me. Especially now."

Leah smiled and reached across the table. Bryce did the same, and the feeling of her hands enveloped warmly in Leah's made her heart melt.

"Bryce?"

"Yeah?"

"I am your friend for life. You call me if you ever need anything, okay?"

"You too…but with me."

They both burst out laughing, and although Bryce knew that both of their hearts were breaking, she also knew that what they had shared together had forged a bond that would connect them as confidantes and best friends for life. She felt a security and fullness in her soul knowing that no matter what happened, Leah would always be there for her.

Chapter Thirteen

Bryce took a deep breath before walking into her house. Pastor Harold's Range Rover was sitting in the driveway again and she knew she was in for another evening of unbearable and patronizing conversion talk.

"No time like the present," she said under her breath and turned the knob, poised to sprint even before the door had started to open.

She took off as fast as she could up the stairs and made it to her room before her father had even reached the first step. She fumbled for the lock and had it clicked into place by the time all of the footsteps had reached her.

"Bryce! Come out of that room this instant!" her mother demanded as she banged on the door.

She backed away from the door and sat down slowly on her bed. Even in her dread of returning home, she hadn't expected this kind of greeting.

She didn't answer and her father spoke with quiet authority. "Bryce Lee Montgomery. Do what your mother says or I'll break this door down."

She knew he wouldn't.

Pastor Harold spoke in a softer voice to her mother, "Cynthia, this is not the way to gain back your daughter's trust. Let me try." In a louder voice directed at her door, he continued, "Bryce, honey, your parents are just worried about you. Mrs. Coulson called them about what happened at the Path of the Covenant meeting, and they want to discuss it with you. That's all."

His voice was saccharine and dripping with condescension. Bryce's stomach curdled.

"Come on out of your room, sweetie, so we can talk with you about it. Don't worry, you're not in trouble."

When she didn't respond her father boomed, "Bryce! We will not allow this kind of behavior in our house! We raised you to be obedient and respectful! Open up this goddamn door!"

To which her mother replied, "Ben! Language!"

Her father sounded angrier than she had ever heard him. She curled up in a ball on her bed and faced away from the tirade. She had decided to not flaunt her sexuality in front of them, but that didn't mean they had to force their bigoted ideas down her throat and treat her like some kind of disgusting insect who had infested their home. Her heart was breaking.

Eventually, after a short while of both shouting and pleading for her to come out of her room, the adults who were making her feel so damn good about herself finally left to go back downstairs. Bryce sat up and pulled her computer out of her nightstand drawer, setting it on her legs as it powered on. When it was up and running she opened the chat software and was relieved to see that both Arati and Jennifer were signed in.

She invited them to a video chat and within seconds she saw both of their faces gazing worriedly at her from her screen.

Arati spoke first. "What's going on with you, Bryce? We haven't heard from you in like five days. Not cool."

Bryce took a deep breath. "Settle in, guys, it's story time."

After explaining the disturbing events of the last week to her best friends, they all decided that Bryce would take turns spending the night at their houses. Bryce wasn't running away from home exactly, but she was going to have to limit her exposure to the viral nature of her parents' behavior until she left for school. Only two weeks to go…

Bryce stayed home that night, but the next morning on her way to the pool she knocked on her parents' bedroom door, knowing her father had already left for work. Her mother had just gotten out of bed and was puffy-eyed as if she had been crying all morning. Bryce's stomach clenched. Still, she knew what she had to do.

"Mom, I just wanted to tell you that Jennifer and Arati have invited me to stay with them for the next two weeks."

Her mother said nothing.

"You know, because we're all about to go to different schools and all. We want to…you know…have more time together…before we all leave."

Her mother's eyes narrowed. "You're going to stay with that awful Leah girl."

Bryce was stunned. "No! No, I'm not. Mom, I had a talk with Leah and we decided that...well, Leah is just a friend. I don't want to hurt you, so I'm not going to see her...like that...anymore." It felt good to show her mother that even though she couldn't stand those brainwashing meetings, she was willing to make some concessions for the benefit of her parents' feelings. She smiled slightly to prove her good intentions and raised hopeful eyebrows even though the indignity of having to go through this charade at all still really pissed her off.

Tears streamed down her mother's face as she sobbed, "What has happened to you? My sweet little girl! What did I do wrong?"

The blood drained from Bryce's face. What was she supposed to say? Apparently compromises were no longer part of this twisted game. Bryce realized that nothing she did would ever be good enough again. She was tainted. She was soiled with the most appalling sin of all in her mother's eyes. She was damaged and would no longer receive the support, the love, and the adoration of her parents.

She wanted to rail at her mother. Scream at her for her ignorance and her hurtful words, but she also wanted to hold her and make the pain she had caused melt away. This angered her more, because she knew deep down she shouldn't have to feel guilty for being gay.

So she just stood there; dumbstruck and shaking.

Her mother tried to regain her composure and then reached out and took Bryce's hands in her own. "Honey, we can get through this. Just tell me one thing..."

Bryce was doubtful of her mother's intentions. Maybe she was finally trying to understand her and could see how hard it was for Bryce to inadvertently hurt her family like this. Maybe she was willing to put in the time and effort that it took to accept her only daughter. Bryce looked with trepidation into her mother's eyes and squeezed her hands, trying to hold back the small spark of hope.

"Sweetie, I want you to think about what will happen to you when you die and have to spend an eternity in the hell of your own creation. Think about what it will be like. Tell me if you're prepared for that and then tell me if you want to continue this disgusting farce of being a...a *lesbian*."

A wave of nausea threatened to overwhelm Bryce as an icy numbness spread from her head to her toes. She swayed on her feet and jerked her hands out from her mother's as if they had been burned.

She looked deep into the eyes of the woman who had given her life, who had nursed her hurts, and who had always beamed with pride at her accomplishments. In them she now saw only a hysterical fervor. Her mother no longer recognized the daughter she had known and loved, but saw her as some kind of demon or lost soul that she couldn't exorcise or save.

Bryce turned around slowly and walked out of the house, her mother yelling after her. She tried not to listen. The only words that filtered through the buzz in her head were "hell," "damned," "ashamed," and "disgusting." She was glad she couldn't hear the others.

The drive to the pool seemed to take hours as the horror of what her own mother had just said to her bored through her brain, driving out all but the most basic thoughts needed to get her safely to her destination. Her body was still numb and although she felt like thrashing about and screaming until she was hoarse, she just sat in a stupor and drove.

She worked a full shift at the pool that day, and even though she was completely drained and sticky with an oversaturation of sunscreen by the time the pool closed, she still dove into the water with relish once she was alone. The cool splash banished the numbness that had plagued her all day, and as she became buoyant, the weight that had been slammed onto her shoulders seemed to lessen. In the water she was free. Free to be who she was, free to dream about her future, and free to entertain whatever thoughts she wanted to have without fear of damnation.

She swam until the sky turned a brilliant West Texas orange and her skin was wrinkled and begging for a dry towel. As she pulled her exhausted body out of the pool and dried off, she tried to decide if she would go home tonight to get clothes or just head straight over to Jennifer's house. Jennifer's summer job was at her mother's law firm, so Bryce knew that she had already gotten off of work several hours ago. She would be waiting for her, but Bryce also didn't want to leave things as she had with her mother.

She would go home to get her change of clothes.

She would tell her parents she loved them.

She would leave for the night.

It was that simple.

Wasn't it?

When she arrived home there were no strange cars in the driveway, but all of the lights in the house were off. It took her a moment to figure out why this made her feel so uneasy. As she parked and got out of her car, it hit her with a wave of despair: the front porch light that was always, *always* left on to guide her home at night was also off. The house was completely dark. Unwelcoming. Cold. This one subtle act of disapproval by her parents was what finally broke her. Bryce leaned back against her car and cried.

Covering her face with her hands, she gasped for air and hiccupped as the tears flowed freely down her face. She scrambled back into her car so she could hide her breakdown from anyone who might be looking, thankful she always kept tissues in her glove box. When her throat was scratchy and she had calmed herself down somewhat, she decided to go ahead and enter the house to get her change of clothes.

Wiping her eyes she trudged up the sidewalk, finally reaching the front door. She put her key in the lock and turned, but the door had been bolted from the inside. It wouldn't budge. Adrenaline shot through her as a sickening fear gripped her. Pretending to be unbothered, she walked around to the kitchen door on the side of the house. It too barred her entrance to the house. She looked through the kitchen window and thought she saw a moving shadow in the living room, but it stilled as she watched.

She didn't want to ring the doorbell only to have her entreaties go unanswered, so she walked around to the other side of the house where a large pecan tree stood next to her bedroom window. She and her father had nailed pieces of wood to the tree when she was a child so that she could climb up onto a small platform he had built for her. Her heart ached with the memory, but she stoically climbed up and sat on the edge of the warped wood. A sharp pang of loss pierced her heart when she saw the weathered carving next to where she sat. *Daddy's Little Girl.* A lopsided heart encircled the words. She turned her head back to the house with effort, and from where she sat she was able to reach out across the empty space to her bedroom window and lift it open. She never kept it locked. She realized now how unsafe that was, but still, it served her well at this particular moment.

She climbed into her room and listened quietly for a minute before moving further. She heard no movement in the house. Instead of grabbing only the intended change of clothes for the next day, she pulled out her largest duffel bag and stuffed all of her favorite jackets, sweaters, shirts, shorts, and jeans into it, not knowing if she would be able to return home before she left for the Coast Guard Academy's Swab Summer.

She had to be prepared for the worst. She also grabbed her backpack and in it packed her favorite books, her computer, her academy correspondence, the plane ticket to New London, her favorite photos, and all of the cash she had been saving from her job. If she had to leave home for good tonight, she was ready. Her bags were filled to the point of barely being able to close properly, but the weight of them had nothing on the weight in her heart that threatened to send her spiraling into a deep depression.

With her backpack slung over her shoulders, she tossed the laden duffel bag out of the window and followed it back to her tree platform, taking one last painful look at her room, her trophies, the leftover photos of her family and friends, and the closed door on the opposite side of the room. She knew she had made a lot of noise, but her parents hadn't come to check on her. Locking the doors hadn't been an accident. Somewhere in the back of her mind she had hoped there was a reasonable explanation, but now she knew she was no longer welcome in her own home.

Fighting the urge to cry again, she slowly climbed down the tree. She hefted the heavy duffel bag over her shoulder and walked slowly to her car. She risked one last glance back at the house and saw two shadowy figures turn away from the front window. It took every bit of willpower she had to straighten her back and walk away. She threw the duffel and backpack into the trunk of her car and, taking a shaky breath, sat back down in the driver's seat. Her heart shattered as she drove away from the house where she had spent her entire life. She didn't look back again.

Jennifer saw Bryce's puffy eyes and immediately hurried her upstairs to her bedroom, waving off her mother as she came to welcome her. When they were alone Jennifer took the heavy bags from Bryce and set them neatly in the corner. Bryce stood like a statue in the middle of the room, unsure what to do next.

"Come on. Take your shoes off and make yourself comfortable on the bed."

Bryce did as she was told, preferring to just follow directions than have to think for herself. She leaned up against the headboard and stared at the far wall, trying to stop the jumble of fear and agony in her head.

Jennifer grabbed her phone and dialed quickly. "Arati, code red. Come over ASAP." She hung up without saying more and turned to

Bryce. "She'll be here in five. Hang on just a sec, I'll be right back, okay?"

Bryce nodded and continued staring at nothing.

When Jennifer reentered the room she carried a box of tissue, a carton of skim milk with three glasses, and a huge bucket of brownie bites. She carefully set everything on her nightstand and then chewed on a fingernail as if she were trying to figure out what else they'd need for the night.

Bryce couldn't help but smile. This was so like Jennifer. Always prepared for any eventuality. She decided her friend was truly missing her calling as a therapist, having chosen to study zoology.

Tentatively Jennifer joined Bryce, sitting cross-legged across at the end of the bed facing her. She opened her mouth to speak, but—

Arati burst into the room. "What happened? What did I miss?" She took one look at Bryce's face and jumped onto the bed next to Jennifer, a worried frown on her normally happy features.

"Bryce?" Jennifer began. "Are you ready to talk about it?"

Bryce let out a huge sigh and told them about her fight with her mother before work and how she was "welcomed" home afterward.

"Wait," Arati said, anger creasing her brows, "your parents kicked you out of the house for good?"

"Looks that way, yeah," said Bryce, emotionless.

"But we've known your parents for years." Arati looked at Jennifer, who nodded in agreement. "They don't seem like they could ever do something like that. They love you more than life itself."

Bryce laughed mirthlessly. "Apparently not."

Jennifer placed a consoling hand on Bryce's knee, "Honey, don't think like that. You know they still love you."

Tears welled unbidden into Bryce's eyes as Jennifer continued, "They're just confused and scared. They've never known a gay person before and they don't understand that you're still their sweet little girl."

Bryce clenched her fists and said through gritted teeth, "What are they supposed to think when their distorted brand of religion has convinced them that their only daughter is an abomination? Jenn, no amount of reason will convince them otherwise. They're not logical or rational like you guys. Hell, they're still pissed about the schools teaching safe sex in health class instead of just abstinence. That with Saltus having one of the highest teen pregnancy rates in the country. Brilliant, if you ask me."

Her friends nodded as one in understanding. Arati ventured, "Do you want us to go with you to talk to them? Maybe if they see that your friends still love and accept you they'll realize that it's not such a big deal."

Bryce closed her eyes and leaned her head back. "It won't work. I gave her some helpful websites to check out, but she couldn't read them for more than a minute before closing them in disgust and locking herself in her room to pray."

The room fell silent. No one knew what else to say, so Arati held up the tub that sat between them and said, "Brownie bite?"

This was why she loved her friends. And this is why being away from them would be even harder than she had thought it was going to be.

"I just have one favor to ask you guys," Bryce said thickly through a mouthful of delicious chocolate.

"Shoot." Jennifer replied.

"Don't tell your parents what actually happened, all right?"

Jennifer gave her a confused look.

"It's just that I don't want any attention drawn to this. One: it's embarrassing for me personally, and two: it doesn't actually show my parents in the best light, does it?"

"That it does not." Arati scowled.

"So anyway, let's just keep this between us, okay?" Bryce held out her pinkie and the other two linked their own with hers. "Okay. Thanks, guys. For everything."

Arati and Jennifer both leaned forward to pull Bryce into a hug.

"You'll get through this," Jennifer whispered in her ear. "At least now we get to hang out pretty much non-stop until you have to leave!"

She smiled and relaxed almost fully into her friends' embrace.

Almost.

Nothing would take the sting away from losing her parents…

"I can't do it."

"Yes, you can. You'll always regret it if you didn't know for sure." Jennifer patted Bryce's knee as they sat in the car.

Bryce looked nervously at her house through the side window.

"It seemed pretty obvious."

"I know, but this is the last opportunity you're going to have before you leave next week."

Bryce took a deep breath. "Okay. But I'm scared shitless."

Jennifer smiled kindly. "I didn't say it would be easy."

Bryce got out of the car and made her way purposefully to the front door. She rang the doorbell and felt a mixture of relief and fear when both of her parents opened it.

They didn't invite her in.

"Mom? Dad?"

"Bryce," they said as one.

She hesitated. "I'm…I'm leaving for the academy next week and…I just can't leave things like they are with you guys." Despite her best efforts to fight them, tears welled up in her eyes. "I love you both so much."

Her mother made a move to embrace her, but stopped short. "Bryce, don't you know how much we love you too? Why do you think we're doing this?"

Bryce shook her head in disbelief. "You're cutting me off because you love me?"

Her mother turned and buried her face in her husband's side as she sobbed. Bryce's father spoke. "We just want you to know that there are consequences to your decisions. This is what happens when you make the wrong one. Your mother and I will always be here for you when you decide to turn your life around and come back to God and to us."

Bryce's fingernails pressed painfully into her palms as she balled her fists in anger. "I don't understand what you're doing, Dad. I don't understand any of this."

He shook his head sadly, but it was her mother who turned to her and answered. "Bryce, we have given you everything. You've wanted for nothing. Everything you have ever done has made us the proudest parents in the world. You were the perfect daughter. And now look at what you've done. You've chosen to be an abomination. You've chosen sin over your own family." The next words came out in a staccato of grief. "We. Are. *Ashamed*."

Bryce couldn't find words.

Sobbing, her mother said one final thing. "You have a choice, Bryce. When you make the right one, come home to us." She placed her hand over her chest. "You have broken my heart."

The door closed slowly.

The sound of it latching shut and the lock being turned into place echoed as loudly as an explosion in Bryce's ears.

She turned around and walked in a stupor back to Jennifer's waiting car.

She didn't have to say anything.

Bryce lounged on the couch in Arati's basement. She had slept at Jennifer's house for a few days and was now staying with Arati to make things fair. Arati was away with her parents for the day, on a shopping spree to buy decorations for her dorm room at CalTech, and it was Saturday so Bryce had the day off from work at the pool. She stared at the number on her phone, trying to get up the courage to call. She was hesitant because Amanda was a stranger, but she also knew she needed to talk to someone who could really understand what she was going through.

She pressed the number and Amanda answered within one ring.

"Hello?"

"Oh. Hey. Um. This is Bryce Montgomery. From the Path of the Covenant meeting."

There was a pause before she heard a surprised "Oh! Hey, Bryce! How are you?"

"Actually, things are kind of shitty with me." Bryce explained everything. "So anyway, I just wanted to know if that had happened to you or anyone you know. Is it normal? Is this how parents normally react? I thought you might understand, so I thought I'd call."

"That sucks, Bryce. I am so sorry. But no, I'm still living at home. It's hard sometimes, but I don't think my parents have any intentions of disowning me. They're not happy that I stopped going to PoC, but at this point we all just kind of ignore each other. I'll be a senior next year and then off to college. I think we're all looking forward to that."

"Oh." Bryce realized then that she was one of the unlucky ones. Why couldn't she have parents that loved her for who she was? Or at the very least tolerated her?

"I'm sorry, Bryce. But it could be worse."

"How could it be worse?"

"Well, I hate to be the bearer of bad news, but remember Benji from the meeting?"

"No, which one was he?"

"The little kid whose parents thought he was too effeminate."

"Oh yeah. He made me really sad." Bryce remembered how scared and confused he had looked.

There was a pause before Amanda continued, "He killed himself last week."

Shock jolted through Bryce. "What?"

"Yeah, he was despondent over how he was treated both by bullies at school, and by his own parents at home. He was told he was worthless and he believed it." Amanda sounded furious. "He stole all of his mother's sleeping pills and…well, went to sleep."

"Oh my God, what did his parents do? What did Mrs. Coulson say?"

"Well, I don't know about his parents. I hope they feel like shit, though! But Luis is the one who told me about the whole thing and he said that Mrs. Coulson acted like she was sad about it, but she takes no responsibility for it. Bullshit!" Amanda spat.

Bryce didn't know what to say. Poor Benji had been made to feel so disgusting and awful by the people who were supposed to love him the most. The thought could barely even register with her, despite how she had been treated by her own parents.

"What's wrong with people?" Bryce asked softly.

"You got me. I don't get it either. So anyway, I'm sure I was absolutely no help at all, especially with news like this."

"No, you helped to put things into perspective for me. I appreciate it."

"Well, just stay strong. I know you're good at that," Amanda said with admiration.

"It's hard, but you're right. We can get through this BS and have happy lives. I'm sure of it. Anyway, thanks for talking to me. You take care, all right?"

"Thanks for calling. And thanks again for giving me the courage to get out of that group. I'm so much happier now!"

"No problem."

"Bye, Bryce."

Bryce ended the call and immediately dialed Leah's number. They might not be a couple anymore, but she needed to talk to her friend. She only had a few days left in Saltus, and she wanted to make every moment count with everyone who still loved her. Her heart warmed knowing that despite all that had happened, she still had the best support group she could hope for in her friends. She was going to be okay. She was stronger than she had ever dreamed she could be.

❖

"Why is it that I'm so nervous now?" Bryce couldn't stop wringing her hands.

"That's a silly question. You know you're ready to go." Leah smiled and put her hands over Bryce's.

Jennifer sniffed and wiped her nose with a tissue. "I just can't believe it's time. Everything went by so fast."

"Promise you'll keep in touch. I mean it. Don't make me come up there and embarrass you in front of all of the hot Coast Guard guys in those awesome uniforms." Arati playfully slapped her shoulder. "Wait…that doesn't sound too bad actually…"

Bryce laughed. "You guys really have no idea how much I'm going to miss you."

Jennifer scoffed. "You'll be too busy to miss us. You're going to one of the best schools in the country you know. Plus add to that all of the running, jumping, push-up boot-campy stuff."

"Jenn, you're not helping." Butterflies had started dancing in her stomach again. "What if I can't do it?"

To her surprise all three of her friends laughed as one, but it was Arati who said, "The Great Bryce Montgomery? Not able to do something? Not possible."

Bryce threw herself at her friends, who embraced her warmly.

She would not cry, damn it. If she started she wouldn't be able to stop, and no one wanted to sit next to a loud, snotty mess on a plane for four hours.

"You'd better go. You'll miss your flight," Jennifer said into Bryce's ponytail.

Bryce pulled herself away from her friends and couldn't help casting a small glance over her friends' shoulders, hoping desperately that her parents had changed their minds and had come to see her off and wish her well as she started this new part of her life.

They weren't there. She knew they would never be there again.

No. No Tears.

"I love you guys. I'll call when I get there."

She lifted her two bags over her shoulder and turned around. She heard her friends sniffling as she walked forward and crossed the threshold of the airport alone.

PART TWO

CHAPTER FOURTEEN

Bryce Lee Montgomery, graduating with high honors, U.S. Coast Guard Cutter Gossett, *Seattle Washington…"*

Even though two and half years had passed since hearing those words, Bryce still smiled as she remembered her U.S. Coast Guard Academy graduation day. She did this occasionally as she was getting ready for another long day of duty, reveling in the fact that she had realized her dream. She wouldn't let herself forget what she had been through to get where she currently was. Four years of grueling but fulfilling work at the academy had prepared her for her current position as an officer in the United States Coast Guard. Her parents hadn't attended her graduation, of course. She hadn't spoken to them in years, actually. She regretted having had to cut ties with almost everyone in Saltus. She missed her family. She missed Daniela. She missed her high school. But it didn't matter (or she told herself that it didn't). Leah, Arati, and Jennifer had all been there to celebrate her commissioning, and it was their pride in her accomplishments that would always mean the world to her.

She still talked with all three of them regularly and they even met up for a girls' weekend somewhere new each year. New York City, Orlando, Santa Fe, etc. Of course, Bryce's duties made scheduling difficult, but they always managed to get together without fail. These last two years Leah had even brought her girlfriend along. They had met at SSU and Bryce couldn't help but like her. She was one of the nicest people Bryce had ever met and she knew that Leah had found her perfect match. She had felt an initial, brief pang of jealousy, but she realized that it was because somewhere in the back of her mind, she still longed for a relationship of her own.

She had undertaken her time at the academy with her usual

single-mindedness that led her to rise to the top percentile of her class, and because of this, she had her pick of assignments. However, she hadn't made many close friends there, preferring to keep most of her interactions professional, but still friendly enough. After what she had been through during her last months in Texas, she had wanted nothing more than to immerse herself into her schooling, and now she was doing the same thing in her career as a U.S. Coast Guard Lieutenant, Junior Grade.

She also hadn't wanted to fall for someone while at school, but she hadn't been without offers. She'd had to turn down the male cadets at the academy right and left. Her good looks had been somewhat of a hindrance to her progress until, after several months of men trying to get into her uniform pants, she finally came out as a lesbian by joining the campus gay-straight alliance, the first of its kind in any military academy. Of course, she had a female cadet or three hit on her after that, and that had proven to be much more difficult to resist. She did have a thing for women in uniform, after all. She had enjoyed a brief romantic relationship with her roommate during her second year, but they both found that it was too much of a distraction to their studies, so they'd broken up and settled back into normal friendship. She had refused to put herself in any kind of position that would jeopardize all she had worked so hard to achieve.

Now, a couple of years later, she was still stationed aboard the Medium Endurance Cutter *Gossett* based out of Seattle with only a couple of brief stints in between at various training schools. She was the training officer as well as the boarding officer for her cutter and she regularly took her team on inspection boardings of various vessels around Puget Sound and the Pacific Ocean. She loved it. Most of the boardings were noneventful and she and her fellow Coasties didn't find anything of interest (drugs, smuggled goods, threats to security, trafficked human beings, etc.), but occasionally they would stop a drug runner or save the lives of sailors in distress and all of the training she had endured would kick in, helping to keep herself, her team, and the U.S. waterways safe.

Because of her by-the-book and logical approach to doing her duty, she was never the life of any off-duty parties, but she was the first one the commander would approach to get something done right the first time. She was a trusted and invaluable asset to her crew and even though she was nice, fair, and the crew liked her, she always kept everyone at a professional distance.

Work made her happy. She told herself she didn't need a relationship at this point in her life anyway. She was far too busy serving at sea and developing her career. Every now and again she would drift off to thoughts of her time with Leah or have frivolous imaginings about a couple of her fellow female crewmembers, but she never acted on anything. She had turned herself into a "Coast Guard nun," just like Jennifer had predicted.

Maybe in a year or two, when she was more comfortable with her position as a junior officer in charge of human lives, maybe then she could set aside some time for a personal life.

Maybe.

Bryce laced up her boots quickly and stood in front of the small mirror in the cabin she shared with another female officer. She ran fingers through blond hair that was now only chin length. After arriving at the academy it hadn't taken her long to figure out that having shorter hair was going to make her life a lot easier in the military. At first she had thought she would be sad to see her long locks go, but when the barber had chopped them off she had felt like a new person.

New hair.

New life.

New Bryce.

It still suited her all these years later. So did the uniform. Her gaze traveled down to look at the blue operational dress uniform she wore almost every day of her life aboard ship. Many of her other shipmates complained about having to wear the same thing all the time, but she loved it. And she looked damn good in it, if she did say so herself.

She turned to the calendar on the wall and marked off day 176. Her cutter had been on a lengthy mission up near Alaska for 150 of those days and was now back in the waters of their homeport of Seattle, waiting to finish up their 190-day deployment.

Almost everyone on the ship was starting to get homesick, but Bryce could have stayed out on the open water for months, years even. It was her home, and her devotion to her duty meant that she never wanted to be anywhere else.

"Lieutenant Montgomery." Commander Hendricks's voice crackled through her radio as she readied the boarding team to lower their quick response boat into the choppy sea.

"Sir?"

"Be careful out there today. There's more traffic for this kind of weather than I'd prefer."

Bryce looked at the water around her, what she could see of it. It wasn't too dangerous to do security boardings, but rain fell heavily, and the morning fog had yet to burn off. Visibility wasn't the best at the moment and she couldn't see any other vessels in the vicinity other than the offshore fishing boat they were currently trailing. Even with the foul weather, this was probably going to be another noneventful mission. She would have to make sure there were no drugs or weapons on board, inspect safety gear, check the logs, check permits, etc. Still, she felt the familiar tingle of adrenaline that she got every time her team prepared for a boarding. It had been several weeks since their last major bust and Bryce was itching for some excitement.

"Aye, sir."

The boat slid into the water and the coxswain pulled away, leaving the cutter behind as he sped toward their target. Bryce couldn't help but smile as the small boat leapt over the rolling waves. This never got old.

The fishing vessel emerged from the fog as they approached on its starboard side. Bryce's boat matched its speed and pulled alongside as she hailed the vessel's skipper.

"Good morning, Skipper. My name is Officer Montgomery with the U.S. Coast Guard. We're here to do a boarding today to ensure that you're in compliance with all federal laws."

The man glanced around. "Okay."

"Without reaching for or touching them, do you have any weapons on board?"

"No, ma'am."

Bryce gave him a quick nod, then motioned for her team to board the vessel. Two fishermen on deck helped them over the gunwale. The inspection of this relatively small fishing boat would probably take no more than an hour and a half. Maybe they could get a few more inspections in today—if no search and rescue cases came up instead, that is.

Bryce moved to the side of the larger vessel and was about to start her climb when she heard shouts simultaneously from her coxswain and team members who were already onboard the fishing vessel. Startled, she looked behind her. A recreational powerboat, way too far away from shore in this weather, had just appeared through the rain and fog and was speeding toward them perpendicular to their starboard side. Bryce jumped away from the fishing vessel and back into her own boat as the coxswain made the split-second decision to immediately throttle down to avoid collision. They didn't have the time or room to attempt to steer away from the powerboat. She fell forward heavily onto the deck as her Coast Guard boat slowed with a jolt.

The powerboat was going too fast, though. Its operator had seen them at the same time they had seen him and he tried to slow down and steer clear, but it was too late. The powerboat clipped the front of her boat just as it slammed into the stern of the fishing vessel.

Time seemed to slow.

Her eyes are squeezed tightly shut, but the cacophony of metal being slammed into metal pierces her skull. It seems like it will never stop.

Suddenly she no longer feels the cold, wet deck below her.

Air rushes past her ears.

Searing pain in her face.

A sickening series of snaps as her flailing limbs collide with something metallic.

A body-crushing impact knocks the breath from her lungs.

Freezing cold.

Water in her eyes.

Water in her mouth.

No air.

She can't breathe.

She can't breathe.

Oh God, she can't breathe!

Pain shoots through her body as she fights for air.

Her lungs scream, but finally draw a knife-sharp breath.

A flicker of red and orange before the world goes black.

She is underwater. Voices, muffled and unintelligible—she can barely hear them. She's on the bottom of her swimming pool. Why are people disturbing her when she's meditating? Something hurts. She tries to tune out the voices. They bring an unwelcome physical pain.

Concentrate on meditation.

Become one with the water.

Consternation creases Bryce's brow. The voices speak with more force, excitement building in their tone. Why won't the voices leave her alone? Why do they hurt so much?

Slowly she is forced upward against her will. Rising from the water that soothes and protects her. Her body is changing; being reborn into a coldness that brings fear and a sharper pain.

Agony pierced her head as her eyes slowly blinked open and light stabbed its way into her skull. Slowly she focused on a smiling woman in medical scrubs. Standing alongside her was a man she recognized but couldn't immediately place through the mist that still surrounded her mind.

Commander Hendricks smiled at her warmly. "Welcome back, Lieutenant."

Her mouth felt like it was full of cotton and sand, but she managed to croak, "Where am I…sir?"

"You're at the Naval Hospital in Bremerton. You were in an accident. Do you remember anything?"

Bryce closed her eyes and saw the powerboat speeding toward her. Her eyes popped open, terrified. "My crew?"

"They're all safe. Your coxswain, Petty Officer MacDonald, is a few rooms down with a broken wrist and various scrapes and bruises, but it's nothing to worry about."

"Fishermen?"

"Also fine." He shrugged. "Their boat has seen better days and will definitely have to be dry-docked for repairs, but it stayed afloat and got them safely back to the harbor."

"The powerboat operator?"

"He's fine, but I'll get to that in a bit."

Bryce hesitated, but finally tore her eyes away from the commander's and looked down at her body lying supine in the hospital bed. Her left leg was in a full-length cast and rested in a sling above the sheets. Her left arm was bandaged but didn't appear to be broken. She tried to take a deep breath, but pain shot through the left side of her chest. When she grimaced, tape and gauze pulled at the left side of her face.

Captain Hendricks watched her physical inventory, and his expression grew somber. "Lieutenant Montgomery, let me first say that we're so glad that you're back with us. Petty Officer MacDonald pulled you unconscious from the water and we all feared the worst when we couldn't revive you. You took in a great deal of water when you were thrown from the boat."

"How bad?" Bryce didn't want to hear the answer.

"I won't sugarcoat it for you. I know you don't want that."

He was right. She was a straightforward person and wanted to know everything.

"It appears that when the coxswain slowed suddenly, you were thrown forward onto the deck at your bow, right into the path of the powerboat. When the collision occurred, you were slammed into the fishing vessel's stern and entered the water from there. You got some pretty deep cuts on your left arm and a lot of bruises. Three ribs on your left side were broken, but the doctors are very confident that they will heal cleanly and quickly." He paused for a moment. Bryce knew that the first injuries were the easiest ones. He cleared his throat before continuing. "When you hit part of the fishing vessel's stern, that cut up your arm, but it also created a significant cut to the left side of your face. I haven't seen it, but the doctors tell me that it extends from your left temple to your jawline. You have several stitches and will have a scar."

Bryce tried to cover up her growing panic with sarcasm as she thought, *So much for being pretty. It's too bad I waited to get a girlfriend.*

The commander still hadn't mentioned her leg. "What about this thing?" She gestured with her unharmed right arm to the complicated sling.

"Your leg was broken in multiple places. That injury will…that one will take longer to heal and may not…"

"Tell me."

"You may not have full use of it again."

"W-what?"

"I'll have the doctor show you later on the x-ray. I think there may also be some nerve damage, but she knows more about it than I do." He smiled at her, but concern showed in his eyes.

Bryce nodded solemnly, a movement that hurt every part of her body. "Thank you for being here for me, sir. You didn't have to leave the ship."

"Well, technically I did. They're getting the inquiry ready and I need to report to Sector. But don't worry about that right now. You'll do fine when they question you. You're trained for it, and from what we observed from the *Gossett*, you and your crew are without fault in this situation. Preliminary reports show that the powerboat operator got lost in the fog and was three times over the legal intoxication limit. You got hit by a drunk driver." The commander's face had a hint of anger in it now.

"Lovely," Bryce said emotionlessly.

"Let me know if you need anything, Lieutenant. I'll make sure the doctor keeps me updated on your condition and I'm sure you'll be up and about in no time." He smiled, but the look in his eyes showed that he didn't really believe that.

"Thanks for coming by, Commander. Tell the guys hi for me, would you, sir?"

"You've got it. Now you just rest and start the healing process. I'll talk to you soon." He turned and left the room, leaving Bryce alone with the woman in the scrubs.

Her eyelids felt heavy, and even though she thought the polite thing to do would be to at least say hello to the nurse and thank her for her care, Bryce slid back into her underwater world of sleep.

After two weeks of lying in the hospital bed, Bryce was growing restless. She had never been so inactive in her whole life. The cold ocean air blowing in her face had become so normal to her that the dry, stale air from the hospital room was starting to make her feel like she was in a sealed tomb. Of course, her shipmates and friends had all sent her get-well cards and flowers, so the room looked more cheerful than it had when she had first opened her eyes to the Spartan walls, but still, she couldn't stand the thought of looking at the same holes in the ceiling over and over again. She had also watched so many documentaries and films from her online movie account that she never wanted to look at a computer screen again.

The doctor had promised her she could get out of bed in another week. She knew that it was going to be a slow, painful process, but she was dying for a change, even if that change brought physical suffering. She had been shocked when the doctor had shown her the x-rays of her left leg. Her femur had broken in two places, her kneecap had cracked, and her shinbone had actually snapped with one end piercing through her skin.

Then there was the nerve damage. There were times when she couldn't feel parts of her leg at all and others where the pain was so intense that she broke out into sweats and almost fainted. It was going to take months of healing and physical therapy to get her back on her feet, and even then the doctor had little hope she would ever be able to walk without a cane or, at the very least, a pronounced limp for the rest of her life.

Depressing music played in her head as it did every time she started to dwell on the fact that her hard-won and precious career in the Coast Guard was most likely over before it had even really begun. No. She wouldn't think about that until she had to. She would concentrate her dependable willpower on recuperating. Who cared what the doctor said anyway? She had yet to meet and be conquered by any challenge thrown her way. She would show them what good old-fashioned Texan stubbornness could accomplish.

A knock on the door interrupted her thoughts. She checked the clock on her nightstand: a few minutes before noon. Almost time for the regular delivery of bland hospital food. Normally the nurses rapped once and then entered, but this time no one came in. A second knock, more hesitant.

"You can come in!" Pain in her ribs still stabbed through her when she raised her voice or breathed deeply, but she could tell the bones were healing.

Three people walked into the room. Joy surged through Bryce, the first bit of happiness she had experienced in days. Her three best friends stood at the end of her bed, nervous smiles on their faces.

"Oh my God! I can't believe you guys are here!" Bryce had spoken to Jennifer, Arati, and Leah on the phone in the days following the accident, but she definitely hadn't been expecting to see them in person. Hours of questioning by Sector officials had taken a toll on her emotionally, and her friends had been her lifelines. She hadn't allowed them to video chat with her, though. Not with the giant bandage on her face and her general unkempt and sickly appearance. But they had talked briefly almost every night until Bryce's strength failed and she had to sleep. Having them standing before her in the hospital room felt surreal.

She noticed their reactions to her condition. Each one of them had put on her "brave face," pretending not to notice the bandages, slings, and mysterious medical equipment.

"Well, look at you, ya big faker," Arati said in her usual jovial style after setting a potted plant and "Get Well Soon" bear balloon on the table by the window.

Bryce played along. "Yeah, I was just looking to take a break. You know, catch some R and R. Figured this was the easiest way to do it without the Coast Guard breathing down my neck."

Leah sat gingerly on the right edge of her bed and grasped Bryce's hand. "How are you doing, sweetie?"

Bryce grimaced. "Oh, you know. Shattered leg, ruined career, giant scar spoiling my otherworldly good looks. Same ol', same ol'. You?"

Leah's eyes misted over.

"But seriously, guys, it's *so* good to see you all here! You never said anything about coming!"

Jennifer spoke this time over an insanely large bouquet of flowers. "Bryce, did you think we wouldn't come to see you? Really?" She smiled kindly. "We don't abandon our best friends."

"But you guys had to come from all over the place to get here, and I can't even leave this room yet to hang out with you."

Arati scoffed. "We didn't come out here to play doubles tennis, Bryce. We just want to see you and hopefully get to spend some time with you…if you're feeling up to it."

Bryce smiled widely for the first time since the accident. Pain seared in her wounded cheek, but it still felt good. "Well, I do kick some ass at playing spades, if you're ready to get owned."

"I'm Bryce's partner!" Leah yelled first and they all laughed.

"Oh, before I forget. These," Jennifer held up the bouquet a little higher, "are from…from someone who is worried about you."

Bryce waited for her to say more, but her friends just glanced around the room at each other, trying not to smile.

"Who?"

Jennifer shook her head. "I was instructed, upon pain of death, to not say. Just know that everyone who has heard is really worried about you and they want to let you know how much they care."

Bryce thought for a moment. Could the flowers be from one of her parents? The last time she had spoken to them was to tell them she had arrived at the academy safely for Swab Summer. Her mother had refused to speak to her, simply handing the phone to her father. He had been perfectly polite when she spoke to him, but that was all. There had been no "I love you," no "Good luck, honey," and certainly no "We miss you." So, no. The flowers couldn't be from them. Or could they?

"Why would someone want to send me flowers anonymously?"

"You'll have to ask when you find out who sent them, I guess."

Bryce knew she wasn't going to get any more information out of her. Jennifer was like Fort Knox with secrets. Still, she was intrigued.

Someone out there, besides her three best friends, still thought about her and still cared. Maybe her relationship with her parents was about to be resurrected. The thought terrified and excited her, but whether it was them or someone else, knowing that someone else cared made the pain and anxiety lessen just enough.

CHAPTER FIFTEEN

Bryce didn't want to open her eyes. She had gotten out of bed for the first time yesterday and her body still ached from the effort. The doctor had told her that if she hadn't already been in such peak physical condition she would have been much, much worse off. At least that was something. But even though she had been dying to move around before, now she just wanted to lie still until the pain subsided. Her sleep had been dreamless and deep, and now the sound of someone watering the plants in her room was disturbing her, bringing her back into the world of the living.

At first she thought that one of her friends was back in the room, but that couldn't be it. They had stayed the weekend with her, playing cards, watching movies, catching up on each other's lives, and reliving past memories, but Arati had to return to graduate school in Los Angeles, Leah had to go back to her girlfriend and her job as a social worker in Tucson, and Jennifer was in the middle of writing her dissertation as well as volunteering for a wildlife rehabilitation center in Austin. They had all wanted to stay longer, but Bryce knew she had already caused them to take too much time out of their busy lives.

She blinked her eyes open and saw a blurry female figure standing backlit against the window, holding a water pitcher over the plants. The form and movement was vaguely familiar, but Bryce's sleepy brain couldn't puzzle it out.

"The flowers were watered yesterday," Bryce managed to mumble as she shifted uncomfortably and tried to wake up properly.

The mystery plant lover stopped suddenly as if startled. Bryce saw her back rise and lower as she took a deep breath and turned around.

Bryce's heart threatened to explode from her tender rib cage as she laid eyes on her mother for the first time in more than six years. Her face was thinner than she had remembered, with more lines around her eyes and mouth, but otherwise she looked just the same. Except this time she wasn't crying and telling Bryce she was going to hell. The ability to speak immediately disappeared from Bryce's mental capacities.

Her mother smiled hesitantly and made her way slowly over to her bed.

"Hello, Bryce," she said as her smile wavered.

Bryce couldn't answer.

"Your father wanted to come too, but he's working on a site for a new elementary school on Aspen and Twenty-fifth."

Bryce continued to stare, unable to have a conversation with the woman who had so unceremoniously severed their relationship years ago. Conflicting emotions tumbled around in her chest. Despite what her parents had done to her, she was still elated to see her mom. Because of what they'd done, she wanted to scream at her and tell her to never come back. The pain of their disapproval and the ease with which they'd been able to disown their own daughter felt like an old scab freshly torn open.

"Bryce," her mother ventured cautiously, "we still love you and have missed you terribly ever since…"

Bryce's eyes narrowed.

"We've discussed it and we think everything will be okay now."

For a moment, she sat stunned.

What?

With effort, Bryce found her voice and it shook with fury. "Everything will be okay now? You kick me out of the house only a couple of weeks before I leave for school, never once try to contact me to wish me so much as a happy birthday or to invite me home for Christmas? You miss my graduation and commissioning after four years of backbreaking work and study, and now you have the audacity to come in here and tell me you and Dad think that everything will be okay? Now that I've lost everything I've worked for? Now that my leg is nearly useless and I'm scarred for life?"

The metal contraption that helped to keep her full leg cast steady vibrated with her anger.

A single tear fell from her mother's eye as she looked at the ground. "Honey, I realize what we did was wrong. We've had six years to regret it."

"But what? You regretted it, but just couldn't bring yourself to reach out to your own flesh and blood? To apologize?"

"You have to understand, sweetie," her mother shook her head sadly, "we were just so…so…"

"Ashamed of me."

Her mother winced. "We were disappointed in your choices."

Bryce deflated like a punctured balloon. "Being gay isn't a choice, Mom. Can't you know that by now? Have you not learned anything since I left? And can't you see that my being gay has absolutely zero bearing on who I've become and what I can accomplish?"

"Bryce, please understand—"

"No. You were never able to see past that one small aspect of who I am. You knew me for eighteen years. Knew what a good person I was. Understood my goals and dreams. And you were always so proud. I will never, *never* understand the kind of backward thinking that would make someone disown their own child for something as small and *natural* as their innate sexuality."

"Honey, our beliefs—"

Bryce huffed out a humorless laugh. "I can't believe that this is the first time you've spoken to me in years and we're picking up the same damn conversation right where we left off. This is ridiculous, offensive, and I honestly don't think I can handle it right now."

Tears fell down her mother's face. "Honey, I'm here now. Your commander called to let us know what had happened to you, and I thanked God for the opportunity to make things right between us."

"You thanked God that I was almost killed and my career in the Coast Guard is most likely over," Bryce deadpanned.

"I don't mean it like that and you know it. I think this horrible thing happening to you may be the answer to our prayers, if only we use it for good."

Bryce squeezed her eyes shut. She knew she shouldn't say all of the things she wanted to say right now. Her mother was obviously trying to repair their relationship and make up for her past mistakes, if only in her hurtful and misguided way. As much as it pained Bryce to admit it, part of her wanted their closeness back too, and if her mother could take a step that was obviously difficult for her, then surely she could at least use some of the courage that had been instilled in her at the academy to give it a shot as well.

Truce, she thought, sighing deeply. "Okay. Okay. I don't want to fight, Mom. Not anymore… It's good to see you." She paused, then forced out, "I'm…glad you came."

Her mother broke down sobbing again and gingerly took Bryce's hand. It wasn't the embrace Bryce craved, but they had to start somewhere.

For the next few days her mother stayed by her side, just like she had when Bryce had gotten the flu in kindergarten or the chicken pox in third grade. She finally had her mom back. Maybe there was some good to come out of the accident after all. Bryce latched on to this thought because dwelling on her ruined career, face, and leg just depressed her.

They had plenty of time to talk, so Bryce caught her mother up on her life up until that point. Winning top awards on the Coast Guard Academy swim team, sailing the academy's tall ship, the *Barque Eagle*, to Europe during her Summer Training Cruise, graduating with honors, going through boarding team training, and the rigors, boredom, and excitement of day-to-day life aboard a Coast Guard cutter. She even described the awful accident, what she could remember of it or what had been told to her. Her mother still acted uncomfortable around her, but Bryce expected nothing less after their painful separation.

It was nice having her there as Bryce spent more and more time out of bed too, gingerly testing out her crutches and trying her best to get some semblance of exercise despite the pain in her ribs, leg, and arm. Her mom encouraged her as best as she could, continuously quoting Bible verses she felt would inspire her daughter. Still, it was better than going through everything alone.

"Today's the day. Ready?" The doctor had the surgical scissors and metal tray prepped.

Bryce attempted a smile. "Not really, no. I guess I have to look at some point, though, huh?" She glanced over at her mother, who wore a stoic expression. Neither one of them had seen how her face looked under the bandages when they were cleaned and changed. Now was the time that the bandage would come off for good.

The doctor smiled kindly. "It's been healing beautifully. I mean, for as deep and jagged as that cut was, I'm really pleased with how it's turning out."

"It's still going to be really noticeable, though, isn't it?"

She nodded, but said, “Lieutenant, I unfortunately have to see some really major trauma in my job. There really are a lot worse things that could have happened.”

Bryce felt ashamed. She knew she was lucky to be alive. How could pride be getting the better of her?

“And you know,” the doctor continued, “it sounds cheesy, but scars tell a story. They prove that you’ve been somewhere. Done something. In time it will become just another part of the story of your life.”

“You’re right.”

“See?” The doctor beamed.

“That does sound cheesy.” Bryce smiled and they both laughed. It helped to take the edge off of the nervousness she felt. “Ready, Mom?”

She nodded silently and the doctor slowly cut the bandages from the left side of her face. Before looking in the mirror that the doctor then held out to her, she looked at her mother.

She wished she hadn’t.

Bryce could tell she was trying to hide her shock, but it wasn’t working.

“Wonderful,” Bryce said.

“N-no! Honey, it’s not that bad!”

Bryce held up the mirror to look for herself.

The jagged scar ran from her hairline through the edge of her left eyebrow and all the way down to her jawline. The skin around the stitches was red and puckered, and the whole left side of her face looked swollen. Her left eye also had an asymmetrical droop where the skin was beginning to heal and come back together.

It was so much worse than she had feared.

Bryce’s stomach dropped to her feet. Yes, she had been beautiful and yes, she had known it despite being far from narcissistic, but seeing her pretty features scarred like this was more of a blow to her ego than she had expected.

No one would find her attractive now. She regretted always having an excuse to delay finding love.

She looked to her mother. It was Mom’s job to console her, to tell her she was still beautiful, to make her feel better about herself.

But she didn’t say anything. She just smiled halfheartedly and patted her shoulder.

“Thank you, Doctor,” she said and forced a smile, the pull of the stitches painfully obvious.

As the doctor explained how to care for the wound and smaller bandages Bryce drifted into a dismayed trance, only nodding when she felt it was appropriate to do so.

Eventually, when it was obvious that she wasn't in the mood for discussion, both the doctor and her mother left her alone in the room.

Poisonous thoughts began to fester in her mind despite her recent progress in coming to terms with her leg and other injuries. She was losing her tenuous grip on the optimism she had desperately fostered in the previous weeks. It was too much to handle.

No. She couldn't lose it now. This wasn't her. She was strong.

Just please, if anyone's listening, give me something to hold on to.

Her mother had been with her for seven days when Bryce finally started the conversation she had been dreading. She raised her hospital bed so that she was in a sitting position and then stated, "Mom, I get to leave the hospital in a few days."

Her mother nodded. "I heard the doctor talking to you about it. I'm glad you're finally getting out of here. I bet you're tired of it."

Bryce smiled. "You could say that."

"Will you be able to go back to work?"

She shook her head as the familiar unease caused an uncomfortable fluttering in her stomach. "Technically I'm on temporary retirement right now. I'll be on crutches with this cast for at least two or three more months, so I've rented a small furnished apartment across from the VA hospital where I'll be doing my physical therapy. In sixteen months or so I'll have to be evaluated by a medical board to see if I'm able to return to duty again. If not…" She paused. The thought scared the hell out of her. "Well, I'm still going to find something more permanent here."

"You're going to stay in Seattle?"

"Yeah, I think so. I like it here. I miss the Texas sun, but I've grown accustomed to this area. It's the prettiest place I've ever seen. You just can't beat the trees and the ocean out here." She turned her gaze toward the window even though she knew she could only see sky. "Anyway, that's what I wanted to talk to you about. I'm really glad you came up to see me, but I know that you can't stay with me much longer. I'm sure Dad misses you too." Bryce paused for a moment and plucked at the blanket covering her legs. "I wanted to ask you about your plans when I leave the hospital."

"My plans?"

Shifting uncomfortably Bryce said, "Well, I mean, plans for us."

Her mom gave a quizzical tilt of her head.

Bryce took a steadying breath. The moment of truth. "You guys cut me off for six years. You can't expect everything to go back to normal overnight. So…what I want to know is…will I see you again after you go back to Saltus?"

Her mother paused and looked at her hands folded in her lap. "Bryce, I came out to see you because your father and I still love you, despite all that happened. Despite what you did. I know we were severe with your…situation…and believe me, it tore us up inside. But the last six years have been miserable." Bryce saw tears glistening in her mother's eyes when she finally looked at her. "Things could have been so different if you hadn't—"

Bryce interjected, "Oh, please. You don't think things were five million times harder for me? Forced to face crazy brainwashing zealots? Being made to feel like I was a disgusting monster? Disowned and left to fend for myself right when I needed you most? And please don't tell me you still think this is all my fault."

With tightened features and a hint of irritation in her voice, her mother continued, "You brought it on yourself, Bryce, with your insistence on going against God and nature."

Bryce's skin prickled and she placed her hands over her face. "Oh my God."

"*Don't* use the Lord's name in vain."

It was going to happen all over again, whether she wanted it to or not. All the progress they had made in the last week was about to be washed away. It felt like her foot had just slipped off one of a ship's spars that reached out over the sea and she had forgotten to clip on her safety harness. She was going to fall, the damage irrevocable. And there was nothing she could do about it. "I thought we had gotten past this, Mom. You do realize that we will not be able to have any kind of real relationship if you continue to hate me for what I am."

"I don't hate *you*, Bryce." Her mother made an exasperated noise as she stood and walked over to the window. She stared at the raindrops hitting the glass for at least a minute before she finally said, "I hate that your friends, or that Leah girl, or the liberal media, or whatever evil thing…I hate whatever has made you think that you're a homosexual!"

Bryce stared across the room at her mother, wide-eyed. How could she have thought that all of these years apart had changed her parents? They would never accept her. She was corrupted forever in their eyes.

Her mother approached Bryce's bed again and continued, "That's why your father and I decided that I should come out to see you! Your accident was no accident, honey!"

Bryce could only continue to stare at her mother with growing dismay.

"Sweetheart, God put you in this situation so that you could see the error of your ways. He's punishing you for your unnatural thoughts. Don't you see?" Bryce flinched as her mother gently grasped her arm. "He has brought us back together. We have a second chance. *You* have a second chance. You can come back home to us and we can work together on saving you. I'm sure that there are great jobs waiting for you in Saltus now that the Coast Guard can't use you anymore. Everyone there loves a veteran." Her mother's tone was more hopeful now. "I know you probably can't see it now, honey, but this is the best thing that could have happened to you. God has given you a wake-up call and now you can start atoning for your sins. And we want you to know that your father and I will be here for your battle every step of the way. We *won't* let this defeat you. We see now that letting you go the way we did was wrong. We thought it would help. Make you realize the consequences of your actions. But now we know that you won't get well if you have to do it alone."

It didn't matter to her mother that she wasn't currently in a lesbian relationship. It didn't matter that she was a highly successful Coast Guard officer risking her life, serving her country, and saving lives every day. It didn't matter that she was her parents' only child. She was broken in her mother's eyes. Bryce now understood that she would never be able to foster a relationship with her parents. Not now that she knew how easily they could discard her based on nothing more than her body's emotional and biological reactions. She had been deluding herself about her mother coming around to any compassionate way of thinking. Still, even though she had known to expect it, her mother's words cut deeply. So painfully and raggedly that Bryce felt something inside her break. Actually, she felt many parts of herself break at once. Her heart, her self-confidence, her tenuous hold on optimism. For the first time since her accident she felt the full weight of her situation. She felt every bruise, every broken bone, every damaged nerve, every opportunity she was about to miss, every single loss she had ever and would ever have.

Bryce's eyes glazed over and the only words she could bring herself to say were "Know that I will always love you and Dad. Good-bye, Mom."

"Bryce?" Her mother's smile fell and a worried frown creased the lines around her mouth.

Bryce closed her eyes and turned her head away from the woman who had given her life.

Her mother's voice morphed from worry to anger. "Bryce Lee Montgomery, God has given you a gift. You will *not* squander it! All you have to do is admit your sin and take him back into your heart. Don't let this beat you!"

Bryce was done fighting. All of her strength had disappeared and she saw no point in anything anymore. She wouldn't argue with her mother. She would do nothing but lie in her bed and be the pawn in the chess game that the universe felt like playing with her. She felt detached.

Her mother tried begging. "Please don't do this, Bryce. You *need* us. What do you have now? You're scarred, your leg is useless, and you have no one. No one except us and the Heavenly Father. We're here for you now, but if you turn your back on us, you'll be lost forever. I won't let that happen."

Bryce let her mind float away from her damaged body and out into nothingness. Every word her mother spoke only had the unintentional effect of breaking her spirit even more. Her soul was wounded and her mom poured salt into it with every cruel word.

Her mother's words grew loud and forceful, but Bryce didn't hear their meaning. She barely even noticed when the pleading subsided and her mother stormed out of the room.

A few minutes…or a long time later, she wasn't sure which, she heard the door open again.

"Lieutenant Montgomery?"

She opened her eyes, but didn't say anything. Her nurse stood by the bed.

"I just wanted to let you know that your mother has been escorted out of the building and has been placed on a list that bars her entrance to the hospital for security reasons."

"What?" Bryce asked, startled.

"Apparently she tried to force her way into the hospital chaplain's office. We don't know why."

"Oh…"

The nurse's eyes flickered with sympathy but she held her bearing, even as her voice softened. "If you would like to override this order, just let us know. However, she won't be allowed to visit you without staff supervision from now on." The nurse paused, studying her face. "Would you like for her to be allowed back inside in a little while?"

It was one of the hardest things Bryce would ever do, but she shook her head slightly. With that one move she broke ties with her parents for good. She had tried to be a good daughter, to be a beneficial and worthwhile person, but clearly they would never be able to see that. Even if she did return home, she would practically have to hide in the shadows, never revealing her true self to her parents or any of their friends for fear of their judgment and hateful words.

She was alone now.

Loved only by her three best friends.

Unwanted by anyone else.

Unable to continue the career she had planned on having. Broken, scarred, and finally defeated.

CHAPTER SIXTEEN

Bryce hobbled up the ramp of the physical therapy building at the VA, her crutches clicking with each step. Her cast had only been off for ten days and her leg felt tender, stiff, and fragile, even in the temporary brace. She was only four days into her physical therapy and it consisted mainly of reminding her leg that it had the ability to bend. She was forced to put only a slight amount of weight on it. It hurt like hell and she would probably have to use her crutches for another month or so before she could graduate to a cane.

Moodiness she had grown accustomed to descended on her yet again. She still had several months before she could be evaluated by the Coast Guard medical board, and her bad attitude wasn't going to help her get to where she needed to be by that time. She couldn't help it. In the months since she had last spoken with her mother she couldn't seem to shake the dread, depression, and hopelessness she had fought so bravely before their second falling-out.

She checked in at the front desk and was sent to a different part of the building this time. As she approached wide double doors, a familiar smell hit her and the corner of her mouth drew up in an unexpected smile. Chlorine. The scent brought back memories of growing up, of high school, of competing, of summer, and of her friends. She pushed one of the doors open with her crutch and her smile broadened as sunbeams from the skylights danced on the surface of an Olympic-sized swimming pool.

"Lieutenant Montgomery. Welcome to your first pool session!"

Bryce's therapist was a graying ex-football player and ex-Marine whose ebony skin was marred by several small burn scars, as if he had been on the wrong end of shrapnel in his younger years. His name was Thomas, and he turned out to be the most unforgiving, the toughest, and the most respectable man Bryce had ever met. She had only been with him since the beginning of the week, but by the end of each session she had been on the verge of tears. He had an aura about him that made her want to push herself to her absolute limits, and he had made sure to give her the shove she needed. She was always exhausted and in tremendous amounts of pain by the time she left him, but his proud smile had left her wanting to do it all over again.

Bryce's smile faltered. "Will I be able to swim at all? I don't think I can kick properly with this leg."

"From what I hear, you were a champion swimmer. I don't think you're going to drown," he said dryly. "And oh yeah, I know what the hell I'm doing, so shut your mouth and get changed." His eyes twinkled despite his harsh words and Bryce couldn't help but laugh.

"Yes, Sergeant!"

When she'd changed and carefully lowered herself into the water she was overcome with something like comfort. Not quite the normal overwhelming calm and euphoria she used to feel, but it was close. It was like a homecoming of sorts. She hadn't been in the water in months, even before the accident. She let out a long sigh and relaxed as the warmth surrounded her.

"Don't get too comfy, Lieutenant. You don't know what I have planned yet." Thomas smirked.

"Tough love again?"

"You got it."

Getting back in the water had been the catalyst she needed. Learning to walk again was still incredibly painful and frustrating, but it was worth it now that she had graduated to walking with a cane instead of hobbling around on the crutches. It had taken two months, but at least she had made some progress. Still, knowing that the limp and the cane were going to be ever-present in her life depressed her. The only time she could move with an ease that came anywhere close to equaling her before-accident condition was when she swam. Kicking in the water didn't seem to be a struggle for her like walking in a straight line had become. She'd never win any races, but she still moved with a freedom and fluidity that made the extent of her injury completely invisible to the untrained eye.

Despite her progress in physical therapy, she was still unable to come to terms with the injury to her face. Every time she looked in the mirror she saw the hideous scar. It had come to represent her entire situation. She was ruined for the two things she wanted more than anything: her career and a meaningful relationship. She hadn't planned for anything else. There was no plan B. She didn't know if she could face what was to come when her physical therapy ended and she had to go before the medical board and show them that she was still unfit for active-duty service.

These thoughts ran through her head as she sat in the hospital waiting room. Thomas was late for their daily session, and that just gave her more time to brood. She absentmindedly poked at the muscles in her left leg. They had atrophied a lot while her leg was in the cast, but they seemed to be regaining strength slowly. Maybe it would at least look normal in several months. Not like her face. She grimaced thinking about the puffy red skin distorting her features.

She had become hesitant to leave her gloomy little apartment knowing that people would stare. Going across the street to the VA was one thing—there were many there who were far worse off than she—but going to the grocery store had become such an ordeal for her that she had signed up for a grocery delivery service. Adults who saw her tended to look away quickly with pity etched upon their faces, but the children stared in horror, ignorantly unaware of the insult they were adding to her injury. She only left her apartment for therapy sessions now. How she was going to be able to stand like a lab specimen in front of a medical board was beyond her.

Approaching footsteps roused her from the despondent thoughts. She looked up and saw a middle-aged naval lieutenant commander in the everyday working khaki uniform glance at a chart and then head directly for her, a sincere smile on his face. Bryce stumbled to her feet, bracing herself on the edge of her chair as she tried to salute and stand at attention.

"At ease, Lieutenant, at ease. Please, have a seat." He gestured at the chair she had just vacated.

As Bryce sat down she noticed with a sickening plummeting of her stomach the gold cross on the officer's left lapel. She tried pointedly to focus on the lieutenant commander's lined face.

The man noticed her grimace despite her attempts and gave her an apologetic look. "Bad history with chaplains, Lieutenant?"

Bryce spoke softly, obviously wary of anyone with a strong religious bent. "No, sir. Just with certain…zealous people. No offense to you, sir."

The chaplain nodded sadly. "You'd be surprised how often I hear that. There are some people out there who give my life's calling a bad name. But don't worry, I'm just here to check on you and the other VA patients. I'm here if you need any guidance, advice, or just want to talk things out. My name is Chaplain Davis." He smiled and held out his hand for her to shake.

Bryce took the proffered hand but otherwise sat still and silent.

The chaplain studied her. "Would you like to chat for a little while? You look like you have a lot on your mind. It might help to have someone who will listen."

Bryce shrugged with noncommittal apathy.

"How do you feel you're coping with your injuries, Lieutenant? Emotionally, I mean."

Bryce swallowed hard as she fought an unexpected flood of self-pity and sadness. "I'm fine, sir."

Chaplain Davis looked at her for a moment before saying, "How are you coping really?"

"If you don't mind, sir, I'd rather not talk about it."

"I understand." He paused and looked out of the window for a moment before adding, "I'll be back around every couple of days or so if you change your mind. Please know that I'm here for you, okay? You don't have to be Christian, or religious at all. I'm here for everyone."

"Thank you, sir."

She was done talking and the chaplain seemed to sense it, so he made a movement for Bryce to stay seated as he smiled and left the room.

Bryce couldn't believe it. After all that had happened to her, both with her church, her parents, and now her body and career, she was going to be confronted by religion again. And religion in Bryce's mind had come to equate itself with bigotry and intolerance. She knew she couldn't handle that in her current condition. Her strength had all but failed her and she felt as fragile as a Faberge egg, both inside and out, the haphazard patterns on her shell masquerading as purposeful decorations barely holding her together. It wouldn't take much pressure at all to cause her to crumble.

She jumped as Thomas spoke only a few feet from where she was sitting. She hadn't noticed him come in. "I got a penny."

"What?"

"Penny for your thoughts."

Bryce sighed. Maybe she did need to talk to someone. She hadn't spoken to her friends in a while, even though they called constantly.

She just couldn't bear to have them hear defeat in her voice for the first time ever. She also refused to speak to a military psychologist, preferring to try to get through everything on her own, just as she had always done. But it didn't seem to be working this time. Despite the exemplary progress with her leg, her bouts of depression were growing stronger and her will to get on with her life rapidly diminishing.

"A chaplain named Davis just came in to see me."

Thomas nodded. "Yeah, he used to come by several times a week to minister to the folks here. He just got back from six months overseas or else you would have seen him earlier. He's a good one, that Davis."

"I'm not religious, Thomas."

He shrugged. "So?"

"I don't know if I feel comfortable talking to someone who…who might judge me." Bryce's lip quivered involuntarily.

Thomas looked pensive. "Sounds like you been treated bad by some of those who call themselves Christian. Am I right?"

Bryce nodded and looked down, pretending to examine a small scar on her left arm.

"I thought so. Now, I have a deal for you."

Bryce looked up at him with watery eyes.

"If we skip the treadmill today and spend the whole time in the pool, will you do me a favor?"

She couldn't help but nod. Thomas knew her weakness.

"Talk to that man."

"Thomas, I—"

"Bryce, he's a good man and a good chaplain. Forget about all the religious stuff. You need to talk to someone and he's the best person for it."

Bryce made a face.

"Do you trust me?"

She nodded again.

"Talk to him, then. Please? For me."

Bryce let the idea tumble around in her brain for a minute before deciding that her fear of rejection and judgment was less than her need to get everything off her chest. And, she did trust Thomas. A lot. "Okay. For you, I will."

"Good girl. Now get your lazy ass up and start doing laps."

❖

Two days later Bryce sat in the same chair in the same room, waiting for Thomas to come and get her yet again. Sure enough, Chaplain Davis entered and gave her the same winning smile. She started to rise, but he again motioned for her to sit down.

"How are you doing, Lieutenant? That cloud above your head doesn't seem as dark and stormy today."

Bryce was determined to keep her promise to Thomas, so she gathered up her courage and settled in for a real conversation. "I got some advice from a friend, so I'm trying to follow it. Having a plan helps me get my thoughts in order, I guess."

"Excellent!" He looked genuinely pleased. "How is your treatment going?"

"Apparently I'm doing better than most for this kind of injury, but it doesn't seem like much when I don't have anything to look forward to."

"What do you mean you don't have anything to look forward to?"

Oh no. She was starting to choke up. She didn't want to show him weakness by crying. "I mean…you know…I'm going to be forced to medically retire…sir."

"Don't worry about the 'sir' thing right now. Right now I'm just a chaplain. Ignore the rank."

"Yes, sir."

Chaplain Davis smiled. "Is that what bothers you most?"

"The rank?"

He smiled warmly, "No, no, the possibility that you'll have to leave the Coast Guard?"

Bryce paused, contemplating. "That's definitely a big part of it. This is all I've wanted for…for a long time. I don't know how to do anything else."

"From what I hear you're extremely smart, talented, and dependable. I'm sure you have a bright future ahead of you, even if it's not in the service. The world needs people like you."

She shook her head incredulously.

"Have you had the opportunity to talk to anyone else about how you're feeling? Your friends? Your parents?"

Crack.

Bryce broke down. She could barely see the chaplain through her tears, but from what she could make out, he looked surprised and worried.

"Miss Montgomery, I'm sorry. Did I say something wrong?"

She tried to steady her breathing, but could only say, "No…sir…it's not…you."

"I'm here to listen if you need to talk about it."

His words sounded genuine and kind. Bryce realized, right then, she was going to tell him everything. She wouldn't be able to help it. Every tormenting memory, every poisonous thought, every emotional and physical trauma she had endured since her senior year of high school was about to erupt onto this poor, unsuspecting Navy chaplain. Well, he'd asked for it.

At least an hour must have passed by the time Bryce stopped talking. She had peripherally noticed Thomas enter and then leave the room, and her throat was dry and sore from crying and spilling her guts. But she had done it. She'd bared her soul to someone who might damn her to hell just as her mother had.

What had she been thinking?

When it was obvious she'd finished her confession, the chaplain placed his hand on her shoulder. "Bryce?"

She blew her nose wetly into her thousandth tissue before replying, "Sir?"

"I want to thank you for trusting me enough to tell me all of those personal things that have been a weight on your shoulders for so long. I'm truly honored."

She shrugged lamely. "I couldn't really help it."

"It seems that these things have been bothering you for a long time. Do you feel better now that you've been able to talk about them?"

Bryce considered this. She did actually feel a little lighter. She nodded.

"Good. I'm glad. I'm also very, very sorry to hear about what your parents did to you. What they and your ex-minister did was most definitely not in the true spirit of our Lord or of Christianity in general. No wonder you were so uncomfortable the first time we met. Please allow me to apologize on behalf of those who misconstrue the words of the Bible to match their own twisted beliefs."

Bryce looked at him in astonishment. Of course, she knew that not all religious believers were bad people; she knew amazing people of almost every religious bent, but having a chaplain be so understanding about her situation shocked her.

"Lieutenant, let me show you something." He reached into his back pocket and pulled out his wallet. After digging through countless credit cards, receipts, and folded money, he finally pulled out a faded and bent photograph. "This," he held the picture up, "is my sister Karen, her wife Michelle, and their daughter Mary, my beautiful niece. They are my family and I will love them no matter what the rest of the world might say." He extended his arm, offering it to Bryce. "The picture is a bit out of date. Mary is in college now, but I wanted you to see them."

She slowly took the picture from him, bringing it close to her face and looking for shame or unhappiness in the eyes of the women, but she saw only joy and love.

"I'm showing you this so that you know that nothing is wrong with you. I know that many of the world's religions get up on a misguided high horse and try to put others down because they're different. This isn't the way it should be and it's certainly not what I preach to those in my care."

Looking at the picture lit a fire inside Bryce's chest. She had let the words of her parents, of Pastor Harold, of that damnable Mrs. Coulson spread like venom for years, and now this one man had just injected her with something that felt uncannily like life. Real, unapologetic, hopeful life.

Tears fell down her cheeks again. "Thank you." She handed the photo back to him and he placed it carefully back in his wallet.

Chaplain Davis leaned forward. "Will you do something for me, Bryce?"

"Of course, sir." She sniffed quietly.

"I want you to start living again. Live on your terms and don't ever let anyone tell you what you can or cannot be."

Bryce protested by gesturing to her leg, but the chaplain cut her off. "I'm not talking about your career, Lieutenant. I'm talking about you. Who you are in your heart. Jobs come and go. Physical ability is fickle and fades with time anyway. But *you*." He pointed straight at her chest. "You have to learn to live your life free from the fear of the prejudices of those around you. There are those out there who love you. You told me about your three best friends, for example. Do you think they're wrong for loving you as you are?"

Bryce shook her head, ashamed.

"Right. Trust in them. Trust in yourself. And never, ever give up." He smiled broadly and sat back in his chair. "Okay. Lame motivational speaker time over now."

With a quivering breath Bryce replied, "I'll try, sir."

Thomas then entered the room again and stood next to the chaplain. "Well, you missed the physical part today, but you surely didn't miss the therapy."

"Sorry about that." Bryce smiled weakly, her eyes still puffy from her break down.

"Hey, don't you worry about a thing. You needed that conversation more than a few extra lunges. Besides, you'll be done with me in a few more sessions."

"Oh no." Bryce felt a surge of fear knowing that she would be on her own after her physical therapy sessions ended.

"You'll be fine," Chaplain Davis and Thomas said as one before smiling at each other.

Bryce only hoped that they were right. She had a long way to go to get there.

Chapter Seventeen

Bear, off the bookshelf. Now." She snapped her fingers and the fluffy dark gray cat dutifully jumped to the floor. As if asking forgiveness, he sprang up purring onto Bryce's stomach as she lay on the couch watching a Modern Marvels marathon, crumbs from her breakfast of chips and salsa littering her T-shirt, couch, and floor.

Named after the Coast Guard Academy's mascot, Bear, a starving stray kitten she had discovered crying for his long-gone mother in the bushes outside of the VA, had been her only companion since her physical therapy sessions had ended three months ago. She never left her apartment and instead spent all of her time working out, watching TV, playing Xbox, and teaching herself how to play the guitar. She had never been so lazy in her whole life and she found that while it didn't suit her, she couldn't stand the thought of trying to integrate back into civilian society with her damaged features and lack of direction.

Two weeks ago she had stood before the medical board and, as she had expected, they had found that her leg had been too damaged to allow her to return to active duty. She had been hoping for the opportunity to at least take a desk job, but her leg just wouldn't bend well enough or move easily enough to pass the physical. After being forced into medical retirement she had lain in bed for two full days, doing nothing but stare at the ceiling and sleep fitfully with dreams of desperately trying to keep her ship on course in huge storms. It was only the pitiful mewling of Bear that had made her finally emerge from her stupor to feed and play with him.

Today, *Modern Marvels* marathon or no, she knew that she had to eventually get up and clean the apartment. Jennifer, Arati, Leah, and Leah's girlfriend Hannah were coming to visit for a full week starting tomorrow. Bryce planned to stay with everyone in a reserved hotel suite downtown, but her friends would still come over to her apartment to pick her up and meet Bear, so it had to look at least halfway presentable. Not like the dark, disheveled, and depressing den of a workout-obsessed shut-in.

Which was pretty much what it was. She hated this place. The bare walls reminded her of everything she had lost, but she couldn't bring herself to do anything with it. The sparse and ugly surroundings suited her current frame of mind.

Bear meowed and rubbed his head clumsily against her chin.

"I know, I know. I'm getting up. I just didn't know how to fit anything else into my busy schedule, you know?" She scratched between his ears before picking him up and placing him back down onto the couch in her place. When she looked around the room, her heart sank. She had zero attachment to this nondescript box of an apartment, and it showed. She'd really let the place go, too, which did nothing to perk it up. "What do you think, Bear? Daft Punk or '80s to get us in a cleaning mood?"

Bear meowed, lifted his back leg into a yoga position, and proceeded to lick his belly.

"You're right. We need some energy around here. Daft Punk it is."

Grabbing her cane, she began by opening all the windows and letting the crisp Seattle fall breeze air out her stuffy hovel. It reminded her of being out on the open water, and although it saddened her, it brought back happy memories that helped to rejuvenate her. She was going to have to try harder for her friends. She didn't want to let them down.

"Bryce! How in the world can you swim in this weather?" Arati's muffled voice came from a tiny hole in the blanket that was wrapped around her whole body. She looked like a shivering cocoon on the lounge chair next to the hotel pool.

"It's heated! It feels great! You should join me!"

"My ass! It's like negative a million degrees outside!"

"We've been in colder pools on the swim team and you know it."

"Colder pools maybe, but they weren't outside in the Arctic!"

"Seattle is much farther south than the Arctic, Arati." Jennifer's reply floated lazily over from amidst the steam of the hot tub where she soaked with Leah and Hannah.

Although she couldn't see her face, Bryce knew that Arati had just rolled her eyes.

Bryce pulled herself out of the pool and goose bumps erupted angrily on her skin as the frigid air made contact. Arati rushed over to hand her the cane that was now her constant companion and Bryce thanked her with an apologetic look. She then made her way slowly over to the hot tub to join her friends, Arati following behind in her tightly wound bundle. At least the cold weather meant that no one else at the hotel was brave enough to be outside at the pool. Bryce was still struggling with being seen in public. The leg and cane were one thing, but she could do absolutely nothing to hide the hideous scar that had altered the landscape of her face.

She lowered herself carefully into the water and Leah put a friendly arm around her trembling shoulders. A long sigh escaped her lips as the hot water washed over her cold skin.

"So, Bryce," Jennifer began.

"So, Jenn," Bryce replied.

"We wanted to talk to you about the benefit."

"Not that again." Ever since her friends had found out about the invitation Bryce had received a month ago to attend a charity fund-raiser benefiting a disabled veterans' association as one of the five guests of honor, they had insisted she accept. The fund-raiser wanted to have a veteran from each branch of the military who had been disabled in the line of duty there to represent their service. Bryce could think of nothing worse than to be paraded around like a broken china doll in front of hundreds of the Pacific Northwest's elite. Bryce involuntarily lifted her fingers to her drooping left eye. "I'm not going, Jenn, and that's the end of it."

"We all think you're missing out on a great opportunity."

Arati joined in. "You'd be doing a really good thing for the charity, Bryce. You know firsthand how hard it is for disabled veterans in this country. You should support your fellow service members."

Bryce was starting to get irritated at this conversation. It had come up at least once a day since her friends had arrived four days ago. She had accepted the invitation in a fit of positive thinking, but as the date drew nearer, her feet were getting more and more mired in a giant block of ice. "I don't...I'm not...I can't handle it, guys."

"Is it the scar?" Leah asked.

She sighed. "That's part of it, yeah. And don't y'all tell me that it's not that bad. I know there are people out there who have it way worse than I do, trust me. I'm not delusional." Her tone softened. "I saw what war can do to the human body and mind in the VA. None of it is pretty. But what happened to me bothers me anyway and I can't help it." She shrugged. "I'm selfish. Yes, I'm embarrassed of the scar and my ugly face. I'm not proud of how I feel. It's just…I'm just struggling with it. You guys don't know what it feels like to have people stare at you with pity or revulsion or both."

Leah removed her arm from Bryce's shoulder, reached into the water to take her hand, and turned to face her. "Bryce. Listen to me carefully. Yes, you have a pretty impressive scar on your face."

Bryce winced.

"Yes, you have to use a cane most of the time. *But* you are still the same beautiful, intelligent, and amazing person we have always known and loved."

Bryce looked at the faces of her friends surrounding her. Arati had even poked her head out of her blanket to smile kindly. "It's not just that stuff, guys. I mean…who am I now?"

"What do you mean?" Arati asked.

"I worked so hard to get into the academy and to prove that I could be a good officer, but what do I have now? I have no job, I'm living off retirement and disability, I'm afraid to leave my cramped little apartment, and I have no idea what to do with my life. I feel lost." She slumped deeper into the roiling water.

Jennifer took her other hand. "Bryce, you're scrambling for a foothold, but I know you. I know how determined you are and what a good heart you have. I honestly think this fund-raiser will be an amazing opportunity for you to help others. That's why you joined the Coast Guard in the first place. You said it yourself, you've seen the damage that can be done to those in the military. Maybe this is your calling. Maybe going to this thing will be good for you as well as being beneficial to your fellow servicemen and women."

Bryce sat pensively for several minutes before saying, "I don't know, guys. I don't know if I can do it."

"You *can* do it. And we'll be with you." Jennifer squeezed her hand and smiled.

"You can't come! The tickets are three hundred dollars a plate!"

Jennifer waved her hand dismissively. "Come on. What's three hundred dollars compared to being there to support our best friend?"

"Besides," Arati began, "there are going to be tons of hot military guys there!"

Bryce couldn't help but laugh. It seemed like she and her friends were still in high school: talking about boys, supporting each other, making jokes to make each other feel better. They were the only good left in her life. Her parents had proven they wanted nothing to do with her, so her friends had become her replacement family. She had no strong ties to anyone in the Coast Guard or in Seattle, so the feeling of safety she got from her friends' visit was not only welcome, but needed.

Bryce took a deep breath and looked in the mirror. Her hair had grown long again since the accident, so she had it up in a tight bun. She wore her formal dinner dress whites and she had to admit to herself, even with the cane, she cut a dashing figure. Her medals hung proudly on her chest and the gold buttons running up the center of her coat were at a high shine. Her friends had pitched in and bought her a pretty black cane with a silver pommel that looked much nicer than the standard-issue gray one she had gotten from the hospital. She admired herself until she got to her face, then any confidence she had gained was immediately destroyed. Tears welled up in her eyes.

"Ohhh no you don't." Arati rushed to her side, trying not to trip on the floor-length skirt that was too long without her heels, and dabbed at the corner of Bryce's eyes with a tissue. "You're not going to ruin that mascara right before you get to the ball."

"I'm not going," Bryce said quietly.

"Yes, you are." Arati replied as she reapplied concealer to the top inch of Bryce's scar.

"Stop it, Arati." Bryce pushed her hand away. "That stuff doesn't help anyway. It doesn't hide the ugliness."

Just then Jennifer walked into the room with Leah and Hannah. Leah and Jennifer both wore cute black strapless dresses and Hannah had on an elegant pantsuit. "Bryce Lee Montgomery, if I hear you badmouth yourself *one* more time, I'll—"

"You'll what, Jenn?" Bryce snapped. "What could you possibly do to me that will make me feel worse?" She sighed when she saw Jennifer's hurt face and bowed her head. She was angry, but it wasn't fair to take it out on her friends. She knew they were trying desperately to help her. "I'm sorry. I'm just terrified of going to this thing. I don't want to be seen and I damn sure don't want to be a poster girl for wounded veterans."

Leah approached and tilted Bryce's chin up. "Do we really have to go through this again? Do you know how many people you'll be helping tonight? Besides, it will be good for you to get out there, talk to people, remember that you're still alive and important to all of us."

Bryce pinched the bridge of her nose and resigned herself to her fate. "Fine. Let's just get this over with."

"Bryce?" Hannah rarely spoke to Bryce directly because she was even more shy than Leah had been in high school, so Bryce looked at her curiously. "You look...*really* hot in that uniform."

Simple flattery or not, Bryce smiled, blushed, and turned to leave the room, considerably more hopeful about the evening.

The muffled sounds of upbeat music drifted through the walls of the waiting room in the downtown hotel where Bryce and her fellow wounded veterans sat quietly, waiting for their turn up on the stage. Next to her sat a Marine who absentmindedly fingered the folded-over portion of his uniform trouser where his lower leg used to be. Across the room, talking excitedly to a sailor whose head and neck had been severely burned, stood a handsome airman gesturing with his prosthetic arm. The only other person in the room was a soldier who sat with her back to the wall, holding the evening's program close to her chest as if it were a shield. Occasionally she wiped nervous sweat from her brow.

What a fine lot we are, Bryce thought sarcastically. *All five services sitting in one room, waiting to show a ballroom full of philanthropists how damaged we are. What do we have, folks? One hundred dollars for a bum leg! Three hundred for no leg at all! Three fifty for no arm! Do we hear five hundred for PTSD? Dig deep into your wallets for a horribly disfigured, burned face!*

The music from the other room grew louder as a great chorus of people ended a song she vaguely recognized on a wall-shaking chord. Bryce glanced down at her program and her eyes fell to the entertainment portion of the evening. The touring cast of a revived Broadway musical had apparently just performed their show's big number for the benefit.

"Damn. I would've liked to have seen that," she said to no one in particular. The Marine to her right made no indication that he had heard her. They had all been invited to sit in places of honor for the whole evening, but when the female soldier and the Marine had declined, preferring to stay in the room across the hall until the last possible second in order to shorten their public appearance time, Bryce, the airman, and the sailor had stayed with them in solidarity.

Just then one of the benefit's volunteers opened the door and let them know that the speeches, and therefore their time to shine, were about to start. Bryce's heart immediately pounded and she felt on the verge of passing out. She couldn't do it. She couldn't stand the scrutiny of all of those people. Panic seized her. She searched for a way out of the situation.

Before she could take any rash action, the door opened again and her eyes popped as she saw Chaplain Davis enter the room. As soon as he saw her his face lit up in a smile. He was wearing his Navy whites and looked extremely handsome. All of the service members in the room struggled to their feet at his entrance, but he just told them to be at ease and pulled up a chair next to Bryce.

"So, Lieutenant, how are you feeling?"

"I feel like I'm going to throw up all over those pretty white pants…sir."

He bellowed with laughter. "Thanks for the warning!"

"You asked." Bryce grimaced and tried to get her breathing under control.

"Listen, I came back here to hopefully help you through it. Should you need me."

"I don't think I can do this."

"Of course you can! You're a Coast Guardsman in our nation's oldest military service. You brave seas that send naval vessels back into port, and as a Navy man, it pains me to say that."

She laughed softly, in spite of her choking fear.

"You protect the country. You save lives every day. What is standing up and waving to a few hundred people for an evening compared to that?"

Bryce was silent for a minute before replying quietly, "I'm not a Coastie anymore, Commander. This"—she gestured to her leg—"took care of that."

Chaplain Davis shook his head sadly. "Do you honestly think that just because you were medically retired you're not the same brave person you always were? That you're no longer Lieutenant Montgomery?"

"I don't know."

"Once a Coastie, always a Coastie. Don't forget that."

Just then the door opened again and the volunteer gestured for them to follow.

Bryce widened her eyes at Chaplain Davis, who nodded and smiled kindly. She took a deep breath and stood with the help of her cane. She was about to take a small boat into gale force winds, but even though she was terrified, she would make herself get through it. Chaplain Davis was right—she'd been trained to handle any situation, and by God, she would handle this.

Bryce stood alongside the other service members, shaking hands with the attendees and accepting their thanks and sympathy for what had happened to her with a grace and dignity that felt false and forced.

After an interminable amount of time and handshakes, the stream of people finally ebbed and Bryce was able to break away from the group to sit. Her leg throbbed and the effort she had taken to smile at each guest made the scar on her face itch.

Suddenly she heard Arati's voice from across the room. "Bryce! Bryce!"

She looked up to see Arati trotting toward her, Jennifer, Leah, and Hannah racing to catch up.

"Bryce! Oh my God, you won't believe who—"

Jennifer caught up with Arati and elbowed her in the ribs.

"Ow! What the hell, Jenn?"

Jennifer gave Arati an exasperated look before tilting her head toward Bryce conspiratorially.

Bryce's brows furrowed. "What was that all about?"

"Nothing! We'll tell you later. Anyway, are you coming outside with us? The band just started playing. They're a Journey cover band. You like Journey, right?"

Bryce continued to look at Jennifer distrustfully. She appeared to be giddy and nervous at the same time. It was odd behavior for their current situation. "Yeah. Journey's fine."

"Well, come on, then! It's a beautiful night. No rain or anything."

Bryce made no move to get up.

"It's an open bar!" Arati offered helpfully.

Bryce rolled her eyes and stood with Leah's help.

"I don't know why we can't just go home. I did my bit."

"And you looked beautiful up there." Leah smiled.

"You're biased, Leah."

She shrugged. "Maybe so, but it doesn't make it any less true."

"Come on, Bryce. This 'dance under the stars' thing is the last part of the evening. People will expect to see you out there. But don't worry. You can sit with us. You don't have to do anything but drink champagne and eat those little puff pastries they're passing out on fancy silver trays."

Bryce shook her head. "You guys just don't give up do you? Fine. Lead the way."

All four of her friends smiled and Jennifer gave an odd little nod to Arati, who beamed.

When Bryce stepped out onto the rooftop terrace she saw a band full of middle-aged men with receding hairlines and ponytails playing Journey's "Separate Ways," people milling about the bar area, and white holiday lights strung beautifully above a small dance floor where a respectable number of white-haired officers and their spouses spun each other around with surprising agility.

A few heads turned to look at Bryce when she and her friends walked to an empty table in the corner, but they just lifted their glasses to her and then turned back to their own friends and colleagues. She calmed a little as she noticed that she was no longer the center of attention. Now everyone just wanted to dance and have fun. The depressing part of the evening was over. She smiled when she saw the burned sailor dancing joyously with his girlfriend in the middle of the dance floor.

"See? This isn't so bad, is it?" Hannah asked hopefully.

"No. Not so bad…I guess." Bryce still warily looked over the crowd of people. "I think I need a drink, though. I feel completely drained." Bryce turned toward Jennifer, who was focused on the far side of the terrace. "Jenn?"

Jennifer's eyes popped back over toward Bryce, surprise on her face. She shot an unreadable glance at Arati, who rolled her hand quickly.

Why were her friends acting so strangely? "Jenn? Is everything okay?"

Jennifer nodded enthusiastically. "Everything's great! I do think, however, that you should go to the bar to get a drink if you want one."

Bryce looked doubtful. She really didn't want to leave her friends' company. She was already on the verge of breaking after all of the attention of the evening.

"Go ahead. It'll be good for you."

"Can't I just wait for the server to come over?" Bryce looked and saw a waiter three tables over taking orders.

"No! No, I think you should go over yourself. It will give you self-confidence!"

"Wow. You are so bullshitting me right now." Bryce was befuddled by her friend's behavior, but she really didn't have the strength or heart to argue. "Fine. If it means you'll lay off for the rest of the evening, I'll go. Deal?"

"Deal!" Jennifer smiled widely.

Bryce stood with only a small amount of pain and picked her way toward the bar through the clusters of people. She tried to hide her face as she walked, feeling guilty and weak about her embarrassment, especially after the bravery and honor shown that night by the disfigured sailor and the other wounded veterans, but she knew that nothing she did would draw attention away from the scar.

She had made it about halfway across the expanse when the panic hit. She stopped dead in her tracks and looked wildly around. No one seemed to be paying any attention to her, but her heart slammed in her chest, and she felt like running straight back to her apartment. Busted leg be damned.

Her anxiety finally overwhelmed her and she turned around, stumbling slightly as she did so, and took a single step to hurry back to her friends at their table. She was stopped when a hand reached out and gently grabbed her shoulder.

"Hey. Bryce."

She stopped, and in the split second it took to do so she tried to place that voice. She had heard it before, but it seemed like a lifetime ago, so the memory escaped her.

She turned slowly, gaze focused on her feet, careful to keep her unmarred right cheek toward the speaker, as if doing this would completely hide the damaged side of her face. "Yes?" Bryce saw a woman's legs in a blue knee-length dress. Not anyone in the military, then.

"It's so good to see you."

Bryce realized she would never be able to see the speaker properly if she kept trying to hide her face, so she looked up slowly, and as the woman's features came into her view the missing pieces of memory fell into place immediately. "Oh my God."

"That's not the greeting I expected, but I'll take it!" The woman laughed melodiously and Bryce felt an immediate stirring in her chest.

"Daniela! Why…what are you doing here? I mean…I'm sorry. I'm just shocked to see you! It's been…"

"About eight years! Yeah." Daniela's smile was radiant. She was still shorter than Bryce, but her sleeveless dress showed off her toned shoulders and she had filled out beautifully since high school.

For a moment Bryce forgot about her damaged face. "What are you doing in Seattle? At this fund-raiser?" Bryce's shock at seeing her old friend had completely stamped out the panic attack she had been on the verge of suffering.

"I'm in the touring cast of *A Chorus Line*. We're playing at the Paramount for a month before heading up to Vancouver and then east across Canada. When the tour started we were invited to perform a few numbers tonight for the fund-raiser so, of course, we jumped at the chance! It's for a good cause."

Bryce was completely speechless. Daniela had always been extremely pretty, but now, at—Bryce quickly did the math—twenty-four years old, she was drop-dead gorgeous.

"Bryce?" Daniela's smile had turned into a worried frown. "Are you feeling all right? Is your leg hurting you?"

Bryce realized she had been staring like an idiot. When she came back to herself she also realized the Bryce Montgomery that Daniela was seeing was a thousand miles from the Bryce she had known in high school. A weight dropped heavily into Bryce's stomach, stamping out the pleasant flutters. She realized how she must look now to her old friend. What must she think of her now? Daniela had admired the beautiful, confident star athlete who had the whole world open to her. The person who stood before her now was broken, scarred, rejected, and spiritually severed. Oh, and she lacked a future too. "No. My leg is fine," Bryce replied impassively.

Daniela didn't look convinced, but continued in a much more serious tone. "I've wanted to see you again for a long time. There are so many things I want to tell you."

Bryce trembled with the effort of acting out some semblance of normalcy for this friend she had lost track of over the years. She felt like such a jerk. Daniela had always been such a good friend to her. How could she have never thought to check on her, to see how her life was going? Just because Bryce herself had been through such an ordeal before she left Saltus? So selfish.

Seeing Daniela now, apparently a successful actress just like she had dreamed of being, still kind, and so beautiful it hurt to look at her, made Bryce feel unworthy and embarrassed.

"I have to go." Bryce pushed past Daniela and, as quickly as she could manage, made her way back into the hotel and down the elevator to the lobby. Once outside, she hailed a taxi and headed straight back to her apartment where she locked the door, discarded her handsome uniform in a messy ball on the floor, and curled up around Bear in her bed, all while crying her eyes out and messing up the mascara Arati had worked so diligently to apply.

Chapter Eighteen

"You really hurt Daniela's feelings, you know," Jennifer said as she scrubbed at the dried makeup on Bryce's face.

Bryce sighed heavily. "I know. I don't know what happened. Seeing her just brought back so many memories and made me feel... like such a loser." She paused, but Jennifer said nothing. "What did she do after I left? Was she mad?"

"No. She came over to sit with us and asked that I give you this." Jennifer handed Bryce one ticket to *A Chorus Line* for the following night's performance. "Bryce, you need to go see her. She was so worried about you after the accident."

Bryce was surprised. She didn't know that Daniela had even known about what had happened to her.

Jennifer noticed the shock on Bryce's face and continued. "Everyone in Saltus knows about it. Don't ask me how. Your parents never said anything. Dani's parents told her right after it happened, and as soon as she found out that the show would be stopping for an extended stay in Seattle, she got in touch with me to find out how you were doing and to see if it would be possible for her to visit you. The cast just arrived two days ago."

"So she knew I would be at the fund-raiser last night?"

Jennifer smiled. "No, actually. I had no reason to tell her about that. Hell, I didn't even know if you would go through with it! That was just happy circumstance. I didn't know that seeing her again would upset you, though. Now I feel awful."

"Oh, Jenn, it's not your fault at all. I just had a mini-breakdown. There's no way you could've known. I just thought about how much I've changed. How awful I feel about myself and how I've been behaving lately. I was just so humiliated."

"What's done is done. Do you think that you'll be able to go see her in the show, though? She really wants you to be there. And"—Jennifer pointed to the ticket held limply in Bryce's hand—"that's front row center. She'll know if you don't show up."

Bryce put the ticket down on the kitchen table and settled her face into her hands. "God. You guys are killing me. I feel like I've been thrown overboard in the waters of the Bering Sea without a life jacket and told to just swim for it."

"Do you ever even think in non-nautical terms?" Jennifer smiled.

The corner of Bryce's mouth lifted as she sat up and replied, "Nautical terms help me keep my compass bearing."

Jennifer laughed loudly. "Dork."

"Landlubber."

"But seriously. We won't be here to help you after we leave tonight. Are you going to be okay?"

"Define okay."

"Bryce, I'm serious. Do I need to worry about you?"

Bryce felt guilty for causing her friends to worry about her so much, especially when they had busy lives of their own. "No, Jenn. I'm fine. Really."

"Does that mean you'll go see Dani's show?"

Bryce couldn't find her voice, so she just nodded.

"Good. I know she'll be ecstatic that you're there. Just be sure to talk to her. She said she'll be coming out of the stage door afterward."

Bryce sighed and gave a wan smile. "I kind of wanted to see the show anyway, before I knew she was in it."

"Good. Text me when you get home, okay? Even if it's really late with the time difference."

"I will. You and the others call me when you get back home tonight too."

"We will." Jennifer walked around the table to hug her. "You take care of yourself. And we had a blast this week. Seattle is an amazing city. Next year our trip is going to be somewhere warm, though, got it?"

Bryce smiled. "Find me a private island in Tahiti and I'm there."

"I'll work on it."

Bryce tapped her fingers nervously on the program as the seats around her slowly filled. The din of conversation in the large theater grated on her nerves and she wanted nothing more than for the lights to dim and to be swept away in the music. She could feel gazes on her damaged face. Instead of letting herself tumble into another panic attack, she opened up the playbill to read the cast biographies. With a pleasant jolt she came upon Daniela's name and discovered that the young woman she had been so impressed with in high school was playing Diana Morales, a character who struggles through acting classes and ends up singing one of the best songs in the show. Bryce couldn't help but smile. She had seen Daniela's talent emerge in *Bye Bye Birdie* all those years ago, and now she was about to see her in a real, professional show. Excitement replaced nervousness.

She decided not to read Daniela's biography. She would rather have something to talk about when they met up after the show. Instead she just stared at the amazing headshot printed in black and white on the page. Daniela really had grown into one of the most beautiful women Bryce had ever seen, and she found that she couldn't tear her eyes away.

Uh-oh.

At just that moment the lights dimmed and the steady A from a single oboe started the tuning of the orchestra. Bryce clutched her program to her chest and tried to slow the beating of her heart. In only a few seconds, Daniela would see that she had been brave enough to come to the show and Bryce would see firsthand how talented…and attractive…her friend had become.

For two solid hours Bryce had felt happy. She had forgotten her self-deprecating depression and had lost herself in the story of desperate triple threats. Every member of the cast was brilliant, but Daniela… Bryce had never been as mesmerized by another performer. Even when she had just stood in her bored dancer's pose, one knee bent daintily forward and hands on her hips, she had owned the stage. Bryce's eyes had run up and down the length of Daniela's body from her muscular legs in dancer's tights to her perfect ponytail. The view had been… titillating.

The best part of the show had happened in the first five minutes, though. As soon as the dancers formed up into their famous line, Daniela's eyes had furtively glanced straight to Bryce's seat to see if she was there. When she had seen Bryce staring up at her, she had forced back a smile and winked directly at her. Bryce had felt light and significant for the first time in a long time.

Now the afterglow was fading. The show had ended and Bryce stood by the stage door with several other fans, out of place and unprotected in this group of people. She kept her back firmly to the wall but felt as if she could lose it at any second. Eyes still glanced furtively her way, taking in the cane and her face. She'd never get used to it.

Fifteen minutes later, Bryce nearly chickened out and left. But even as she considered it, the stage door opened and actors, orchestra members, and crew filed out. The actors smiled, signed autographs, and posed for pictures with their fans before jumping into the backseats of their chauffeured cars. From her semi-hidden spot against the wall Bryce could only see the backs of everyone's heads, but eventually an actress slightly shorter than the rest exited and Bryce recognized Daniela's dark, straight ponytail. Young girls flocked around her and Bryce watched with amazement as she posed with her arms around her adoring followers. The timid girl Bryce had babysat and taught to swim had become a celebrity.

Instead of following her cast mates into the waiting car after signing all of the autographs, Daniela hesitated, scanning the crowd with a frown replacing her movie-star smile. Bryce stood up a little taller and stepped from the shadows into the stage door light. Daniela saw the movement out of the corner of her eye and turned around quickly.

"Bryce. You came! Thank you *so* much." She approached cautiously—probably afraid of scaring her off again.

Something appeared to be caught in Bryce's throat, but she managed to speak around it. "No, thank *you*, Dani. You didn't have to comp me a ticket."

"Yes, I did. You're part of the reason I'm here."

Bryce's confusion made Daniela laugh.

"We need to do some catching up. Feel like joining me for a late dinner?"

Bryce's heart skipped a beat. "Yeah. Sounds great."

They walked a few blocks to a late-night diner and sat down at a booth by the window. They perused the menu in silence for a few minutes before Bryce said, "You know? I'm not really hungry." She was too nervous.

Daniela replied, "I'm starving. Doing that show every night really takes it out of me."

"I imagine so."

The waitress approached and took Daniela's order of egg whites, a whole-wheat English muffin, veggie sausage, milk, and sliced fruit. Bryce ordered a coffee.

When she had gone, Daniela stared at Bryce for a minute, then finally said, "So."

"So," Bryce replied, unsure of what to say.

"I'll start. I have so many questions about your life since high school."

Bryce smiled, but was dying to know everything about Daniela. She was entranced by what her friend was doing with her life. "Okay, but you first. I mean, I can't believe you're an actress."

"Well, I have you to thank for a lot of that, Bryce."

"Me? What did I do?"

"Well, you were pretty much the only person who ever made me feel truly special. You supported me whenever I needed the encouragement. My parents never wanted me to do this. Dad always said that he didn't move to America from El Salvador for me to waste my life pretending to be someone I'm not, embarrassing myself in front of thousands of people."

"That must have been difficult."

Daniela shrugged.

Bryce understood having to deal with unsupportive parents, so she let it drop. "Well, I didn't do anything special."

"Not true. You made me feel talented and worthwhile. You complimented me on my role as Rosie, remember? When I told you that I wanted to be an actress you said, 'Then that's what you're going to do. And you're going to be amazing.' You also said that you couldn't take your eyes off me when I played her." She smiled in a pleased way.

"You remember all that?"

Daniela's cheeks reddened. "I remember pretty much everything you ever said to me, Bryce."

"Wow."

"Why so surprised? You have to realize that you were the coolest girl in the school and I worshipped the ground you walked on."

Bryce snorted. "I wasn't Miss Popularity, Dani."

"True, you didn't run with the 'popular' girls, thank God. They were all bitches. You were that girl who's nice to everyone so everyone loves you. And being a super-hot swimmer sure didn't hurt."

Bryce flushed from the compliment and sat pensively for a moment. "You know, it just didn't feel like that from my side, I guess. I mean, yeah, I tried to be nice to everyone and I did well on the swim team, but there were always girls more beautiful, more popular, and way cooler than me."

"I beg to differ."

The flattery warmed Bryce…and embarrassed her. "You make me sound like I was the prom queen or something."

"No, I mean, I differ with you on two of those points. I thought you were ridiculously cool and you were definitely the most beautiful."

It was Bryce's turn to blush, but not before her stomach dropped. "Well, I'll still claim cool, but beautiful…" She gestured to her scar and drooping eye, then shrugged it off. "But we were talking about you. How were the rest of your high school years? What happened after you graduated?"

Daniela frowned quickly, then said, "High school was normal, I guess. I continued to do theater in school and community productions. Shakespeare in the Park and the like. I figured out pretty quickly that I had found my calling."

"It shows. You were fantastic tonight."

Daniela blushed. "I've always been a pretty shy person, but when I'm onstage I can be someone else entirely. It's an amazing feeling. I can be anyone and it's really cathartic."

"Well, once again, I couldn't take my eyes off you." Bryce gulped as she tried to force the words back into her mouth, but Daniela's eyes lit up as her face broke out into an enormous smile.

"See? That's what I'm talking about! You were always so complimentary and supportive of me. Thank you."

Bryce coughed, trying to cover up her embarrassment. The waitress rescued her by setting her coffee and Daniela's milk on the table. Bryce took a good two minutes doctoring her cup before she asked, "What about after you graduated?"

"Dad tried to pressure me to go to medical school, but I kept thinking about your encouragement to do what I wanted with my life, and I really wanted to act. I had secretly applied to all of the best acting program colleges and, after a terrifying live audition, I got accepted to the musical theater program at NYU and earned my degree there."

Bryce slowly settled down again. "NYU? That's really, really impressive, Dani."

She shrugged. "I had a great time. It was a lot of work, but it was the best decision I've ever made. After I graduated I just started auditioning like everyone else. I wanted to make it on the Great White Way."

"Well, it looks like you're doing really well!"

"Right *now*. It took forever for me to get a good role. I worked for TKTS as my day job and only got bit roles for the first two years in New York. Off-off-off-Broadway stuff, bloody murder-victim extra in a film student's thesis project, crowd scenes…This"—she pointed at Bryce's playbill—"is my first big role! I had to really work on my dancing to get this. It's definitely not my strong suit."

"That's your voice."

"What?"

"Your voice is a-frickin-mazing, Dani. I've always thought so. That's what puts you ahead of the rest."

"I knew that finding you again would be good for my ego."

Bryce was pleased to see a distinct redness coloring Daniela's neck and cheeks.

Daniela's food was brought over and set in front of her. "Do you mind?" She gestured toward the food.

"Of course not. Go ahead." Bryce silently sipped her coffee and watched as Daniela tore into her post-show meal.

When she had slowed Bryce asked, "How is it being on tour? Do you miss being home in NYC?"

Daniela leaned back in the booth. "Nah. This is what I've always wanted. I have no strong ties there, and although I love New York for being what it is, I don't really like living there. It's just too loud and chaotic. I'm thrilled to be on the road, seeing new places."

Bryce swallowed tentatively before asking, "Don't you miss… anyone there? Someone special?"

"I miss my friends, but no, there's no one special. I've dated people on and off in school and in the city, but I mainly know theater people and they can be kind of…dramatic. Most of my relationships don't last very long because of that. Two theater people in one tiny New York apartment is *really* tiring."

"I can imagine."

"And anyway, I was always way more concerned with my career than my love life. Besides, not many people can meet my high standards." She smiled shyly at Bryce.

For some reason the knowledge that Daniela wasn't seeing anyone made Bryce incredibly happy. "Do you have a roommate? New York is expensive, isn't it?"

Daniela scoffed. "Right now I'm actually sharing a tiny one-bedroom apartment with *three* other people! All starving-artist types just like me. It's a nightmare even though it's pretty convenient. At least one of us is usually out of town on a job somewhere, so it's not *always* crowded and rent is a lot lower for each of us this way. The one thing I really, really miss, though, is a view. Our apartment's windows look out onto a brick wall. No sky, no greenery, just dull red brick. It's so depressing."

Bryce sipped her coffee as Daniela finished her meal. "What about your family in Saltus? What happened there after I left for the academy? I never…I haven't been back."

There was silence for a minute and Daniela looked uncomfortable. "I am glad to be out of Saltus. I visit at Christmas, but that's about it. My parents and my brother are well. Dante is at SSU finishing up his BS in engineering, and Mom and Dad are still the same." She rolled her eyes as she said it. "They've come around a *little* about the acting thing, though. They came to see me in my last show at NYU and I think Mom was really impressed. Dad was reluctant, but I think he liked it too. But otherwise, I haven't really been to Saltus much since I graduated."

"Did anyone…ever talk about me?"

Daniela rubbed the back of her neck. "You know our moms are close, right?"

"Yeah."

"Well, I guess your mom told some…stuff…to my mom. I never heard the whole story, but from bits of conversation I overheard from them and some people at school I gathered that you and your parents had a falling-out because of something that happened between you and Leah and that you were…kicked out…I guess."

"That's basically it, yeah."

Daniela leaned forward, concerned. "Do you mind my asking what exactly happened? I mean, you don't have to tell me if you don't want to, but I'd like to know. It was like you fell off the face of the earth and it really upset me for a long time."

Bryce took a steadying breath. She might as well get it over with. For some reason Bryce wanted Daniela to know everything about her. They hadn't talked in years, but she felt like she had just rediscovered a kindred spirit, a connection to her past. She knew she could trust her with the truth. "I hope you've had your coffee, because this is a doozy."

It took Bryce almost two full hours to recount the entire story of everything that had happened to her over the years. Both good and bad. To her credit, Daniela never looked appalled or shocked by anything Bryce told her. On the contrary, she appeared to empathize completely with Bryce's feelings on the varying situations.

By the time Bryce was finished, she was surprised to realize that she hadn't even noticed Daniela take her hand across the table in a gesture of comfort. For some reason this caused a surge of fear in Bryce's chest. How could this beautiful woman who had idolized her as a teenager possibly still think as much of her in her current condition? She was injured, not only physically but mentally.

She shakily pulled her hand away and laid it in her lap.

"That brings me to sitting in a diner with you in the wee hours of the morning."

"Wow. That's a lot to process after eight years."

Bryce's ears felt like they had just caught on fire. "Oh my God, I'm sorry. I didn't mean to unload onto you. That was rude and…I'm an idiot." She rose to leave. She didn't know why, exactly, but she felt humiliated and exposed. Why had she just spilled her guts to this girl for *two hours*? What right did she have to dump all of her problems on her after just reconnecting?

Daniela looked scared. "Where are you going?"

"I can't believe I just made you listen to all that. I'm so sorry. You just got done with an exhausting show and…" She stepped out of the booth and grabbed her cane. "You deserve better than me sniveling all over you the first time we actually get to talk. I don't know what came over me."

"No! I didn't mean it that way! I wanted to know! Bryce, I—"

"I'm sorry. I don't…feel well. Thanks so much for the show." She placed a twenty on the table to pay for Daniela's meal. She knew she was acting erratically, but every nerve in her body told her to flee.

She had taken a few steps outside into the drizzly Seattle night when she heard Daniela ask almost frantically from behind her, "Did you like the flowers?"

The oddity of the question made Bryce stop in her tracks and turn around. "What?"

Daniela stood a few paces behind her, lips trembling. "Did you like the flowers I sent while you were in the hospital? I sent them with

Jennifer and told her not to tell you who they were from. I was…too self-conscious to put my name on them. Especially since we hadn't talked in so long."

Seconds ticked by as it sank in. "*You* sent that giant bouquet?"

Daniela smiled feebly. "Yeah."

"I…I thought they must have been from my mother."

Daniela's smile faltered. "Oh. I didn't consider the possibility of you thinking that. That was pretty insensitive of me. I'm sorry."

"No! I mean, I'm glad to know they were from you. How did you even know?"

"Word spreads fast in Saltus. Everyone there…well, almost everyone, apparently…thinks you're a hero. 'Local Golden Girl Swim Star Gets Injured in the Line of Duty' stuff. You know how patriotic Texans are."

"Huh." Bryce paused. "Well, thank you…for the flowers…and everything." She hung her head.

Daniela walked forward and stood only inches from her. "Bryce, when I heard that you had been hurt…that was the first news I had heard about you in years. I had been too shy to contact Jennifer or Arati before that, and I couldn't find you online—"

Bryce shifted uncomfortably. "I wanted to stay anonymous after high school. I was humiliated by what my parents did to me. I got rid of all my social network accounts and crap. Sorry."

"Well, losing contact was really hard for me. I've missed you."

"I've missed you too." Bryce smiled as she realized how much she meant it.

There was a moment of silence before Daniela said, "You know, our show is here for a while. Do you think you're up for hanging out sometime? I mean, I don't want to intrude on your life or bother you, but I really would like to see you again."

Bryce smiled and warmth spread through her abdomen. "Yeah. Okay."

Daniela brightened and her perfectly white teeth dazzled Bryce. "Awesome! Here's my cell number. Will you call me tomorrow? I may have another ticket for the show and I can get you backstage if you'd like a tour."

"You don't need to bribe me." Bryce playfully punched Daniela in the arm. "But yeah, that sounds amazing."

"Cool. Well, I guess I should get back to the hotel now."

"Is it far from here?"

"No, only a couple of blocks."

"Let me walk you back. I want to make sure you get there safely." Bryce didn't know exactly what she could do in her current situation to protect Daniela, but she knew that nothing bad was going to happen to her friend on her watch.

It didn't take long before they stood outside of Daniela's downtown hotel.

"Are you sure you'll be okay to get home?"

"Definitely. My car is parked down the street."

Bryce noticed Daniela's hair sparkling with the drizzle of the evening. "You'd better get inside. I'm sure getting a cold sucks for a singer."

Daniela smiled. "It does indeed."

"Thanks again, Dani. It really is amazing to see you again."

Daniela seemed reluctant to leave, but finally leaned in for a hug.

Bryce embraced her awkwardly. The feel of Daniela's body pressed tightly to hers sent long-forgotten waves of warmth and longing through her. She felt tall and strong, and she knew she wanted Daniela in her life from that moment on.

CHAPTER NINETEEN

Did you go to the show? Did you talk to her?" Jennifer asked like a strict parent.

"Yes, Jenn."

"Well?"

Bryce grinned into her computer's video camera. "It felt like we've never been apart. You wouldn't know all this time has passed. I felt so comfortable with her. Just like old times."

Jennifer smiled back and relaxed. "Good. I was worried that you'd get cold feet."

"Thanks for the vote of confidence," Bryce said wryly.

"Hey, it's not unfounded and you know it."

"Shut up! I've been dealing with shit."

Jennifer shook her head sadly. "Bryce, you need to do something. You can't just sit around and mope forever."

Bryce's eyes narrowed. She knew she was trying to help, but it irritated her beyond belief to know Jennifer was right. "I'm enjoying my beer-drinking, burrito-eating time off, thank you very much."

"Bryce."

"Jenn."

She sighed. "Listen, I'm not going to force you to do anything you don't want to do, but just consider it, okay? Getting out of the apartment will be good for you."

"Thanks, *Mom*." Bryce regretted it the moment she said it. It broke her heart to think that her best friend had to be the one to give parental advice instead of the real thing. She softened her tone. "Look, I'm getting out of the house tomorrow. Happy?"

"Yes. But I hope you do something worthwhile."

"Does seeing Dani again seem worthwhile?"

Jennifer looked delighted and she gave a small golf clap. "More than worthwhile. I know she's been dying to reconnect."

"Thanks, Jenn. I'll talk to you later, all right?"

"Yeah. Have a good time for once, okay?"

Bryce smiled. "I'll try."

Despite the lateness of the year the weather wasn't too cold, few clouds were in the sky, and Bryce reveled in the sun beating down on her face. The park bench outside of one of the downtown office buildings had seemed like the perfect place to take Daniela for lunch. A day like this in Seattle was just too rare to spend indoors.

"This," Daniela said as she swiped her finger across the iPad's screen, "is my dorm room at NYU. And this," another swipe, "is me as Maria in *The Sound of Music*. Okay, your turn." She put the iPad down and turned to see the pictures on Bryce's phone.

"Are you sure I'm not boring you with this? My pictures are nowhere near as interesting as yours. How can I compete with a picture of you screaming, covered in blood, and chasing down a football player?"

Daniela laughed. "*College Carnage 3*. That paid all of fifty bucks. *Plus* catering, I should add."

"Well, that's something."

"The catering was peanut butter and jelly on stale bread with a brown banana."

Bryce looked thoughtful. "But think of the amazing footage they'll be able to use when you're famous and on the talk show circuit in the future."

Daniela pointed at her. "See? I knew someone would get it."

Bryce showed her pictures of herself out on patrols, at her academy graduation, at Coast Guard balls, and on the podium at swimming competitions.

"Girl, I don't know how you think those are boring. Hot blond chick in a uniform? That's kind of a *thing* for a lot of people, you know."

Bryce couldn't help but laugh. "Yes. I *do* know. Firsthand."

"Will you walk me back to the theater?"

"Of course! As long as you don't mind going slowly." Bryce grimaced and stood up from the bench where they had eaten their takeaway Chinese food.

"I'm in no rush. I'm just glad you agreed to have lunch with me today. If you're not careful, I just might try to blackmail you into joining me every day while I'm here." Daniela said it jokingly, but Bryce caught her as she cast a quick glance in her direction.

Bryce purposefully bumped into Dani as they walked. "No blackmail necessary. I had almost forgotten what it felt like to just sit and enjoy the air and good company."

"Promise?"

"Promise."

Bryce could tell Daniela was happy. After walking in silence for a while Bryce said, "This seems almost like the old days, doesn't it? I could be walking home from school with you."

"Don't you dare bring up the babysitting thing." Daniela poked Bryce in the side.

"Oh, I would *never*!"

"Thank you, *Miss Montgomery*."

Bryce laughed loudly. "Oh, *hell* no. We're not doing that again. One more comment like that and I might just have to have lunch by myself for the next four weeks."

Daniela threw her arms up in surrender. "Fine! Fine. The thought of missing out on your company for the show's entire stay in Seattle fills me with abject fear." She smiled up at Bryce. "Better?"

Bryce was pleased. "Better."

For the next week Bryce made good on her promise and had every possible lunch and dinner she could with Daniela. Bryce was able to show her around the city she had fallen in love with, and Daniela was able to get her back into the world. Bryce was starting to relax into this new way of living and found that being around Daniela both calmed and excited her. Their conversation now flowed more easily and they laughed often. Bryce still tried to find seats in the corners of each restaurant to hide her face from the other patrons, but Daniela didn't seem bothered by the way she looked.

Every day Bryce spent with her pulled her deeper into an affection from which she knew she wouldn't be able to surface. It was happening fast, but she was falling for Daniela. No question in her mind. How could she deal with this on top of her already unstable emotions? What would she do when the tour moved on? The thought terrified her.

Putting it out of her mind as best she could, Bryce had decided to take her friend on a whale-watching cruise to show her the beautiful waters of her old patrol areas. Now, as they sailed slowly out of the harbor, they settled into the normal easy banter they had spent the last week cultivating. "Tell me about your worst audition or most embarrassing moment onstage." Bryce smiled with a wicked twinkle in her eye.

"Oh, you *would* have to bring that up, wouldn't you?" Daniela smiled and leaned back against the bench on the upper deck of the boat. "Well, I do have a good one…"

When she didn't elaborate, Bryce playfully bumped her with her left shoulder as they sat snuggled up next to each other under a blanket to keep warm. "You're not getting out of this one. Spill it."

Daniela turned to her right and pretended to look put out. "It's not fair having to tell you my stories without getting one from you." She turned her gaze forward again and leaned in closer to an immensely pleased, but flustered Bryce. "So, you first. I'm listening."

"Okay fine. Let's see." Bryce thought back on her days at the academy. "I was standing in formation for inspection one day during my first year, right before the important spring regimental review, wearing my salt and peppers—the cadet parade dress blues." Daniela shrugged, so Bryce elaborated. "The awesome-looking ones with a black jacket and white pants."

"Nice."

"So the inspecting officer stands right in front of me and says, 'Cadet Montgomery!' I say, 'Yes, sir!' and he goes, 'Would you care to explain to me why you are standing here about to go out onto the parade ground in front of God and everyone with your uniform worn improperly?' So I say, 'Sir?' because as far as I knew I was just as shipshape as it was possible to be."

Daniela grinned.

"I can't help it. I'm really anal about my uniform. It's always clean and pressed and the buttons are shined up. So anyway, he just looks me dead in the eye and points downward. I look down and see that my fly is *all* the way down. You can even see my baby blue striped underwear through the hole."

Daniela almost snorted her Diet Coke out of her nose laughing.

"Oh, thanks a lot! Laughing at my trauma." Bryce looked at her friend in mock astonishment. "Fine. Your turn, Little Miss Perfect."

"Okay, okay," Daniela said, trying to stifle her laughter. "My worst audition isn't really embarrassing as much as it was just bad on my part, so I'll just skip to my worst moment onstage."

"Got it."

"I was in this crappy little play written by one of my fellow students at NYU. It was more of a performance piece depicting romantic relationships in the digital age. We had a lot of Christmas lights strung up all over the place, glowing LED tape lining the backdrop, flickering LCDs and TVs littering the stage, and strobe lights flashing at random intervals. It was a really bizarre representation of people hiding behind their computers and smartphones and the falseness of human interaction nowadays."

"Sounds interesting."

"*Well*, my role was as an underage girl getting propositioned online by a child molester pretending to be a high school senior. So I walk out on stage in a little schoolgirl uniform, a skirt that only reached mid-thigh and a white shirt with the buttons open to my stomach showing off my black bra underneath—very 'Oops, I Did It Again,' if you know what I mean."

Bryce swallowed hard and wiped the sudden layer of sweat from her brow despite the chill air.

"I sashayed on at my cue, trying my best to look sexy but innocent, and right in dead center stage I tripped over one of the damn strings of Christmas lights and *crash*! Down they all came, right on top of everyone's heads. Not only that, but I fell flat…on…my…face. Knocked myself out cold on the edge of one of the random computer monitors sitting on the floor."

"Oh no!"

"Oh, yes. When I came to the rest of the cast was still trying to untangle themselves from the lights, and the audience—full house, by the way—was laughing riotously. It was then that I noticed that what little fabric of my skirt there was had flown up over my back. Yeah, I was wearing tiny black bikini underwear and was basically mooning the audience. *That* was the worst experience I've had onstage."

Bryce laughed because she was expected to, but the mental visual of Daniela's exposed skin caused her to shudder with desire. Luckily she was saved from further embarrassment by the captain of the vessel announcing a small pod of minke whales off the port side of the boat, the same side on which they were sitting.

Daniela let out a squeal of delight and whipped out her camera to take pictures. Bryce, of course, had seen whales with great regularity during her ocean patrols, so she just sat back and enjoyed the sight of Daniela enjoying herself so much.

By the end of the tour Daniela, delighted at her introduction to Puget Sound and its wildlife, sat huddled close to Bryce, who'd slung her arm around Daniela's shoulders to keep her warm.

As the boat was returning to the dock Daniela, voice muffled under the blanket and against Bryce's chest, asked, "What are you thinking?"

Bryce took a moment to consider how she felt. "I'm thinking that this is the first time I've been out on the water since my accident, and it feels really good."

"Anything else?"

Bryce couldn't tell her the full truth about other thoughts drifting through her head. She didn't want to believe them herself. "I'm thinking…that it's really nice having you here."

It was the best she could do.

Daniela snuggled in even closer. "Funny. I was thinking the same thing."

Daniela hadn't been able to get Bryce another ticket to the show, but after two weeks of spending time together pretty much nonstop, she was finally able to convince the theater's security and crew to let Bryce backstage to watch a show from the wings.

"And this," Daniela motioned proudly like someone showing off a shiny new car, "is my dressing room."

Daniela held the door open for her and as she entered, Bryce took in all of the tins of stage makeup, the two brightly lit mirrors, rolls of athletic tape, flowers, and multiple pairs of dance shoes that were strewn about the floor. It looked comfortable and lived-in. High-energy music pulsed from the portable iPod speakers in the corner and Daniela waved to a woman lying down reading a fashion magazine on the single threadbare couch.

"Bryce, this is Kate. She plays Judy Turner in the show and has quite the penchant for watching the male dancers."

The redhead on the couch just smiled slyly and said, "Can I help it if I'm attracted to tight little butts and a well-turned calf?"

Bryce laughed. "It's very nice to meet you, Kate. You're amazing onstage."

Kate stood up and shook Bryce's hand. "Oh, she *is* the charmer. You were right." She winked at Daniela. Turning back to Bryce she said, "Daniela and I are roomies on this tour. Both dressing room and hotel room. It's like living with my little brother. She just does *not* understand the meaning of folding or putting away clothes."

"Hey, can I help it if things are easier to find in that pile over there?" Daniela pointed to a mound of crumpled clothes. "Or that one? Or that one behind the door?" She continued pointing at piles as Kate and Bryce laughed.

"So. Bryce Montgomery. You're the one who's been kidnapping our little Daniela every day…and night. I've heard an awful lot about you," Kate said with a glimmer of mischief in her eye.

Bryce looked warily at Daniela, whose face had immediately turned a dark shade of red. "Oh?"

Kate laughed and turned to Daniela. "Don't be shy now, Dani." She looked back at Bryce and whispered conspiratorially. "She's been talking about you *constantly* since we got to Seattle. I'm just glad she had the guts to meet up with you again. Of course, now she just talks about you even *more*."

"Okay, thank you, *Kate.* I think that's enough," Daniela said through gritted teeth. "Aren't you supposed to be getting your new leotard in wardrobe right about now?"

Kate winked at Bryce. "Oh yeah. How could that have slipped my mind? I guess I'll go do that, then. I'll leave right now and I won't be back for…fifteen minutes or so. Just sayin'. Okay. I'm off. Don't do anything I wouldn't do, girls." She chuckled to herself as she left the room, closing the door behind her.

"What was that all about?" Bryce wondered out loud.

"Nothing!" Daniela was even more flushed than before. "Would you like to sit with me while I put on my makeup?"

"Of course." Bryce sat, glancing around. "This is all so cool. I've never been backstage at a big musical before."

"Well, this one is pretty bare bones. No impressive sets, costumes, or props, but I love it. Sorry I couldn't get you a seat, by the way. I hope you don't mind watching from backstage."

"Are you kidding? This is even better. You have the coolest job ever." Bryce smiled brightly. "I'm just so glad that you asked me. With my recent…issues…it's really good to get out of the house so much."

"You do seem to be doing better with that."

"It's not easy. I'm still self-conscious." She gestured to her face. "But seeing and hanging out with you is...more important." Bryce's stomach flip-flopped again as she gazed at Daniela's perfect profile. She was using a soft sponge to paint a layer of foundation along her jawline and Bryce watched the movements like a person possessed.

Daniela giggled. "I just love having you around."

Bryce gulped.

"So. Have you started to think about getting a job?"

Bryce bit her lip. She knew she couldn't live as a hermit on disability and retirement forever. Sooner or later she would have to put herself out there and figure out what to do with the rest of her life. "I...I've thought about it. It's just that I don't know what to do. I mean, I literally have no idea what I could do. I know how to be a Coast Guard officer. I know how to perform law-enforcement duties. I just don't have the physical ability to do those things anymore."

Daniela finished putting on her blush and then turned to look at Bryce, a fiery look in her eyes. "Tomorrow is my day off. Will you come and do something with me? I know I've been bogarting all of your time, but there's something I want to show you."

"Dani, these have been the best weeks of my life since the accident. I feel like a new...or at least less damaged person when I'm with you. I'll go wherever you want me to go."

"Good. It's a date." Daniela coughed. "I mean. It's not a date...I mean the date is set..."

"Dani?" Bryce said, suppressing a smile. She couldn't quite suppress the flutter in her stomach...

"Yeah?"

"Chill."

"Right. Chilling." Wide-eyed, she turned her chair back toward the mirror and hastily began to apply her eyeliner and mascara.

When Kate returned to the dressing room, Bryce stepped outside and grabbed a chair in the green room so the two performers could change into their costumes and start their pre-show rituals, stretches, and vocal warm-ups.

After another thirty minutes or so Daniela poked her head into the green room. Bryce looked up from a tattered copy of *Entertainment Weekly*. "Hey."

"Hey. Show starts in ten. Come on, I'll show you where you can sit where you won't be in anyone's way."

Bryce followed her, nervous about possibly being a nuisance to the crew, but Daniela showed her a folding chair against the wall, stage left, where she'd have a direct view down the line of dancers and would be completely out of the way of the props and wardrobe crew and curtain operators.

"Can you see from here? Will your leg be okay?"

Bryce sat slowly, placing her cane on the ground behind her. "Absolutely. This is so exciting."

Daniela smiled and squeezed Bryce's shoulder, leaving her hand there longer than Bryce expected her to. "Cool. Well, I'll see you at intermission." She turned around and started walking to the stage as the orchestra warmed up.

"Hey, Dani!"

She turned around, smiling.

"Break a leg. But don't break it too badly." Bryce patted her left knee and they both laughed.

Bryce settled in for another evening of listening to Daniela's beautiful voice and watching her perfect body move flawlessly to the music, all while making the audience laugh with tales of trying to become objects like a table or an ice cream cone. She sang passionately about feeling "nothing" and as Bryce watched Daniela, her heart felt like it could burst at any moment. She found that she just couldn't identify with that song at all.

Bryce frantically kicked the wayward socks under her bed in preparation for Daniela's first visit to her apartment, realizing for the first time just how sterile it appeared. She had spent most of the morning cleaning, but tufts of gray cat hair, a few dirty glasses, and a full bag of recyclables were still visible. As soon as she bent to pick up a clump of cat hair the size of a whole kitten she heard the knock at her door. Panic. Daniela was—Bryce looked at her watch—nine minutes early. She left her cane propped up against the wall in an effort to wean herself from it and limped to the door.

When she opened it Daniela stood before her, smiling and mind-numbingly cute in a pair of ripped jeans, tight gray tee, and open flannel shirt. Her hair was down today instead of in its usual ponytail and she was wearing stylish sunglasses that reflected Bryce's dumbstruck face back at her.

"Ready?" Daniela asked as she bounced a little.

"Huh?" Bryce replied, still in a stupor.

"I wanted to take you somewhere, remember?" An edge of worry worked its way into Daniela's smile.

"Oh. Yeah. I know. Sorry. Come in first?"

"Sure, but only for a few minutes. We're actually on a schedule."

"A schedule? What are we doing?"

Daniela walked past Bryce into the apartment and turned around as she took off her sunglasses. She had a pleading look in her eyes. "Promise you won't be mad?"

"Mad? Why?" Bryce shut the front door and steadied herself on the side table.

"Well, there's actually someone I want you to meet."

"Okay," Bryce said hesitantly, waiting for the bombshell she sensed was coming.

"It's just that I know that you haven't been your normal outgoing self in a long time and I don't want you to be too nervous."

"Right, but I'm not agoraphobic or anything. Just… embarrassed."

"You shouldn't be. And we're going to work on your self-confidence too." Daniela smiled warmly, then glanced around. "So. This is your place?"

"Yeah," Bryce said on an exhale. "I haven't…really decorated much."

"I like it," Daniela said. "Roomy compared to where I live in New York."

"Still no view, though." She gestured to the front window, which looked out on the parking lot and the hospital beyond. "It's not much, but Bear makes it feel like home." Bryce scratched the cat's head since he was standing on the coffee table meowing for attention as if he knew he was the main attraction.

"He's beautiful." Daniela joined in the petting, occasionally running her fingers over Bryce's. "Just like his mom."

Wait. What?

Bryce looked wonderingly up at Daniela, but her gaze was still on Bear as if what she had just said hadn't rocked Bryce's world. Surely it was nothing. Obviously she had misheard or was misinterpreting what Daniela had said. She let it pass. "Well, let me grab my keys," Bryce said. "I'm ready when you are."

"I hope this meeting isn't a total letdown," Daniela said. "But I think it's important for you to hear this person out."

Bryce frowned. This day was beginning to deviate from how Bryce thought it was going to go, but she trusted Daniela. She followed her out of the apartment and into the parking lot, the cane gripped firmly in her hand. Daniela kept walking until they reached the crosswalk at the stoplight.

"My car is the other way," Bryce said.

"We're not taking a car. We're going over there." Daniela pointed to the VA.

Bryce frowned. "What could you possibly want to show me at the VA? I guarantee you I've seen plenty of that place."

"I told you, there's someone I want you to meet."

The crosswalk signal turned to walk and Daniela strode purposefully away, almost like she was afraid to give Bryce time to back out.

When they got to the VA building Daniela turned to Bryce. "Okay. I don't know where I'm going from here. Can you take us to the swimming pool area? It's apparently near the physical therapy department."

Bryce smirked. "I think I can find my way. I've only been there…oh…a few million times."

She followed the path to the part of the building that held her old—well, she supposed it wasn't technically her "stomping" ground. They walked in the door and checked in with a nurse Bryce had never met and were sent back to the pool area. As they walked Bryce pointed out the different rooms to Daniela and expressed her loathing for certain exercises and machines that made her life hell during her therapy sessions.

When they entered the pool area, the strong smell of chlorine welcomed Bryce home once again. She would never stop loving that scent, and she wanted more than anything to just jump into the water, fully clothed, and paddle around contentedly. She hadn't been in the water since that day, two weeks earlier, in the hotel pool with her friends. She felt like Daryl Hannah in the movie *Splash*, and two weeks was a lifetime for a mermaid. Her body felt painful, scaly, dry, and so very heavy.

As she gazed longingly at the pool she saw Daniela wave to someone who was approaching from across the room. She reluctantly turned to look as well and saw a tall, muscular man with a crewcut. He wore black athletic shorts emblazoned with a skull and crossbones and a tightly fitted Navy SEAL T-shirt. Gray speckled his short dark hair and he had weathered lines around his face. Bryce placed him in his early fifties even though he had the body of a much, much younger man.

"Miss Cordova. I'm so glad you could make it." He reached out and shook her hand firmly. She stretched her fingers afterward, as if she was making sure she could still move them.

"Hello, Jack. Here she is." Daniela gestured toward Bryce. She gazed up at her, "Trust me…okay?"

Despite her trepidation, Bryce decided she'd do just that.

"Lieutenant Montgomery, I'm Jack O'Malley, Captain, U.S. Navy, retired." His accent was thick and Southern.

Bryce smiled, indicating the pirate symbol on his shorts. "Captain Jack."

"And proud of it." He smiled back and offered his hand.

Bryce shook it.

Captain Jack tilted his head toward a doorway. "Let's sit. I have a proposition for you, Lieutenant."

Daniela looked nervously at Bryce, but made a shooing motion to make sure she'd follow.

"Come with me?" Bryce whispered.

"Of course."

The three of them sat at a small desk in an unused office next to the pool, Bryce and Daniela next to each other and Captain Jack across the table from them. Bryce stayed silent, waiting for the superior officer to take the lead. Military habits died hard, even for those who had retired early.

"You're probably wondering what you're doing here."

"Yes, sir."

"Well, I met this lovely young woman," he gestured to Daniela, who beamed back at him, "at the veterans' fund-raiser two weeks ago. She's really something, don't you think?"

Bryce turned to look at her, her eyes softening with complete adoration. "Yes. She is."

The lovelorn look in her eyes must have been pretty obvious because Captain Jack chuckled and cleared his throat. "Well, I congratulated her on her performance after the fund-raiser—don't tell anyone, but even some badass ex-Navy SEALs like going to the theater every now and again—and we got to talking. She told me about knowing you in high school and how she was hoping to get to know you again. She actually couldn't stop talking about you." He winked at Daniela. "She had been shocked to see you up on that stage with the other veterans."

"Not a place I'd ever planned on being either, sir."

He acknowledged that with a slight nod. "She did most of the talking, but I did eventually get to tell her about my recent move to Seattle."

When he paused, Bryce thought he was waiting for a response. "And why is that, sir?"

"I'm glad you asked. When I retired from the Navy seven years ago, I didn't really know what I wanted to do with my life. I ended up working in a stuffy office at a weapons manufacturer for three years, and I tell you, that dog just wouldn't hunt. I couldn't stand it."

"I can imagine."

"In my free time I ended up getting involved with a nonprofit group called Diving Veteran Rehabilitation, or DiVeR. Being a SEAL and a divemaster made it a perfect fit for me." He fell silent.

After a moment, Bryce cleared her throat. "It sounds great, sir, but—"

"There are a couple of groups like it in the U.S., but basically, it's a free program teaching disabled veterans how to scuba dive." He smiled. "Well, damn if I hadn't found my calling. I quit at the firm and have been working for DiVeR for four years now. It's a nonprofit, so it doesn't pay well, but I can't imagine doing anything else."

Bryce looked at him quizzically, but with curiosity and excitement. "How can disabled veterans scuba dive, sir?"

"You'd be surprised. You, for example. I've read your files. Champion swimmer in high school and at the academy, correct?"

"Yes, sir."

"Do you walk very well without your cane?"

Bryce's face darkened. She hated being reminded of it. "Not very well. No, sir."

"How do you feel when you're in the water? How do you move?"

Bryce didn't have to say anything. Her face told him everything he needed to know.

"Exactly. And if soldiers are missing limbs or are paralyzed, it doesn't matter. They might need a little extra help from their buddy or some modified equipment, but being in the water is always, always a freeing experience for them."

She nodded, mesmerized.

"No matter what's wrong with their bodies or minds on land, they can fly underwater. They become weightless. It's a universe where they have a freer range of motion, a quiet world where their stress disorders are placated and they can calm down and relax. Understand?"

She felt Daniela's eyes on her, and because a rock had formed in her throat, she simply nodded. Bryce understood very well. She herself took refuge in the water, and it now meant even more to her since the accident. Every word he said was true for her.

"Excellent. So that's why I asked you to come here. I had to leave the fund-raiser before the afterparty, so I gave Miss Cordova my card in case she did get in touch with you. After I read your bio in the program I knew you were the person I needed."

"Excuse me, sir, but…do you mean that you want me to join the DiVeR program?" The prospect excited her. She had always wanted to learn how to dive, but she hadn't had the time and since the accident she figured that she would never be fit enough to do it. Now this man was saying that it was not only possible, but also beneficial for her to be successful at it.

"Yes, I do. Not only that, but I want to hire you for the program."

Stunned, Bryce blinked.

He held up a palm. "Like I said, it doesn't pay much and the actual divemasters and trainers will be unpaid volunteers, but we'd still love to have you."

"But, sir…I'm not scuba certified."

"That's not a problem. I don't need you as an instructor…yet…I just need someone with your qualifications to help me set up and run the new Seattle branch."

"What exactly are my qualifications, sir?"

"Well, for one, the championship swimmer thing sure doesn't hurt. You're comfortable in the water and you'll be an excellent diver one day."

Bryce hoped so.

"For another, you're a well-respected and competent Coast Guard officer. I've done my research. You know how to get things done properly and efficiently. Your commander couldn't recommend you highly enough. I've read the files of many, many retired officers and you are by far my first choice."

"I'm flattered."

"So, what do you say? Do you want to learn to dive and help other veterans do the same?"

Bryce smiled broadly. "Hell yes, sir."

They spent the next hour and a half going over the specifics of the job that Bryce would start in a month. She was excited about getting scuba certified and gaining a job that would allow her to be in the water every day if she wanted to. She wouldn't be in charge of getting donations, but would be the veteran liaison. That meant visiting all the VA hospitals in the area, spreading the word about the program, maintaining the website, answering calls and e-mails, and keeping track of all equipment and facility requests and reservations. The classes would be conducted right there at her VA pool, and open water certifications and dives would be reserved in advance on local dive boats. She'd be busy.

By the time she and Daniela had walked back to her apartment, it still hadn't sunk in that she had just gotten a job—the first job since her forced retirement. She'd get to work with soldiers, sailors, Coasties, Marines, and airmen that had been put into horrible situations and she'd be part of their healing process. Not to mention the fact that she'd finally learn to scuba dive and would live part-time in her liquid world. She couldn't believe that Daniela had done this for her.

"So. I know you said you're excited about this, but are you really sure this is something you want to do?" Daniela asked once they had opened up two bottles of Alaskan Amber Ale and plopped down on the couch back at Bryce's apartment.

"Absolutely. I mean, it's not the Coast Guard, but at least I'll still be doing something worthwhile. I don't think I'll ever be able to thank you enough," Bryce said honestly. She held her bottle out to clink with Daniela's.

"Good. I'm just glad to see you with something positive to do. Something that will get you out of the house. And you'll be helping people too. That's the Bryce I know and love."

Bryce's cheeks warmed. She wished Daniela would stop throwing the l-word around. It sliced like a knife in her chest every time she heard it.

"I just want to make sure you're going to be okay after I leave. We're only here for another week and a half, you know." Daniela's lip trembled almost imperceptibly when she said it.

Bryce nodded, a surge of sorrow blocking her ability to speak. She had grown so accustomed to having Daniela around. She had a new career path now, but she had also fallen head over heels in love for the first time in her life. Her heart ached with every thought of Daniela. Her breath caught and her belly tingled with every late-night imagining. Seeing her sent waves of love and desire rippling through Bryce's scarred body. And now the person to whom she'd become so addicted would be leaving to finish a tour that would keep her away for another two months. After that, an entire continent would separate them when Daniela returned to New York. Any relationship that Bryce dreamed would form was doomed from the start. Not to mention the fact that even if, miraculously, Daniela could love her back, Bryce still felt she wasn't good enough for Daniela. She wasn't pretty enough, wasn't stable enough, and there was no way she could ask Daniela to swap New York and her burgeoning career for a poor veteran in Seattle.

Bryce jumped when her mobile phone rang and pulled her out of her pensiveness. She held it up to look at the screen and her despair grew.

When she forced it to go to voice mail Daniela asked, "Who was it? You look like someone just spit in your beer."

Bryce paused, still staring at the phone. "My mother."

They both sat in silence for a moment as the implications set in. Daniela finally said, "Maybe you should listen to the message. It could be important."

Bryce thought about it. What if something had happened to her dad? What if her parents had decided to treat her like a human being?

She squeezed her eyes shut and gripped the phone tightly. "I thought I was done with her."

"They're your family. Is it possible to ever truly cut them out? Do you really want to?"

Bryce opened her eyes and sagged. "It wasn't exactly my choice, was it? I only said what I did in the hospital because she gave me no choice. It was either that or continue to let myself get abused."

Daniela moved closer so their legs were touching. "That's one of the reasons I admire you so much."

Bryce looked at her suspiciously. "I don't follow."

Daniela put her hand on Bryce's knee.

It felt like electricity shot through her body.

"It takes an insane amount of courage to stand up for yourself like you did. To refuse to be insulted and belittled. I know it must have been agony for you to do that."

Bryce grew misty-eyed. "I didn't feel courageous. I felt…hollow and beaten."

Daniela shrugged. "But you still did what was best for you." She gave her leg a small squeeze.

Bryce didn't know how to respond to Daniela's warmth, so she said, "Okay. I'll listen to the message. My expectations are basement level, though."

She pressed the button for her voice mail and put the phone up to her ear. After a few seconds of silence her mother's voice came through. "Hello, Bryce." Pause. "I don't know what I wanted to say. It's been a long time. Your father said that…that I shouldn't let things end the way they did when I left Seattle. Maybe…maybe you could come home to see us. We would really love that."

Bryce knew what was coming next.

"Pastor Harold has counseled us to never give up on you. What kind of parents would we be if we did?"

The predictability of her mother made Bryce so very weary.

"So…so that's what I wanted to say. We love you, honey. Please come back to us. Bye."

Bryce didn't speak for a while.

Finally, Daniela asked, "Well? Good news? Bad news?"

Bryce shook her head sadly. "Same ol' shit." She couldn't help it. She leaned her head down onto Daniela's shoulder. "God, I love them so much. I mean, they're my goddamned parents. But I just…can't… handle this. Especially on top of everything else."

Daniela sighed. "I don't know what to say. Your parents have really reached a monumental level of asshole-ocity…in a warped, altruistic sort of way. No offense."

"None taken."

Bryce realized that Daniela's hand was still on her leg, and the sudden surge of desire combined with her insecurity and now her parents' reemergence in her life made her disintegrate inside. Every time she thought she had a handle on her emotions and her psyche, something would happen to tear her down again.

She couldn't have the woman she had fallen in love with. She couldn't have her family. She was simply no longer the woman she wanted to be and she could think of nothing that could rescue her from her fragmented life.

Unable to stand the growing grief in her chest, Bryce said, "I think I need to rest now. Do you mind? I'll call you tomorrow."

Daniela looked disappointed, but finished her beer and stood, bending forward to hug Bryce. As she pulled away she held Bryce's hands for a moment. Her touch sent painful and exquisite flames dancing over Bryce's skin.

"Are you coming to the theater tomorrow night?" Daniela asked hopefully.

Bryce wanted nothing more than to go to the theater tomorrow night, but it hurt too much. "I…think I'll take a rain check."

Daniela's face fell. "Oh. Okay, then. How about lunch? You promised to take me to that brewery at Pike Place Market and on the Underground Tour before I leave." She smiled hopefully.

"I will take you. I promise. But I don't know about tomorrow. I have…errands to run." Bryce's heart was breaking. The words coming out of her mouth were defensive, meant to distance and protect them both. But another part of her brain screamed at her to keep Daniela close, to wring every last second out of their time together. Instead, panic seized her, causing her to retreat—something she rarely did. Her tough veneer had cracked in the last year, exposing her weaknesses, which had begun to prey on her.

"Okay." Daniela let go of Bryce's hands and walked slowly to the door. "I guess I'll talk to you later?"

Stop her, you idiot.

"Yeah. I'll call you."

Daniela walked out of her apartment and Bryce curled into a little ball and started crying. Why did she have to fall in love at the exact moment in her life when she felt the most worthless? She hadn't even been able to get out of the house long enough to find a job for herself. A friend she hadn't seen in eight years had to find one for her. So lame. What in the world did she have to offer in return?

Nothing.

She had nothing. She was nothing.

Hours passed slowly as she tried to get her thoughts together. Eventually she uncurled herself from her ball of pathetic self-pity and stumbled to her bedroom, wondering what in the world she was doing. She had hurt Daniela's feelings and she knew it. It wasn't Daniela's fault she was having a minor breakdown. How was Daniela supposed to know that the woman she had reconnected with after so many years had fallen madly in love with her? How was she to know that loving her was causing Bryce to doubt herself and her condition even more?

She flopped down on her bed, Bear following her, and buried her head under her pillows. She would have to apologize to Daniela. She would have to explain at least some of what was going on in her head. It was only fair. Maybe she wouldn't profess her undying love, but Daniela needed to know more about how she was feeling and what she was struggling with every day.

But not tonight.

Tonight Bryce needed to get the poisonous emotions out of her system. They had been simmering for a while and it had surprised her how quickly they had erupted. A single call from her mother, and bam—there it was. She had to stay away from her friend while her viral neurosis was still at its peak.

A tear fell slowly down her cheek as she took a shaky breath. Bear seemed to sense her angst and walked up to her from the foot of the bed. Purring loudly, he curled up against her left side as she ran her fingers through his soft fur.

"Thanks, buddy," she whispered to him in the dark.

Chapter Twenty

The next morning Bryce awoke after a sleepless night of tossing, turning, and unbidden provocative thoughts about Daniela. Bear had long since gotten irritated by Bryce's restless movements and was elsewhere in the apartment, leaving his mother feeling alone and still massively depressed. Still, she knew she had to get up and talk to Daniela today. She couldn't leave things the way she had yesterday afternoon. She dreaded the conversation. It would be humiliating and probably wouldn't change anything for the better. But despite her anger, hurt, and doubts, Bryce prized honesty and kindness above most things and she hadn't been completely honest with or kind to Daniela yesterday.

Of course, she wasn't about to just prostrate herself and confess her true feelings for Daniela either. She didn't want to make things weird between them, and she was mortified by the possibility of Daniela realizing that someone with so many issues was in love with her.

Sighing, she pulled herself wearily out of bed and checked the clock on her nightstand. It was still too early to call Daniela, so she limped to the shower to make herself look as presentable as she could. When she was dressed in her favorite pair of jeans and a long-sleeved white thermal under a Coast Guard Academy T-shirt, she paused in front of the full-length mirror. The ever-present cane was in her hand at her side and her scar stood out red and swollen against the smooth pale skin of her face. She quickly leaned the cane against the door and pulled her hair down from its ponytail. This was something she had found herself doing more often of late. It helped her to think that her long blond hair could somehow hide the left side of her face if she looked down at the right angle.

She picked up her cell phone and was sickened to see that her mother had left four more messages early that morning. She shook her head. What was she going to do?

Trying to put the unwelcome thoughts out of her mind, she took a deep breath and dialed Daniela's number.

"Bryce!" Daniela's excited voice came from the earpiece.

"Hey, Dani."

"I thought you weren't going to call. I was worried about you."

Bryce felt a stab of guilt. "It seems like I'm good at that. Making you worried, I mean."

"That's not what I meant, and don't be like that. Of course I'm going to be worried. Some days you seem almost happy and others, like yesterday…well, I wonder if it's me." She sounded anxious.

"No way, Dani. You're the best thing that's happened to me in a long time." Bryce was thankful that Daniela couldn't see her. She continued quickly, embarrassed. "I'm sorry about my little shutdown last night. I've been…struggling with some things."

"I know, but I also want you to know that I'm here for you."

"I know you are and thank you. So how about that beer? Are you still up for going to Pike's?"

"Absolutely!"

"Sweet. I can be there in about thirty minutes."

"Bryce?"

"Yeah?"

"Thank you for calling."

Bryce smiled. "I'll see you in a bit."

She parked in the Pike Market lot and slowly made her way down to the brewery where she knew Daniela would be waiting. Her skin tingled in anticipation of seeing her again. It didn't matter that she had seen her every single day for the past two and a half weeks. It was only getting worse as she fell more and more in love with her.

Sure enough, as Bryce carefully made her way down the stairs, her first sight of Daniela caused her to miss her cane placement and almost tumble down. Daniela leapt off the bench and sprang up the stairs to steady her.

"Well, that was graceful," Bryce said as her ears flamed red.

Daniela just smiled and held on to Bryce as they descended the rest of the stairs and approached the check-in podium. Despite her embarrassment, Bryce couldn't help but love the feel of Daniela's strong arm around her waist.

The hostess led them to a corner table in the back of the pub where they could easily see the Seahawks game on the TV above the bar. They ordered draft beer and two orders of mac and cheese as soon as they sat down.

Bryce looked up to check the game score, but noticed Daniela watching her. "Not interested in football?"

She smiled. "I like football just fine, I am from Texas after all, but I'm more interested in you right now."

Bryce swallowed. "You want to talk about yesterday afternoon."

"Yep."

"I don't know if…" She paused. "It's complicated."

"Are you mad at me for setting up that meeting with Captain Jack?"

Bryce shook her head vehemently. "No. Absolutely not. That was an insanely cool thing you did for me. I really can't thank you enough."

"Still worrying about your mom?"

"Well, yeah." Bryce paused. "But that's not the only thing."

"Okay. What then?"

Bryce stalled, but had to tell her something. "You know that I've been having a hard time with…my situation."

"Yes."

The words spewed forth. "I just can't seem to get over what happened to me. I know it's vain and it could have been so much worse and I'm lucky to be alive and all that shit, but Jesus, it still pisses me off. And the fact that it pisses me off pisses me off even *more*. I'm not used to not being in control or letting myself down or feeling weak." Bryce leaned her forehead onto her fist. "I don't like *me* anymore."

Daniela didn't say anything so Bryce looked up at her, abashed. "God, I'm sorry, Dani. Buzz-kill Bryce strikes again. But see? This is what I mean." She slumped back into her seat. "I don't know who I am now. I'm not who I used to be, that's for damn sure, and I feel like…I feel like I'm letting you down."

"You aren't."

Bryce waved her words away. "I'm a big disappointment after all those years you spent looking up to me. It just…it kills me to see how wonderful, kind, and amazing you still are and I can't be the same for you."

The waitress chose this inopportune time to bring their food to the table. Her chipper smile made Bryce feel even worse.

When she left Daniela was still looking deeply into Bryce's eyes with an unreadable expression.

"I won't blame you if you want to leave now," Bryce said sadly.

Daniela let out a long sigh. "Bryce, you could never, ever, disappoint me. You were always there for me when I was younger. You were my idol. Right now you need to know that none of that has changed." She leaned in closer and said her next words with perfect clarity. "Now that I've got you back in my life, I'll be damned if I let you go again."

Bryce's chest pounded. Words that could mean so much to her might not mean the same thing to the beautiful woman across from her.

No. She wouldn't let herself get pulled into some lovesick fantasy only to have her heart broken. She was tired of the pain.

God, she needed help.

She had expected the rest of lunch at the brewery to be awkward and forced, but true to form, Daniela had made her feel at ease once again and the afternoon ended on a high as they sat together and watched the Seahawks win their game. She would never in a million years know how Daniela managed to make her feel so much better just by her presence. Yes, she was smart, funny, playful, and a great conversationalist, but it was more than that. She just had a glow about her that drew Bryce in and wouldn't let her go.

Bryce drove Daniela to the theater with the promise of taking her on the Underground Tour tomorrow and was now on her way to a coffee shop near the VA where Chaplain Davis waited for her. She had called him as soon as she'd let Daniela out at the curb, and he had immediately agreed to speak with her. She couldn't think of anyone else she could go to for help.

She arrived, and when she entered the building Chaplain Davis stood and waved her over to a set of cushy chairs partially enclosed by a wall where they could talk in relative privacy. He wore his blue patterned navy working uniform with the sleeves rolled up despite the cold weather outside.

"Hello, sir."

"It's good to see you again, Lieutenant. I must admit I was a little surprised that you called. You didn't seem like you wanted to talk much a few weeks ago at the charity ball."

Bryce smiled halfheartedly. "I was a little nervous."

The chaplain laughed. "Yes. I could see that. I was relieved that my 'pretty white pants,' as you called them, made it out unscathed." He leaned forward to rest his elbows on his knees. "How are you now? It looks like something is troubling you."

Bryce's lips trembled, but she refused to cry in front of this man who seemed to have made it a personal mission to help her.

Attempting to keep her emotions in check, she told him everything that had happened in the last three weeks. He looked incredibly pleased when she told him about her new job with DiVeR, but grew somber again when she explained about falling in love with Daniela and feeling unworthy of her. When she mentioned how her mother had been trying to get back in touch with her, he looked troubled.

Bryce's voice shook as she said, "It's just too much. I don't know what to do."

Chaplain Davis looked pensive for a moment before saying, "Let's deal with these one at a time. First, Daniela. She sounds like a very special woman."

"She is."

"And you're sure you're in love with her?"

"Yes."

He paused and sipped his cappuccino. "I think she deserves the truth. From what you told me, she's gone above and beyond to welcome you back into her life and has even helped you feel better about yourself."

Bryce thought about how she felt when she was with Daniela. "I'm torn. When I'm around her I feel whole again. Like I can do anything. Almost like the old me. But at the same time I feel like a burden, and I can't shake the feeling that I'm just not good enough anymore. It's like I'm at war with myself. It's illogical and infuriating."

"Do you actually consider this a war?"

Bryce looked at him, confused. "I don't know. It's just an expression."

"I don't think so in your case. It's actually pretty telling."

She cocked her head to the side. "How so?"

The chaplain raised his left hand. "On one side you have your normally indomitable spirit, your strength, and your love. On the other," he raised his right, "the caustic relationship with your parents, your fear of being helpless, and the self-imposed shame of your condition. Love versus hate, to put it simply. You're just currently in a tougher battle than most."

"Which side will win?"

He smiled kindly. "That depends on you."

Bryce sighed. "You know, I could sure use a push in the right direction."

"Okay. How do you feel about calling your mother back?"

Bryce sat bolt upright and her eyes popped.

"I'll take that as terrified beyond belief." He chuckled. "What if I call her with you? Moral support?"

"Do you think it's necessary?"

He shrugged. "I don't think it's right to not try to reforge that connection if she's reaching out."

"But, sir, she hasn't changed."

"What about you? Have you changed?"

Bryce motioned to herself incredulously.

Chaplain Davis shook his head. "No. I mean, have *you* changed? Really think about it this time. You've spent the last thirty minutes telling me how different you are now. How you don't know yourself. But all I've seen and heard is a passionate young woman still trying to do what's right for herself even though her road just happened to get a lot more complicated. I've seen nothing but strength."

"I wish I could be so sure."

"You do realize that doubts, fears, and self-pity don't make you weak? Succumbing to those things does. Fighting them, asking for help, and working through them as you're doing now takes courage and a willpower that amazes me. I see it in many of the injured veterans I minister to and I see it in you." He paused. "So answer me again. Have you changed?"

Bryce sat in stunned silence, her eyes filling with tears. His words had cleansed the murky waters of her mind. She felt warmth and pride. "No."

"Who are you?"

"I'm Bryce Lee Montgomery."

"You're a fighter."

"Yes."

"You're strong."

"Yes."

"You're going to win your battles, no matter how tough they get."

"I don't know. But I'll try."

"Good." He sat back in his chair. "Call your mother. Don't let her belittle you. You know who you are. I'll be with you."

Bryce took out her phone and dialed with a shaking hand. Her mother picked up before the second ring.

"Hello?"

"Hi, Mom."

"Bryce." She took in an excited breath. "Thank you for calling."

"How is Dad?"

"He's fine. He misses you."

"I miss him too."

"Are you coming home?"

She paused. "No."

Her mother's voice sounded smaller. "Why not?"

"Why do you think?"

"Honey, we're only trying to help you. I just don't understand how you don't see that."

Bryce let out a weary sigh. "I do see that, Mom. Really I do. But you're never going to get the daughter you want."

"We don't believe that. You *are* the daughter we've always wanted and loved. Why else would we go to the lengths we have to protect you? To lead you back to God? I know our methods weren't pretty, but we didn't know what else to do. If only you would come home we could—"

"No." Bryce cut her off. "Let me talk now. I will come home if you can do something for me."

"Anything."

"I want you to admit you were wrong. I want you to tell me you love me unconditionally like parents should. I want you to say you're sorry." Bryce looked over to Chaplain Davis, who smiled and gave a thumbs-up.

Her mother was silent on the other end of the line, so Bryce continued, "I want you to think about everything I've done in my life and then I want to know if you can still think that I have shamed you, that I've done something truly wrong. Can you do any of these things?"

"Bryce…" Her mother's voice cracked. "We have always been proud of you, but…this isn't something we can forgive."

Bryce's stomach plummeted. "You realize what you've done, don't you?"

"Honey, Pastor Harold said—"

"Mom, I don't give a flying fuck what Pastor Harold said!"

"Bryce, how *dare* you? You see? This is exactly what we were afraid of. You've given in to the repugnant lesbian lifestyle and now you're a foul-mouthed, unrepentant sinner. How could we ever think we could help you?" she added, almost to herself.

Bryce glowered and opened her mouth to speak.

"Do you mind?" Chaplain Davis interrupted. He held out his hand for the phone and she slapped it into his palm. She listened intently, but could only hear his side of the conversation.

"Hello, Mrs. Montgomery," he said more gently than Bryce would ever have managed to. "This is Chaplain Davis of the U.S. Navy here in Seattle. Bryce has explained the situation between you two, and I wanted to let you know that Bryce is one of the most capable, goodhearted, and significant people I've ever met. It is my professional opinion that you seek guidance from someone other than your current pastor. I fear that he isn't giving you the best or the kindest advice in regard to your daughter's life."

A pause. Bryce could hear her mother's angry voice on the other end, but couldn't make out her words.

"I'm not going to debate with you, Mrs. Montgomery. Just know that the information is out there for you to discover for yourself. I highly recommend that you do so because if you don't, you have lost your daughter forever. She doesn't deserve the abuse you and your husband have imposed on her."

More anger carried across the line.

Bryce watched Chaplain Davis shake his head sadly and hold up his hand. "Thank you for your time and God bless," he said through the torrent.

He held the phone back to Bryce, who was beaming at him. "I ended the call. I hope you don't mind."

"Not a bit."

"She makes me sad," the chaplain said, frowning.

"Why?" Bryce asked, surprised.

"It's obvious she won't listen to anyone else. You can tell she loves you, but those horrible people have just led her down such a judgmental path." He paused. "Please know that's not the way of our Lord. It makes me sad to see people like her victimized by that kind of bigotry."

Bryce took a moment to let that sink in. Her parents *were* victims, just like she was. It was a vicious cycle that led to nothing but pain and heartache. Bryce stood to leave, her cane firmly grasped in her hand. "Chaplain?"

He stood too. "Yes?"

"I have no words to thank you enough for what you've done for me."

He smiled broadly. "Words aren't necessary. Actions are. Are you going to tell Daniela the truth?"

"I'm still afraid."

"Tell her that too."

Bryce shrugged. "I'll try. It's hard to admit your shortcomings and fears to someone you're madly in love with, you know?"

"I know." He clapped her on the shoulder. "But you just showed me how strong you can be. Use that strength to just get it all out there. She deserves it."

"Yes, sir." She saluted him as a sign of respect, and after saluting her back, he took her hand and shook it firmly.

"I'm here whenever you need me, Bryce."

"Thank you." She smiled again, left the coffee shop, and went back to her apartment. She had a lot to think about.

Chapter Twenty-one

It turned out that Bryce had more trouble than she had anticipated on the Underground Tour because of the stairs and uneven flooring, but she got through it and was glad she had finally decided to make good on her promise. Daniela had been entranced as the tour guide told the group about Seattle's colorful, resourceful, determined, and amusing history. It turned out Daniela was a history buff, and seeing the original floor levels of businesses buried under the current walkways of the city intrigued her. At the end of the tour she bought one book about the history of the Seattle underground and another about the seedier aspects of Seattle's old red light district.

"I have one more place to show you over here," Bryce said as they left the tour building. "You still have time, right?"

Daniela looked at her watch. "Yeah, I have two hours before I need to be at the theater."

"Excellent." Bryce headed toward the end of the block and jumped slightly when Daniela slipped her hand into the crook of her elbow. She pressed herself closer as they walked, and adrenaline exploded through Bryce's body. The air was chilly, but Bryce didn't think it was cold enough for her to be snuggling in solely for warmth. She had longed to get physically close with her, and this friendly gesture only increased the craving. She concentrated on walking in a straight line.

They turned the corner and Bryce's voice cracked as she said, "This is it."

Daniela looked from Bryce's face to the storefront where they had stopped. "Seattle Mystery Bookshop?"

"Yeah. It's kind of a book lover's paradise. It's pretty famous for being an awesome independent bookstore. I thought you might like it. I saw all of the old paperbacks in your dressing room. Thought you might need some new reading material for your downtime…other than books about local prostitution," she said, gesturing to the new books in Daniela's bag.

Daniela surprised Bryce by standing on her tiptoes and kissing her cheek. "You're brilliant, you know that?"

Bryce gently touched the spot on her cheek where Daniela's lips had just made contact. "Why?"

"You're observant, for one. I've read through the books I brought with me on tour about ten times each. I definitely need new ones. Let's go see what they have." She turned and walked into the store, Bryce trailing on a cloud of stupefied bliss at her heels.

By the time Daniela had finished perusing the store's ample collection a full hour later, she had a bag of no less than fifteen new books.

"Think that will last you?" Bryce said sarcastically.

"Hmm. I don't know." She put her hand on her chin as she considered it. "Before I came to Seattle and started hanging out with you, I finished a book every two days."

Bryce's smile fell. "Damn. Sorry."

"No, that's okay. I still have my computer and some ebooks, and I won't have time to read my last week here anyway. That is, if you can still stand my company," Daniela teased.

Bryce sighed. It was time.

"Will you come sit with me?" Bryce motioned to a bench in front of the Pioneer Building.

"Oh! Your leg. You've been on it all day. Of course we can sit down."

That wasn't it. Sure, she had been fighting the pain in her leg as the day wore on, but she barely noticed it compared to the emotional turmoil that disquieted her. Still, she couldn't help the groan of relief that escaped her throat when her left leg bent as she sat down.

Daniela looked worried. "Better?"

Bryce let out a grateful breath. "Yeah."

"We can sit here as long as you need. We have a whole hour to just sit and chat."

"You're too good to me, Dani."

Daniela snorted. "Don't give me that. I haven't done anything but kidnap you into hanging out with me every hour of every day. I'm sure you have other things you need to do besides act as a tour guide for a poor actress."

"I don't, actually. But I do kind of need to talk to you." She paused, braced herself. "I didn't say everything I needed to yesterday."

Daniela laid her palm on Bryce's knee. "Whatever you need. I'm all ears."

"I got some good advice from a friend after I dropped you off, and I think I have the proper perspective on things now. But what I have to say is…difficult for me."

Daniela looked nervous, but said simply, "Okay."

Bryce took a deep breath and looked at the ground. "I told you yesterday that I feel like a disappointment, but it's…it's more than that."

Daniela stayed silent.

"God, this is going to sound so stupid, but I don't want you to feel like you have to do things for me. To make sure I'm okay all of the time." She grimaced. "I feel like…I feel like I'm causing you to get trapped in my messed-up life."

"Bryce, I—"

"Seeing you again after all those years and getting to know you the way I have in these last few weeks…I feel like I might need you or want you around *too* much. That scares the hell out of me. I don't want to be a burden on you, especially when you'll be leaving in a week."

Bryce looked up to see confusion and hurt on Daniela's face. When Daniela finally found her voice she said, almost defensively, "Do you think I feel obligated to watch out for you?"

"I—"

"I know who you are, and you're the strongest woman I've ever known. I'm sorry if you feel like I pity you or something. That wasn't my intent."

Fighting the urge to cry, Bryce waited a moment before speaking. "Why in the world would you want to spend so much time with me, then? I'm not the person you knew in high school. I'm nobody. I don't exist." She twirled her fingers in the air as if dissipating smoke.

Daniela spoke with a slight tremor in her voice. "Of course you exist. You're very real to me and to so many others. Bryce, what in the world are you talking about? What's making you think like this now? I know you've been struggling, but you seemed to be doing so much better. What happened?"

Bryce couldn't hold it in anymore. Tears streamed down her cheeks. "I've lost my parents. I'm not fit for duty in the Coast Guard.

And this." Bryce turned her head so that Daniela had a full view of her scarred features. "This represents everything I've lost. I want to hold on to something, to someone…to you, but I can't ask you to carry my weight."

Daniela made shushing noises and pulled Bryce into an embrace. "Hey. Stop."

Bryce's shoulders jerked as she tried to calm herself and stop the flow of tears. She couldn't tell Daniela how much she loved her, even though her words would make more sense if Daniela knew the extent of her feelings. But she still didn't have the courage to make that leap.

Unable to speak without great gasps of air, Bryce said, "Dani…I am so…glad…that we've become…friends again."

"Me too, Bryce. You honestly have no idea." She squeezed her tighter and then pulled away to look into Bryce's eyes.

"But…you'll be leaving soon and I…I don't want you to have to worry about me. I'm not worth the energy you're putting into helping me."

"That's not true." Daniela sounded exasperated, and Bryce didn't blame her. "Of course I worry about you, Bryce, but it's not because I don't think you're capable or because I think that you need rescuing. I worry because I care about you so much."

Bryce shook her head.

Daniela continued anyway, "Bryce, I've waited so many years to get to see you again. I really don't think you understand what it means to me to have you back in my life."

"I appreciate that, really I do. You don't know how much. But…I just can't shake the way I feel about this. I feel like an anchor that will do nothing but drag you down if you tie yourself to me."

"*Tie* myself," Daniela repeated. She narrowed her eyes. "There's something you're not telling me."

"What do you mean?"

"I know you, Bryce. You've been hiding something from me. Have I done something wrong?"

Bryce had never seen Daniela on the verge of tears like she was now. She felt like such an asshole. What in the hell was wrong with her?

"If I've offended you in any way or…or…God, if I'm bothering you—"

"No! Dani, I swear, you…you honestly have no idea…"

"Tell me, then. Please!" she pleaded, the tears falling unchecked down her flawless cheeks.

"I…I can't."

"Yes, you can." She put her hands on Bryce's shoulders and forced her to face her. "You have to."

"You don't understand."

"Damn it, Bryce! Help me to understand! I'll never understand if you don't just tell me—"

"I've fallen in love with you!" Bryce's heart stilled. There it was: the truth. But as she stared into Daniela's red eyes, she knew only the absolute truth would do for the woman she had grown to love with all of her heart.

Daniela gasped and put her hand over her chest, breathing fast. Bryce looked up at a cloudy sky that had started to sprinkle small droplets of rain onto her face, mixing with her salty tears. She had said it. Now Daniela would know why she was pulling away, why she didn't want her to get too attached.

She felt Daniela's hand gently guide her face back down. "Oh, Bryce. I have been in love with you from the moment I saw you. How can you not have seen that?"

"W-what?"

Daniela laughed with obvious relief through her tears. "I never thought…oh my God, I really never thought that you could love me back!"

Bryce's jaw opened in stunned disbelief, and she completely forgot how to form or utter words. Elation as powerful as she had ever felt surged through her whole being.

Daniela laughed gleefully at Bryce's stunned expression and pulled her into a tight hug. Bryce didn't return the embrace. When Daniela noticed, she pulled away carefully. "What's wrong?"

Bryce tried to think of some way to express her emotions eloquently, but all she came up with was, "Dani…I don't know."

Daniela's smile fell immediately and fear filled her eyes. "Don't know what?"

Bryce rose from the bench, frustrated and insecure. "I don't know if I'm good enough."

Fiery determination replaced the terrified expression. Daniela stood. She took Bryce's face in her hand and tilted her head to look down into her eyes. "You listen to me, Bryce Lee Montgomery. I have been in love with you my *whole life*. Don't give me any of this bullshit about you not being pretty anymore or being damaged. You were and still are the single most beautiful woman in the world."

Bryce made a doubtful face.

"Do you think I give a damn that you have a limp? That you have a little scar on your face? Bryce, I love you. I love *you*. I've never loved anyone else because no one has *ever* been able to compare to you. You were everything to me when I was growing up." Her voice softened as she ran her palm down the scarred side of Bryce's face. "When you went off to the academy and no one back home ever heard from you again…Bryce, I couldn't stand it. Not knowing what you were doing with your life, not knowing how you were."

"I'm sorry," she said quietly.

"For years I heard nothing, just the rumors about you and Leah and your parents. And then, out of the blue, I hear you were in a life-threatening accident in the Coast Guard, and my world came crashing down. I panicked until I was able to track down and talk to Jennifer and find out you were okay. And later when I learned that our tour would be in Seattle for four weeks? Well…let's just say I made it my mission in life to meet up with you again. I would never have been able to forgive myself if I hadn't gotten to see you at least one more time."

Several tourists emerged from the Underground Tour building, laughing and paying no attention to the life-changing moment occurring only yards from them.

Daniela smiled. "And now look at us, standing in the rain like some kind of old romance movie, professing our love for each other, and all you can say is that you're not good enough for me. *Me*! An unknown actress sharing a closet of an apartment in New York with strangers? Not a penny to my name?"

"You're more than that, Dani."

"Yes, I am." Her eyes narrowed with passionate fire. "I'm someone who has loved you from the moment she laid eyes on you. Someone who knows the real you and not the person you've deluded yourself that you are. I *am* more, yes. And so are you."

"I'm—"

"Not the lost soul that your parents see," Daniela said, shaking her head. "You're not the loser you've convinced yourself you are. You are Bryce. *My* Bryce. And I will love you more than anyone in this world until my last breath."

Bryce stood flabbergasted, her face still cupped in Daniela's soft hand. "But…" was all she managed to say.

Daniela placed her left hand on Bryce's other cheek. "You just said that you had fallen in love with me. I have never in my life felt as happy as in that one split second."

"Yes, but—"

"Is it true? Do you love me?"

Bryce just stared. She had never seen Daniela so resolute about something.

"Damn it, Bryce!" She quieted her voice. "Do you love me?"

A tear ran down Bryce's cheek and she said simply, "Yes."

Daniela let out a sob and then pulled Bryce's face to hers, kissing her with the passion of years of pent-up desire.

Bryce's world exploded. She had spent every waking hour of the past three weeks imagining what Daniela's lips would feel like, but no amount of daydreaming could have prepared her for what she was feeling now. Heat flamed in her stomach and she couldn't help but drop her cane and pull Daniela tightly to her body.

She moved her tongue greedily over Daniela's lips and was rewarded with the same from her. Daniela moaned and wrapped her fingers in Bryce's now-wet hair. It wasn't until they got a catcall from a passing teenager and his friends that they pulled apart.

They both breathed heavily, electrified by the contact, and Bryce felt as if she would never be able to remove her hands from Daniela's back.

"I love you too, you infuriating, wonderful woman," Daniela said breathlessly.

Bryce couldn't help but smile. It took every ounce of willpower she had to not bring Daniela in for a kiss again. Instead she simply said, "Dani, are you sure this"—she put her hand over the one Daniela was using to cup her damaged cheek—"doesn't bother you?"

Daniela actually laughed. "Oh, Bryce. Chicks dig scars."

Bryce rolled her eyes but moved Daniela's palm to her lips, kissing it gently.

"I think we should get out of the rain," Bryce said reluctantly. It was falling more heavily and their clothes were soaked.

"God, how am I going to do the show tonight? Knowing that you're waiting? I just want to...*feel* you."

Bryce blushed deeply. "Geez, Dani!"

Daniela laughed again. "You'd better drop the shy thing and get used to it. This has been building for...how many years now?"

Bryce pulled her close and bent down to kiss the side of her neck softly. The pleased gasp from Daniela made her tingle all over. "You'll stay with me tonight?"

"I'll stay with you forever."

The two women smiled at each other and held hands as they walked to Bryce's car. There were so many things that they were going to have to talk about, so many logistics to work through, but tonight would be just for them. Nothing would ever hurt again as long as they were entwined in each other's arms.

Epilogue

Bryce put a large black line through her wall calendar. It had been three months to the day that Daniela had left Seattle to finish her tour and get back to New York. Three months of nothing but phone calls, video chats, texts, and a near-debilitating lack of physical contact.

But that would end tomorrow night.

Daniela was coming back. Bryce had no doubts that they would pick up precisely where they had left off, and it didn't involve ever leaving the bedroom…or getting dressed, for that matter.

A knock on her office door made Bryce jump as she fought the rising heat in her stomach. "Come in." Her voice cracked with embarrassment.

Captain Jack entered the room.

"Captain. It's been a while. Good to see you."

"Likewise. It looks like things are going well here." He gestured to the pool outside her office door where wounded veterans were getting scuba lessons from volunteer divemasters.

Bryce smiled. "We're getting so many new students that we're going to need more staff. It's amazing what this program is doing for them. They love it!"

"And what about you?"

"Well, obviously I love it. I got my advanced certification last week and will be working on my rescue certification in the next few months."

He nodded. "That's good to hear."

"Please sit." She gestured to the chair.

As he sat, he pointed to the picture on Bryce's desk. "Miss Cordova?"

"She's…she's my girlfriend."

His face broke into a wide smile. "Damn fine work there, Lieutenant. Damn fine."

Bryce laughed and sat down.

"What's she been up to these days?"

Bryce's chest swelled with pride. "She's auditioning for Broadway shows."

"New York, huh?"

"Yes, sir."

"I bet it's tough having to do the long-distance thing."

"It's just like being in the military."

He chuckled. "Settle in, Lieutenant, I have a proposition for you."

She looked at her foot, annoyed that it was tapping so insistently. The computer screen in baggage claim was showing that Daniela's flight had landed five minutes ago. Bryce imagined her girlfriend waiting behind the infinite line of passengers pulling heavy bags from the overhead compartments on the plane. She tried not to pace, instead focusing all of her attention on the escalator that would bring the love of her life back to her.

Just then, standing behind a very large man in an ill-fitting Hawaiian shirt and a woman holding a screaming baby, Daniela came into view. All of the extraneous noise of the airport silenced as Bryce's breath caught in her chest. Seeing Daniela in person literally made Bryce weak in the knees. Thank God for the cane. Daniela hadn't seen her yet and Bryce watched with obvious pleasure as the woman she loved looked from right to left, biting the corner of her bottom lip as she searched the crowd. Her hair was pulled back into its usual ponytail and she wore the fitted Seattle Coast Guard T-shirt Bryce had given her as a reminder of who waited for her.

When Daniela was halfway down the escalator, her eyes finally found Bryce's and she took a relieved breath and smiled. It took an eternity for her to descend to the ground floor and make her way through the crowd, but when she finally reached Bryce she dropped her duffel bag and threw herself into her arms.

Bryce buried her face in Daniela's hair, breathing in her scent deeply. "God, I missed you."

Daniela sniffled. "I don't ever want to leave you again."

Bryce laughed. "You know I won't let you give up your opportunities in New York for me."

"I know. But you'll come with me next time, right?"

Bryce squeezed her tighter. "I don't think I could do three months apart from you ever again." She paused, breath shallow with excitement. "I have some good news on that front."

Daniela pulled away and looked up at Bryce with happy tears in her eyes.

"I was talking to Captain Jack yesterday…" She allowed for a suspenseful pause.

Daniela waited. "And?"

"And…DiVeR is expanding. To the East Coast." Bryce winked.

Daniela's eyes widened. "Where on the East Coast?"

Bryce cupped the back of Daniela's neck, caressing her soft skin. "He said it was up to me as long as there are veterans in need nearby. I'm going to be in charge of the whole thing. On both coasts. We can live in both places."

"Oh, my God." Daniela's face broke into an enormous smile.

Bryce gleefully pulled her into another hug. "I feel so damn… lucky. We'll never have to be apart like this again."

Daniela pressed her body closer to Bryce's. "Thank God. I thought I was going to explode if I didn't get to touch you soon."

Bryce shuddered as a ripple of lust coursed through her body. She was disappointed when Daniela pulled away.

"I have some amazing news too. Ready?"

Bryce nodded.

"The producer of a brand-new musical saw me in *A Chorus Line* and called me in for an audition when I got home. I didn't tell you about it," she said when she saw Bryce's confused look, "because I didn't want to jinx it. And I wanted to surprise you."

"Well?"

"I got the part! Bryce, this is like a, possibly my big break, big deal. It's a big-budget musical…like along the lines of *Wicked* or *Rent*. I'm part of an ensemble cast, but it's still a really important and prominent role. Way bigger than Morales. And the paycheck…" Her eyes were glittering.

Bryce was thrilled. "You're going to be famous!"

Daniela blushed. "Maybe. God, I love you so much."

Bryce looked at the ground, but smiled. "I still don't know what you see in me, but I'm sure not gonna argue."

"I will proudly show you off. My brave, beautiful Coastie. You're going to turn heads and make people jealous when I take you out in public." She gazed adoringly at Bryce. "I never want to forget how I feel right this second. Everything is perfect."

Bryce restrained herself from taking Daniela right there on the floor of the airport. Instead, she offered a hand, which Daniela took gracefully. "Daniela Cordova, soon to be Broadway star, please come with me. I have a surprise for you."

"No peeking, okay?" Bryce said, making sure that Daniela's eyes were closed.

"For the hundredth time, I'm not looking," Daniela said with an excited smile on her face.

"Okay, just hold on to me." Bryce turned and started walking as Daniela held on to her shoulders.

"Not a problem." Daniela moved one of her hands down to Bryce's hip and then slowly slid it forward.

"Dani!" Bryce exclaimed in mock outrage. "Behave!"

"Never."

Bryce giggled and led her outside. Daniela shivered when the chilly night air touched her face.

"Okay. You can look now."

Daniela opened her eyes and gasped as she looked down upon the entire city of Seattle, lights burning brightly and the ocean beyond sparkling with the reflection of the brilliant full moon.

"This is...beautiful. Where are we?"

Bryce reached down and popped the cork from the expensive bottle of champagne that Jennifer had sent as a housewarming gift.

"Welcome home, Dani...the West Coast version, anyway."

Daniela looked behind her into the new condo, dumbfounded. "This is yours?"

"No. This is ours." She poured two glasses and handed one to Daniela.

"But...how?"

Bryce smiled. "I got a great deal from a retired Coast Guard commander. She moved away and"—she gestured toward the room—"I bought it. You said you always wanted to have a good view." Bryce looked out over the city. "Well? What do you think?"

Daniela threw back the champagne in one gulp. "I think I'm about to do things to you that will make you forget your own name." Her voice was low and sultry and the look in her eyes animalistic.

Bryce shifted uncomfortably in jeans that now seemed far too tight and coarse.

"Bryce?" Daniela said, putting down the glass and wrapping her arms around Bryce's waist.

"Yeah?"

"I want you to know that I love you more than anything. I'm so in love with you it hurts. And I am so proud of you. I'm proud of both of us."

Bryce shook her head and smiled. "Dani, you're the best thing that's ever happened to me. You're my family. You've made me live again. I will spend every last second of my life showing you how much I love you."

Daniela pressed herself up against Bryce's trembling body. "If you don't make love to me right now, Miss Montgomery, I will spontaneously combust right here on our fancy new balcony."

Bryce obliged by kissing her with all of the lust, the passion, and the love of years of longing. Never had she felt something more true, more perfect, more transcendent. The woman she loved was safely in her arms, and she knew that from that moment on, they could weather any storm. Their course was set.

Bryce melted into Daniela's embrace. She was finally home.

About the Author

M.L. Rice was born and raised in the plains of Texas. She graduated with a degree in Radio/TV/Film from the University of Texas at Austin where she was a proud member of the Longhorn Marching and Basketball Bands. After college, she moved to sunny Los Angeles, where she currently lives with her wife and three cats. She enjoys scuba diving, hiking, kayaking, swimming, spending too much time on video games, going to the theater, and playing in Disneyland. She volunteers for various nonprofit organizations, travels whenever she can, collects and plays multiple instruments including the trumpet, cello, and great highland bagpipes, and is also a member of the U.S. Coast Guard Auxiliary.

Books Available From Bold Strokes Books

Crossroads by Radclyffe. Dr. Hollis Monroe specializes in short-term relationships but when she meets pregnant mother-to-be Annie Colfax, fate brings them together at a crossroads that will change their lives forever. (978-1-60282-756-1)

Beyond Innocence by Carsen Taite. When a life is on the line, love has to wait. Doesn't it? (978-1-60282-757-8)

Heart Block by Melissa Brayden. Socialite Emory Owen and struggling single mom Sarah Matamoros are perfectly suited for each other but face a difficult time when trying to merge their contrasting worlds and the people in them. If love truly exists, can it find a way? (978-1-60282-758-5)

Pride and Joy by M.L. Rice. Perfect Bryce Montgomery is her parents' pride and joy, but when they discover that their daughter is a lesbian, her world changes forever. (978-1-60282-759-2)

Timothy by Greg Herren. Timothy is a romantic suspense thriller from award-winning mystery writer Greg Herren set in the fabulous Hamptons. (978-1-60282-760-8)

In Stone by Jeremy Jordan King. A young New Yorker is rescued from a hate crime by a mysterious someone who turns out to be more of a something. (978-1-60282-761-5)

The Jesus Injection by Eric Andrews-Katz. Murderous statues, demented drag queens, political bombings, ex-gay ministries, espionage, and romance are all in a day's work for a top secret agent. But the gloves are off when Agent Buck 98 comes up against the Jesus Injection. (978-1-60282-762-2)

Combustion by Daniel W. Kelly. Bearish detective Deck Waxer comes to the city of Kremfort Cove to investigate why the hottest men in town are bursting into flames in broad daylight. (978-1-60282-763-9)

Ladyfish by Andrea Bramhill. Finn's escape to the Florida Keys leads her straight into the arms of scuba diving instructor Oz as she fights for her freedom, their blossoming love…and her life! (978-1-60282-747-9)

Spanish Heart by Rachel Spangler. While on a mission to find herself in Spain, Ren Molson runs the risk of losing her heart to her tour guide, Lina Montero. (978-1-60282-748-6)

Love Match by Ali Vali. When Parker "Kong" King, the number one tennis player in the world, meets commercial pilot Captain Sydney Parish, sparks fly—but not from attraction. They have the summer to see if they have a love match. (978-1-60282-749-3)

One Touch by L.T. Marie. A romance writer and a travel agent come together at their high school reunion, only to find out that the memory of that one touch never fades. (978-1-60282-750-9)

Night Shadows: Queer Horror edited by Greg Herren and J.M. Redmann. *Night Shadows* features delightfully wicked stories by some of the biggest names in queer publishing. (978-1-60282-751-6)

Secret Societies by William Holden. An outcast hustler, his unlikely "mother," his faithless lovers, and his religious persecutors—all in 1726. (978-1-60282-752-3)

The Raid by Lee Lynch. Before Stonewall, having a drink with friends or your girl could mean jail. Would these women and men still have family, a job, a place to live after…The Raid? (978-1-60282-753-0)

The You Know Who Girls by Annameekee Hesik. As they begin freshman year, Abbey Brooks and her best friend, Kate, pinkie swear they'll keep away from the lesbians in Gila High, but Abbey already suspects she's one of those you-know-who girls herself and slowly learns who her true friends really are. (978-1-60282-754-7)

Wyatt: Doc Holliday's Account of an Intimate Friendship by Dale Chase. Erotica writer Dale Chase takes the remarkable friendship between Wyatt Earp, upright lawman, and Doc Holliday, Southern gentlemen turned gambler and killer, to an entirely new level: hot! (978-1-60282-755-4)

http://www.boldstrokesbooks.com
Bold Strokes
BOOKS
victory
EDITIONS
Drama
LIBERTY
EDITION
AEROS
e
BOOKS
e-Books
Mystery
C
CRIME
Sci-fi
SPEC FIC
Sf
HE
erotica
Erotica
BSB
SOLILOQUY
Young
Adult
MATINEE BOOKS
Romance
BS
BOLD
STROKES
BOOKS
WEBSTORE
PRINT AND EBOOKS